PROFESSOR ROMEO

Also by Anne Bernays

Short Pleasures
The New York Ride
Prudence, Indeed
The First to Know
Growing Up Rich
The School Book
The Address Book

PROFESSOR ROMEO

Anne Bernays

Weidenfeld & Nicolson
New York

Published by Weidenfeld & Nicolson, New York
A Division of Wheatland Corporation
841 Broadway
New York, New York 10003-4793

Published in Canada by General Publishing Company, Ltd.

Library of Congress Cataloging-in-Publication Data

Bernays, Anne.
  Professor Romeo.

  I. Title.
PS3552.E728P76   1989   813'.54   88-33965
ISBN 1-55584-218-6

Manufactured in the United States of America

This book is printed on acid-free paper

Designed by Paul Chevannes

First Edition

10   9   8   7   6   5   4   3   2   1

For Jean Baker Miller and for J.N.D.

PART ONE

Chapter One

Everyone behind the mossy walls of Harvard University—
as well as several hundred scholars beyond this academic
pale—knew that if you wanted to communicate with Professor
Jacob Barker the most efficient path was across the desk or
into the telephone of his secretary, Miss Emily Compton.
Emily was the professor's eyes, ears, and—some said—his
wet nurse as well. Few people had reached Barker directly in,
oh, a decade or so, and even then Emily had in some way
deflected their trajectories. So that when, one bright fall afternoon in the year 1985, an envelope arrived on Emily's desk,
addressed to Barker from the Dean of Arts and Sciences with
the words STRICTLY CONFIDENTIAL stamped across its
face in what looked like blood, she started, as if stung on the
nose by a bee. For the briefest of moments she considered
ripping it open anyway, then said to herself, "We Comptons do
not stoop so low." Sighing, she placed the envelope on top of
the pile of the day's correspondence, duly read by her and
recorded (for Barker received at least a dozen letters a day
from psychologists in as many countries, most of them asking

him do to something). Then she called the vet to see if Louie, her schnauzer, was ready to come home.

Emily Compton had been the Psychology Department's secretary for seven years. Of the four faculty members who shared her services, Emily liked Jacob Barker best.

"I'd like to leave a tad early, Professor Barker," she said, as she brought in the pile of correspondence and laid it on his "in" box. "There's a letter for you from Stanley Mustin that should please you, and—oh yes, there's a letter from Dean Fromme marked 'Strictly Confidential.' " Here she raised her eyebrows and rolled her eyes.

"Thank you, Emmy," Barker said, raising his own eyes just far enough to take in the lower half of his secretary's torso. Women over fifty made him sad, with their low breasts, their soft jaws. "Leaving early, are you? The pooch okay?"

"Louie's just fine. I'm going over to Angell now to pick him up. Is there anything you'd like me to do before I leave?"

Jacob Barker fought the urge to grab Emily around her stout waist and hang on for dear life. While every clean inch of her proclaimed *spinster, old maid, unmarried lady, maiden,* to him she was undeniably Mother.

Although both of them knew she did not need it, Barker gave his secretary permission to leave early.

"Good news first," he said, as he scrambled through the mail for Stanley Mustin's letter, which, in fact, told the recipient that he was on the short list for a MacArthur. Mustin had ended his letter with a caveat: "If you tell anyone that I have written to you with this bit of news, I will not only deny it but will string you up by the gonads." Had Emily read this? No matter; she had seen worse in her years with him.

"Now for the bad news," Barker said, for he knew Dean Fromme well enough to assume that a sealed envelope from him had to be ominous. The letter inside read:

4

Dear Jake,

It has come to my attention that serious allegations have been made against you by certain female students and former students.

As Dean, I'm obliged to investigate these allegations, as there is no way on earth they will disappear by themselves.

Accordingly, I am asking you to call me at your earliest convenience to set up a meeting so that this little matter can be cleared up. I have known you for almost twenty years and have always found you to be a man of the highest principles and stoutest character. Frankly, I find these charges both ludicrous and baffling. Hopefully, this matter will be dead and buried by Thanksgiving.

> With cordial good wishes,
>
> Edward Fromme
> Administrative Dean, Faculty of Arts and Sciences

P.S. In the unlikely event that you have not seen the University's policy statement dealing with sexual harassment, which my office sent out last spring, I'm enclosing a copy of it at this time.

Fromme had drawn a bold line through his name and title and penned in "Eddie."

Barker unfolded the four-page enclosure, his head swimming. Its language, while predictably stiff and formal, pulled no punches; in fact, each sentence penetrated to Barker's soft tissue. There seemed to be some question as to what precisely constituted harassment; phrases like "unwelcome sexual advances," "inappropriate personal attention," and "physical contact or verbal comments" swam into his focus. But the main thing, the crucial thing, was that an official apparatus had been put in place specifically to deal with people who persisted in engaging in this most "inappropriate" behavior. As for punishment, Barker was surprised to find that this, too, was left mysterious, although it was clear that for "grave misconduct" anything was possible—including "severance from the University." Still, it appeared that they were not altogether sure what to do with the poor bastards they snagged. Small comfort.

As Barker's eyes trailed off the page, tears sprang up. He felt the icy weight of a sword across the back of his neck. "Holy shit," he said, "They're after me. I must pray for a miracle."

Sensing his doom, Jacob Barker called forth his personal history, which began to scroll in front of him as he sat in the afternoon shadows of his untidy office in the Science Complex of Harvard University, in the city of Cambridge, Massachusetts, on the east coast of the United States. Not everything that had happened came back to him, for that would have taken forty-five years. Rather, special people and events came bobbing to the surface. Was it to mock him? Perhaps, for Jacob Barker was a man tainted by weakness, plagued by wayward hungers, unable any longer to trim his own sails or steer his own boat.

Looking back, Barker saw himself as a Harvard graduate student, with a head of lush, sandy-colored hair. And his eyes, wickedly blue eyes that fixed themselves upon a target, nailing it. He had read that the great men of history—Hitler, Peter the Great, Charlie Chaplin—had extraordinary eyes, irresistible, penetrating, transmitting a powerful language that couldn't be spoken. Once pinned by Barker's eyes, most people—especially girls—seemed willing to relinquish their freedom of choice. His eyes represented the luck of some divine draw, for they were nothing he had selected or even trained—they were simply there for him to use, as a singer uses her voice, an athlete his muscles. Barker was trim, too, with no suggestion of the paunch that would begin to threaten in his early forties and with which he would do battle with regular exercise and careful diet. His body was important, its value to him rivaling that of his mind. He maintained on his features a fresh and open expression, which reflected a justified optimism. Jacob Barker was considered to be not just ordinarily bright, but shining with brilliance, like the polished brass knockers on the front doors of Brattle Street houses. His mind wandered into nooks and crannies hidden to most, retrieving things of surprising and immense worth. He had published three monographs in scholarly journals by the time his second September in graduate school rolled around. He was easy to get along with and seemed blessed with the kind of judgment that gave his work both clarity and elegance.

The whispered words "Nobel Prize" frequently made his ears prick as he left the room. Barker was the son of a man who taught secondary-school math and a mother who was wasting a perfectly good Wellesley education by working part-time as a lunch-room monitor at the local high school. At this point, in the early sixties, both Barker parents were tucked away in Orlando, Florida; Barker thought about them once a week, when he dutifully called them on the telephone.

Barker had been tapped by the venerable Professor Otto Von Stampler, a hairy Austrian born just as the twentieth century began and an early disciple of Freud. Much to his master's disgust, Von Stampler abandoned the fold and lit out on his own, founding a modest school of psychology, one that relied on hard evidence, like tables of figures and gauges that measured and calibrated. While not entirely rejecting Freud's notions concerning the unconscious, oedipal conflict, and other arcane what-have-you's, Von Stampler dismissed them as tools inadequate for the curing of mental illness. He had asked—not once but many, many times—"How is it possible to make use of such vagaries as infantile sexuality, latency, *und so weiter* under clinical conditions? Are we not on much surer ground if we see what is precisely what in the laboratory?" Here he stressed the second syllable, in the British manner. It was said—primarily by those who found the eminent man to be an insufferable windbag—that in the late thirties or early forties he had shoved the Von between his first and last names in a gesture of self-elevation equal to his own bloated self-esteem.

Between Jacob Barker—actually, he preferred the name Jake to the longer form—and Von Stampler, it was a matter of both intellectual and emotional rapport, Von Stampler the master and Barker the youthful disciple. They eyed each other, warily at first, then with considerable warmth. Von S. sensed in Barker not only a spark of genuine originality but a willingness to hold back in order to help shed glory on his teacher—a rare enough quality.

During his first year in graduate school, Barker became Von Stampler's preeminent student. He often visited the Von Stampler home on Washington Street, where the doctor's Frau fed him overcooked lamb and mashed potatoes and inquired after his parents. He was made a teaching assistant at the age of twenty-two. "I'm the youngest T.A.," he told his mother over the phone. "I have my own corner in Von S.'s lab. The other day I overheard him telling this big-deal biologist that if anyone could do it, I would be the one to decipher the basic differences between male and female. I don't know if he really meant it, but it sure set me up."

"Dear boy," Von Stampler said to him one morning as they sat in Von S.'s office sipping bitter coffee laced with powdered creamer out of heavy brown ceramic mugs, "I understand you are losing that nice apartment of yours on Athens Street. Verna and I have discussed this and propose that you come and be a part of our little household on Washington Street, no rent. We have a charming bedroom on the third floor which is empty since Lucy went to New York to be a big-shot copywriter. We can as well offer you what I believe is known as kitchen privileges—providing, of course, we do not interfere with one another in the preparation of a meal. Naturally, we would expect a few chores in return—the garbage cans must be brought around to the front of the house on Thursday mornings, snow shoveled from the front walk, a few windows . . ." The older man paused and smiled expectantly at his pupil.

"I don't know what to say, Professor Stampler. That's a generous offer. I'm really tempted." Von Stampler beamed and poured some more coffee down his throat.

Barker was, in fact, tempted. Rent-free. But what a price! Cambridge's winter snowfall often exceeded forty inches, heavy wet stuff, backbreaking to lift on a shovel and move elsewhere. Kitchen privileges with Mrs. Von S.? It would be like living with your grandmother. But most of all, Barker feared the disruption of a heavy sex schedule. He could not see bringing a different broad up to the Von Stamplers' third floor, three or four times a week, the way he did now. His mathematician friend Bennie Goodrich, parodying a *National Enquirer* headline, called his habits a running "sexcapade." Maybe, Bennie said, he would make the *Guinness Book of Records* for the most number of girls fucked in the shortest time span.

How to get out of this without making the old guy mad? Barker invented an errand, went down the hall to the men's room and shut himself inside a cubicle to think.

"I'm really grateful to you and Mrs. Von Stampler," he said on his return, "but Aunt Bessie has this house in Watertown and my mom and dad want me to move in with her and sort of keep an eye on her. You see, she gets these seizures and sometimes falls flat on the floor in the middle of the night and can't get up—"

"Stop!" cried the gray-hair. "Please, I have enough problems of my own, I can't bear it. I'm sorry you won't be moving in with us. . . ."

Now Barker was obliged to look for a place in Watertown. In the end it worked out for the best, as the rents in this Boston suburb were far below those of Cambridge and even

Brookline. And he acquired in this city a taste for Near Eastern cuisine—hummus, baba ganoush, pita bread—food that was both cheap and delicious.

This bit of serendipity was typical of Barker's rush through life; everything he did glowed, and he fairly shone with success. The girls he bought dinner for at the local Chinese eatery and then screwed were thin, pretty, bright, and responsive.

Whenever Barker saw, on the faces and in the hearts of his fellow graduate students, the tarnish of envy—either because of his uncanny success with women, his mental agility, or his status with the powerful and quixotic Von Stampler—he did his utmost to wipe it away. This he did by giving frequent parties to which the guests were not invited to B.Y.O.B. "It's my party, isn't it?" he said. "I provide the booze and the munchies. If you guys want to smoke a little dope, you'll have to bring your own. Otherwise, everything's on me." He didn't really have the money to do this and was forced to eat soup and crackers for dinner more than once. It was important for him to keep, if not their friendship, at least the respect of his fellows. It wasn't all that easy being teacher's pet.

To make up for his generosity at party time, Barker tutored students less able than he was. Some of them bitched about how much he charged them—two seventy-five an hour—but they paid it nonetheless; he was good. Barker was convinced a few of them had cotton batting for brains.

"Are you a scamp?" he asked his mirror image one morning as he ran the edge of his razor over his right cheek, covered in foam. The face he saw raised its brows, then lowered them noncommittally. And what, in fact, was a scamp? Was it merely an acceptable name for something extremely disagreeable, like, say, "prick"? One could forgive a scamp far more easily than one could a prick. Undifferentiated, a one-celled thing, the scamp in Barker revealed itself through circuits no scanning device, no X-ray could have detected. It simply made itself known to him, as a woman knows when she's pregnant long before tests confirm it. Scamp, prick, what did it matter so long as he got what he wanted—though Barker would have been at a loss to define exactly what it was he *did* want.

During his second year as a graduate student—this was 1963, before everything hit the fan—Barker ripened and matured: most importantly, he understood that people and events contained elements both seen and unseen, and that, unlike Freud, the man Vladimir Nabokov had recently called "that Viennese quack," he was unwilling to give that much more credence to the latent than to the manifest.

Barker glanced at his watch, saw that if he didn't hurry he would be late, and trotted off to catch the bus to Cambridge, where a typically full day's activities awaited him: a nine o'clock class of freshmen to teach (Early Motor Development), one to take (Statistics 304b), a lunch date (Gloria, lapsed Catholic, enormous boobs), an appointment with Stuart (floundering in Advanced Methodology), a couple of hours solo in the lab working on an experiment of his own creation, a squash date with Bennie, a quick shower, and then dinner with his newest girl, Nancy Swan, and, if he was lucky, a roll in the hay with her at her place. It was amazing: the more he did, the more energy he seemed to have.

Nancy Swan was a knockout, a beautiful girl. If it came to that, none of Barker's girlfriends were dogs—unattractive women turned him off, he wasn't interested in them—but Nancy was extraordinary. Her face radiated both sex and intelligence; he couldn't describe how this was accomplished, the way her eyes were set in her face perhaps, the slight suggestion of moisture on untinted lips, the way she flared her nostrils when she opened her mouth. Her light brown hair was on the thick side; she carried a small brush with her and brushed it frequently to prevent it from going haywire. He thought her shoulders were too broad, but he could overlook this as her breasts made up for the shoulder flaw. Her breasts were spectacular, they sent him into a frenzy. He begged her to undress whenever they were alone so he could look at them. That first split second when she showed their full whiteness, each studded with a nipple the same shade as her untinted lips, caused Barker to quake.

"Do they remind you of chocolate chip cookies?" she teased, turning this way and that.

"No," he said, figuring one of her other boyfriends had described them thus. "They're too white. Though I do want to put them in my mouth."

"Men are weird," she said, advancing on him.

Nancy Swan was a graduate student in anthropology. Her research topic was the nomadic tribes of central Africa. "I am an explorer," she declared. "I'm going to Africa someday and live with these people." He told her she'd have a rough time without her hair blower. Nancy scoffed.

Nancy had a swarm of friends, some of whom Barker actively disliked. They were too . . . too what? What was it about them that put him off? He pretended not to know when Nancy asked him why he didn't seem to like her friends. Then he thought of a good answer.

"Because they don't like me."

"Are you by any chance projecting?" she said.

"Absolutely not," Barker said.

Nancy was crazy about him. He could tell from the way she looked at him, a melted look he had seen before, in other girls, telling him he could do with them anything he wanted.

"You like me a lot, don't you?" he said.

"I'm crazy about you," she said.

"Why?"

"Oh, come on, you know why."

"No, I really don't," he said. He licked her cheek. "Tell."

"Because you're so smart. Are you a genius, Jake? Polly says you are."

"You like me because I'm smart?" Barker wasn't sure this made him feel as good as she seemed to think he should.

"That's only part of it. I like you because you make me feel great in bed, because you have a good shit detector, because you read books that have nothing to do with your work, because you remember jokes, and because you know who you are. And then there are the little things."

"Like what?"

"Oh, I don't know. Your fantastic eyes. Your taste in food and socks."

"Now you're putting me on."

"Maybe," she said. "Do we have to do this conversation anymore?"

As far as he was concerned, Nancy was his creature. He began to think that perhaps he should stop seeing his other girlfriends and concentrate on Nancy. She was mucho smart and ambitious, although he realized this might cause problems later on. She knew how to dress, and she didn't mind eating alone in a restaurant, something not many girls wanted to—or could—do. It was a measure of her self-confidence. She had told him this herself.

"When did you say your parents are coming to visit?" Barker asked.

"In a couple of weeks," she said. "Why?"

He wanted to see if her mother had run to fat. "Oh, I don't know, I'd just like to meet them."

"They're perfectly nice," Nancy said. She climbed out of his bed and stepped into a pair of tiny nylon underpants. He caught a glimpse of the sticky hair between her legs. He suppressed a groan of excitement. "But they're not your type."

"What does that matter?" Barker said. "Whose parents are, after all?"

"They voted for Nixon."

"So did my old man," Barker said.

Nancy smiled, a signal to Barker that she knew—however dimly—the shape of the questions that had begun to preoccupy her brainy lover. Should he abandon his other girls and concentrate on her alone? Should they live together? Could he

13

make this tremendous sacrifice without regretting it? Nancy appealed to him in many ways Barker could identify but also in ways he could not, and it was this mysterious element that intrigued him so much he decided to call it Love. "I must be in love," he said after she had left his place to go back to the library and no one was around to hear him.

A thorough scientist, Barker needed to test his theory. He called Bennie and suggested a walk by the river on the next Sunday morning.

"How can you tell the difference between wanting to fuck all the time and being in love?" Barker said, but when Bennie started to answer, he realized he didn't need to hear what Bennie had to say. "I think I may just be in love with Nancy Swan. I mean, enough to consider getting married. Jesus, listen to me."

"Believe me, I *am* listening and I know you well enough, kid, to know you'll never be able to stick with one lady. You've got too generalized an itch."

"That's what I thought. But so far Nancy seems to be able to take care of it all by herself."

"Yeah? And how long has it been?"

"About two months." The dirt path they trod had been formed by years and years of shoes scuffing away the grass on the riverbank. A man in a single scull glided upstream, his arms pumping in a rhythm so regular he looked like a wind-up toy. Barker shivered; the man in the boat was naked except for a tank top and shorts.

Bennie guffawed. You could trust Bennie to come right out and say what was on his mind. "You're too young to get married. Think about it, pal. Same face across the breakfast table every morning for the rest of your life."

"Nancy doesn't eat breakfast," Barker said. "She says it makes her nauseous."

"But still, why buy a cow when milk is so cheap?"

"I can't answer that," Barker said.

"I read in the *Globe* some society girl from New York just

married the Prince of Sikkim—man, that's at the end of the world. Pretty, too—I mean the girl's pretty. Now, why do you suppose she went and did a thing like that?" Bennie said.

"You ask the damnedest questions, Bennie. Why don't you write her a letter and ask her?" It was freezing where they walked; the wind, skimming over the water, hit them full on.

"Let's go get some coffee," Barker said, and they headed for Pearl's, a cafeteria near the middle of town. Barker's trained eyes took in the scene all at once, a visual vacuum cleaner picking up human dust: an elderly woman alone, eating beef stew out of a bowl with a spoon; a man in a sports jacket and his wife or girlfriend reading the *Globe* and dropping sections of it on the floor as they finished with them; a street person in a greasy black overcoat secured by a rope around his middle, snoozing and snoring in a corner, his mouth hanging open. Pearl's smelled like refried oil with an overlay of cigarette smoke. "You like this place because it doesn't care," Bennie said. "It isn't making any statement." They held mugs under the coffee spout; Bennie took two things of cream. They sat at a table near the front window, opaque with steam. Then, briefly, they analyzed the legs of a girl who was talking with theatrical intensity to a bored woman who looked like her sister, while a plate of waffles went cold in front of her. The legs were okay, but the ankles were definitely on the thick side. Then Barker said, "Marriage isn't something I have to do, you understand, it's just an option, one I've been considering along with all the others—there's absolutely no urgency about it. I can have Nancy any time I want—the girl is nuts about me."

"Then what the fuck are we talking about?"

"For once, I don't know. For once, I haven't the faintest idea what I'm talking about."

"It's been almost two months since my last period," Nancy told Barker over spareribs and Vegetarian's Delight. It had taken several months, but Barker had managed to slough off his lady

15

friends one by one. And it hadn't been all that easy. For instance, Gloria had taken it into her head to swallow a handful of tranquilizers, and he had had to take her to Cambridge City Hospital at three in the morning and stay there while she had her stomach pumped. While he was relieved that she hadn't croaked, Barker was so revolted by the idea of this procedure that he failed to get even the tiniest jolt of pleasure from the fact that a girl would try to kill herself over him.

"What do you mean?" he asked Nancy.

"This needs interpretation?" she said. Lately, Barker had begun to detect in the love of his life a disturbing edge of sharpness.

"Sorry," he said, putting down his chopsticks and leaning back in the plastic chair. "I guess I meant, exactly what are you trying to tell me? You've been late before, haven't you?"

"And I might be pregnant," she said. He noticed that her cheeks were very pink.

"Let's hold on there before you get all hysterical," he told her.

"I'm not hysterical," Nancy said. "My God, it's hot in here. I'm burning up."

"Shit," he said through his teeth, "I thought you were on the pill."

"I skipped a couple of days," she admitted, ducking her chin.

"You what?" Barker shouted. "Why did you do that?" The man and woman at the next table looked at them and then at each other, smirking.

"You think I did it on purpose?" Nancy said. "I forgot. I just forgot! Why is it always the woman's fault and never the man's?"

"It's the woman's fault because it's the woman who uses the birth control. You told me yourself you wouldn't sleep with me if I used a condom. You can't have it both ways, honey."

"I can't stand it in here," she said as she got up and bolted

16

from the table, hitting the neck of the man at the next table. She left Barker sitting alone, feeling conspicuous, and when the waiter came over with the check, he said, "My girlfriend suddenly felt sick; she's gone outside to get some air."

Barker was sure Nancy would be on the sidewalk, waiting for him, but she wasn't, and when he finally caught up with her, three blocks away, he was out of breath, aquiver with fright. "Listen, Nancy," he said. "Please don't worry. I'm crazy about you and I can't stand it when you get angry. I guess what you said about maybe being pregnant sort of threw me for a loop. I didn't mean to be so hard on you. Please, Nancy, stop scowling at me. Please, honey, I apologize. . . ." He was sweating with the effort to hang on to her.

Nancy burst into joyful tears, snapping shut the trap.

Barker felt good for the first time that evening, even though he was beginning to get a headache that almost blinded him.

Two days later, Nancy said, "How about we get married? I don't believe in abortion."

"What do you mean, you don't believe in abortion? Abortion is a fact, not a concept or a theory. You can approve of it or not, but you can't believe or disbelieve in it."

"Jake darling, you're nit-picking again. You're not listening to what I'm saying."

"I am listening to you. You just told me you don't approve of abortion and so we should get married."

"That's right," she said.

Bennie couldn't see it. "Girls get knocked up all the time, but they don't necessarily get married," he said. Bennie had come over to the Psychology Department, the left wing of a huge brick bird near the edge of Harvard Yard. This edifice, constructed in the 1860s, had recently been gutted and refitted with late-twentieth-century direct and indirect lighting, desks, laboratories, bathrooms, pay phones, benches, bulletin boards illuminated from above, and mailboxes. The rest of the building housed the departments of Anthropology and Sociology.

"I don't think I can ditch her now, Bennie," Barker said. "Her parents are all bent out of shape."

Bennie shrugged and said, "Suit yourself." He was in one of his mean moods.

Barker went on anyway. "Nancy won't get an abortion. She doesn't believe in it."

"That's her problem, isn't it?" Bennie said. "Hey, what's this gizmo?"

"Shit, Bennie, don't touch! It's delicately balanced. It measures eye movement."

"I'm impressed," Bennie said. "I wish I could use something like this." He slid his chin into a cuplike depression suspended between two iron rods and tapped a gauge with his right index finger, sending a needlelike arm into a pendular motion. "I said don't touch," Barker said, in a rage.

"Sorry, man, I didn't mean to jiggle it."

It took Barker half an hour to readjust the instrument he had invented, while Bennie (who never picked up his feet) shuffled off into the collegiate afternoon. It struck Barker that several things, stable up to now, had begun to wobble. Tremors of failure, sickness, panic, and frailty continued to turn up and make him uneasy and unsure. His father—a man with whom he had never gotten along the way he would have liked to (though which of them had started the war was a moot point)—was having some sort of circulatory problem down in Florida. Most worrisome of all, Barker had twice spied Von Stampler drinking coffee and munching Danish in the snack bar with a frizzy-haired, intense girl from New York named Perry something, who wore the shortest miniskirts Barker had ever laid eyes on; you could see the edge of her panties. The old goat— it occurred to Barker that his mentor might just be engaging in a little flirtation as well as mentoring. But what was more ominous than the hint of sex was the possibility that Von

Stampler might have bought himself a new star and was about to bestow on this Perry person all the love and attention that Barker had enjoyed for more than two years now. Barker recognized this chilling notion as paranoid, for his work had, if anything (and in spite of the setbacks), increased in complexity, suggestiveness, and brilliance. He was getting somewhere very interesting—everyone said so. Von Stampler himself had told him, "My boy, you may do more for the women of this world than even you suspect." So why was he worried?

In the middle of August 1964, Jacob Barker and Nancy Swan were married in a modest ceremony in the Von Stampler garden on Washington Street. Having refused to have anything to do with the wedding and indicating that they were not even planning to be present, Nancy's mother and father showed up at the last moment, throwing—at least in Barker's opinion—a pall of gloom over the proceedings. Barker's parents had arrived the night before, his father walking with the assistance of a cane. Nancy had stage-managed the entire event herself—hired the minister, arranged for food, music, flowers, and sent out the forty or so invitations; Verna Von Stampler had made it clear that she was contributing the house and nothing more. She seemed to think she was doing them a favor the size of a megaton bomb. "You poor children, you are no better than orphans."

This remark, dropped so casually, rankled. Barker was not an orphan; he had a perfectly viable set of parents and so did Nancy. But he held his tongue, not wanting to risk making the woman change her mind; the garden was spectacular and the house was on a grand, not to say distinguished, street.

Barker and his bride spent their one-week honeymoon based at a motel in Eastham, on Cape Cod. Nancy was not exactly thrilled by the accommodations—she had pushed for a hotel in town—but put up with it and with the weather (it rained four out of the seven days) and complained no more than he felt she had a right to.

"This mattress feels like a hammock," Nancy said, getting out of bed and arching her naked back, a maneuver that pulled her breasts ceilingward. You could hardly tell she was pregnant; her long body absorbed the subtle roundness she insisted on calling fat.

"Two hammocks," Barker said. "One for you, one for me. Come back to your hammock, child."

"Later," Nancy said. "What are we going to do today?" She began to brush her hair, the same place over and over again, trying to flatten it.

"How about a walk through the bird preserve down the road?" he said. He was desperate. There was nothing to do when it rained, and it was now raining steadily; water hitting the roof sounded like the far-off applause of a polite audience and was, in its relentless sound, somewhat reassuring: hooray for Jacob Barker and his beautiful bride, may they live forever. But it also depressed him because this was his honeymoon and he was drowning. Listening to the rain and to the crackling noise made by Nancy's hairbrush in their flimsy love nest made Barker think about how poor he was and how far he had to go. His pride was bruised: he was unable to offer his wife of three days anything more than a walk in the rain. Suppose they had a fatal accident on Route 6 today or the next day? Not for nothing was this known as the most murderous stretch of road on the entire East Coast. The end: none of his colleagues would ever cheer and reward (with money, plaques and scrolls, newspaper profiles, honors, fellowships, unscheduled sabbaticals, and—when he was much much older—testimonials and festschrifts) his important, his unique contribution to the field of psychology. Barker was used to thinking in such bloated terms, enjoying his fantasies as if they carried the weight and force of reality.

"Birds?" said Nancy. Her face did a tricky number, then

settled into a study in surprise and disappointment. "Are you serious? No, you've got to be kidding."

"Why not?" he said. "I understand they have green herons there. Have you ever seen a green heron?"

"I don't think so," she said. "Why don't you go? I'll stay here and do some reading."

From time to time, whenever his mind was on idle, Barker wondered whether he should blame the rain or Nancy for the fact that his first marriage began on an unresolved chord, one his ears kept unsuccessfully trying to correct. That walk he took all by himself—for years it ticked him off that Nancy had not joined him. He had stayed out longer than he planned to, getting thoroughly chilled, and sucking a sourball of loneliness and hurt that refused to dissolve.

Chapter Two

AFTER they returned from their moist honeymoon, Jacob Barker moved his wife's possessions, in a van borrowed from a cousin of Bennie's, from her place to his, in Watertown. It was just large enough for the two of them. After the baby arrived it would be too small. Nancy said, "We can keep him in the bedroom with us—at least for a while." Barker didn't think too much of this idea—at the very least it would put a crimp in their lovemaking—but they agreed to postpone what seemed like an inevitable argument over where to park the baby. Barker put dibs on his old study, a windowless area the size of a cloakroom. After all, as he said, "I've already got my stuff in there." Nancy's books and papers, her boxes of file cards and piles of anthropology journals, her Smith-Corona typewriter, paper clips, ball-points, rubber cement, and color photographs of lean black male bodies posed against azure skies all got stowed in the bedroom, the spillover shoved into a closet off the kitchen. They were crammed in so tightly Barker had to pick his way across the bedroom, high-stepping over cartons and piles of books. He told her it reminded him of the stateroom in *A Night at the Opera*. Without smiling or missing a beat Nancy said, "Is there anything we can do about it? Should I give my clothes to Goodwill and my books to City Hospital? Is that what you want?"

"We can move," he said. In fact they had begun to look on two Saturday mornings but so far had not found the right place. There was an apartment in Waltham that Nancy liked and about which Barker said, "Over my dead body," thus closing the discussion forever. Nancy's parents refused to help them, and as for Barker's mother and father, their monthly gift of fifty dollars—"they think it's princely," Barker said—was deposited in the account he had planted in the Cambridge Savings Bank for the baby.

The two of them were getting along amazingly well, considering, and Barker began to enjoy the rhythms of domesticity. The only shadow that fell across them was Nancy's tendency to insist on emotional engagement. She was a fighter. "I just can't let things go," she explained. "If something's bothering me and won't go away unless I talk about it, then I'm going to talk about it. Why should I suffer?"

"Why should *I*?" Barker asked.

One day, a little over a month after they had set up housekeeping together, Nancy went double, opened her mouth, and yowled like a cat in heat. She sat right down on the linoleum in the kitchen, where she had been washing a pan in the sink, and rocked back and forth with her forehead touching her knees. Barker's comfortable postbreakfast repleteness was replaced by terror.

"Nancy," he said, getting up, "what's the matter? Here, let me help you." He extended his arm for this purpose.

"Don't touch me," she shrieked. "I'm bleeding, I'm dying. I feel like I've been shot in the stomach."

"Don't be silly," he said, taking a step backwards. "You're not dying"—although he wasn't sure about this himself—"I'm going to call Dr. Listner. Stay right where you are."

Nancy groaned. "Where would I go?" she said into her knees.

It wasn't Nancy dying but a three-ounce male infant. Or, to be precise, the baby was already dead when Nancy began to bleed. The doctor told Barker that it wasn't all that unusual for a woman to lose a baby after the third month: "Happens all the time, unfortunately, but you young people, you seem to weather adversity awfully well these days—get right back up in the saddle, eh?" He winked at Barker. The doctor's vague statistic didn't help Nancy, who acted as if the remainder of her own life was being numbered in days rather than years. She lay on their bed—fully dressed except for shoes—in the kind of torpor Barker associated with fictional women suffering an extended menopausal episode. It drove him nuts. She also refused to talk about anything to do with the baby.

Barker went to Bennie. "Talk about irony," Bennie said. "I mean you marry her because she's pregnant"—Bennie had begun to say "knocked up" but apparently changed his mind midway into the first word—"and then she goes and loses the kid. That's what I call an Early-American irony, the real thing."

"I feel like shit, Bennie, I feel as if I knew that baby. He was a person, he was my son. We were going to name him Nick." This admission pulled unexpected tears from Barker's eyes. "Jesus," he said, "I'm crying. What's going on?" He drew in as much air as he could, swallowed hard, shook his head, shot out of his chair, and went over to the window in Bennie's office; meaning to rest his brow against it and instead cracking a long thread into the pane of glass. "I broke your window," he said. "I broke the goddamn window."

Bennie leaned into his swivel chair so far he seemed about to fall over backwards. There was a smile. Was he angry or amused? Bennie said, "Don't worry about it, man. How's your head?"

Barker tried every which way to cheer up his wife. Nancy said she couldn't help it. He said she wasn't trying. She said her

24

hormones were out of whack. He told her she should make an attempt to snap out of it, a suggestion that had an effect exactly opposite to what he had in mind, for she crumbled into a mess and then shut the bedroom door in his face. He heard her banging things around behind the door. "What are you doing?" he said.

"Packing. I'm going home for the weekend."

"You must really hate me," he said. He wanted their marriage to work, saw no reason why it shouldn't. Her anger hurt him.

"Jake," she said, still behind the locked door. "Will you please go away and leave me alone?"

The only time he felt like the Jake of yore—light-stepping, energetic, prodigious, magnetic, luminous Jacob Barker—was when he was working; although each time he looked at one of his babies sitting passively on its mother's lap, he was overwhelmed with sadness—why couldn't it be his? Then he would throw an image on the screen tacked up to the lab wall or play a sound—a beep, a hiss, a thump, a crack—and he would begin to feel that old surge of energy, like freshly oxygenated blood. Work did wonders for his mental health.

Barker sat next to Nancy in the movie theater watching *Hud*. He wanted to rip off the arm between them; it dug into his side when he tried to get closer to Nancy. He liked the way Patricia Neal used her face. Not subtle but convincing; she communicated in a sexual language that made a lot of noise. She was miscast, of course, but still it worked, and maybe it was the miscasting that made it work—the whore named Victoria, the Princess of Wales called Conchita. Melvyn Douglas overacted, but that was nothing new; he was interesting to watch, too. Barker held onto Nancy's hand and began to kiss her mouth, their passion, for once, meeting not only in the same measure but on the same note. "I love you," he whispered into her hairline, and when she smiled, her teeth caught light from the screen and radiated like Halloween makeup. For the moment Barker was happy. He didn't even think about the dead baby or Nancy's bad moods.

Life with Nancy Swan was . . . what? Constant turmoil, feelings splitting and creating new feelings, emotions spilling every which way—the glamour girl had turned into a nervous wreck. Could it be his fault?

Determined to get her Ph.D. in three years, Nancy was an academic athlete. She studied almost constantly and even took a book along with her when they went on a picnic to Walden Pond with some friends. She stayed in the library until they doused the lights at 3:00 A.M. Anyone else he might have suspected of cheating on him, but not Nancy; she came home pale and bleary-eyed, having sat on a hard chair in bad light, grinding up the stuff and ingesting it in industrial quantities. He suggested to her that maybe she should take a rest, take some time off, and she, misunderstanding his motives, blew up, accusing him of envying her dedication.

"You don't want me to succeed," she said.

"Not true," he said. "Why wouldn't I want you to succeed? I love you."

"You want to be the only star in the family," she said.

"Nancy," he said through a sigh, "what can I do to convince you I'm on your side?"

"Maybe you can't convince me," she said to him. "Maybe I wouldn't believe you no matter *what* you said."

There was something terrifying about the way Nancy went after the gold medal. She organized a study group of fellow Ph.D. candidates. The four men and three women (including Nancy) met every Wednesday night after supper in Barker's living room, sitting crouched over the coffee table, spilling papers and notes all over the floor and interrupting each other until long past Barker's bedtime. Sometimes he just went to bed while they were still there; maybe they didn't need sleep, but he did. Their voices, melted together, came through the wall in a blur. Occasionally he would be jolted from sleep by an especially loud-voiced fellow named Harry something, to whom he had taken an instant and intense dislike. This was because whenever Harry came to a study session, he would march right in and sit himself down on Barker's couch without even saying hello to the couch's owner or in any way indicating that he knew Barker existed. When Barker complained to Nancy, she said that he was overreacting to Harry's style, the result of his preoccupation with things of the mind.

"Harry's rude. He's a pig," Barker said.

"Harry's got the clearest, most far-reaching head of the whole bunch of us." Was Nancy including Barker in the "us"? He couldn't tell.

"Does that excuse his inexcusable manners?" Barker asked.

"Come off it, Jake, just don't pay any attention to Harry. What's the big deal here? Okay, so he doesn't get an A for politeness, so fucking what? That's not what he's here for." Nancy's cheeks were coloring up, not a good sign.

"It's my house," Barker said. "I mean *our* house."

"You're impossible," Nancy said.

It was an argument Barker suspected could not be resolved. So trivial on one level and so profound on another, it uncovered the dull nugget that created the pain between them, that thing that made them so different from one another. Still, Barker was profoundly hurt whenever Harry showed up. Am I too proud? he asked himself. Why should I care so much that Harry won't say hello to me?

Barker watched, baffled and concerned, as his wife worked out; he worried as she went to lectures that were not required, read books not on any syllabus, studied too long and too hard for exams. It seemed to him that the more lather she generated, the clearer and more desperate the panic in her eyes. Her effort wasn't paying off.

One afternoon Barker found Nancy stretched out on the bed, eyes shut. She stiffened as he entered.

"Hi, honey," he said, sitting beside her. "You're wearing that green thing again. Bad news?"

"My shirt has nothing to do with it," she said. She half sat up, shifting her weight from her back to her elbows. "I didn't get it."

"The fellowship? You didn't get it?"

She swung her head slowly back and forth. "You said I would."

"What do *I* know?" he said. "I thought you had a good chance at it, but what do I know about the politics of the anthropology establishment? It's not my field."

Unexpectedly she said, "It's because I'm a woman!" Clever girl, she was making it easier on herself by blaming the other guy. He grabbed at it eagerly. "Yes, of course," Barker said, "I'm sure that's it. How many times has it gone to a female?"

"As a matter of fact, never, not once. I feel a little better. Not good, you understand, but better. It's so typically male." Nancy sat up for real and swung her legs over the side of the bed. He hated that green shirt; she always wore it when something had gone wrong for her. It had once belonged, he thought, to her father. "It still hurts terribly. I was counting on it. I know, I shouldn't count chickens, but sometimes you just can't help it."

She mustn't cry again. "I know, Nance," he said, "I know." Barker felt wonderfully compassionate; his empathy warmed his blood and suffused his skin.

"I don't think you do, but thanks anyway," she said.

Chapter Three

IT WAS in the year 1968 that Jacob Barker first noticed that the smooth face he was accustomed to greeting in the mirror above the bathroom sink first thing in the morning had started to break up like parched soil. He was too young for this, but there it was, a crack here, a pucker there, a tiny vertical line between the eyes. He decided to grow a beard; oddly, it came in a shade lighter than the hair on his head. It itched like blazes for three weeks, then stopped. Barker thought the beard enhanced his appeal, and apparently he was right, for more girls looked at him with open desire than ever before. The beard was as effective as a sex pheromone. The beard below the eyes: the face of a lover.

Twenty-eight years old, an assistant professor, Jacob Barker was teaching a survey course attended primarily by freshmen. He liked this class, as he knew the material cold and his memory could deliver fact and theory without having to consult his notes more than once every fifteen minutes or so. He also liked the dramatic set-up of the lecture hall. An upholstered amphitheater of steeply banked seats with foldout arms (designed for right-handed people), it was located in one of

Harvard's newer buildings, Stuyvesant Hall. The room itself (so one learned by reading a bronze plaque affixed to the wall) was the gift of Laurence J. and Miriam K. Levine, June 1964.

Harvard's campus seethed like a volcano about to blow its stack. Overnight, it seemed, every single thing that people like Otto Von Stampler, Barker's high school principal, his mother and father, the editors of *Time* magazine believed to be true, namely that the statue in the main square—a somewhat androgynous figure representing the Spirit of American Freedom and thought to be made of bronze—was in fact, composed of filthy clay, stones, and gilt and threatened to collapse during the next rainfall. "But," cried the *Time* editors and the others, "we have always been told, it is so written in the history books, all public statues in this country have been certified as bronze. No inferior materials have ever been employed." However, the left arm of the statue was clearly melting off, the forehead was pocked and spongy, the boots looked like rotten bandages; one wanted to avert one's eyes, they were so disgusting. But now students had discovered their voices and were yelling at the top of their lungs. Barker was fascinated. Still wearing the mantle saved for golden boys, a new father (for the unpredictable Nancy had recently given birth to a cranky baby boy they named Guy after nobody in particular), he found the current unrest almost unbearably exciting, even—he was ashamed to admit—when Cambridge cops punched the breasts of female protestors and brought billy clubs down over the skulls of young men sprung from so-called best families. It speeded up his pulse; and in his heart he could not sympathize with the authorities, for they had egregiously put something over on the young for years and years, for centuries. He thought it extremely clever of these kids to point to the statue and demand an explanation in a youthful exhibition of outraged consumerism. As for some of their methods—well, Barker felt funny about the basement bombings, the Molotov cocktails hurled without specific target, buildings trashed, cops shot on purpose. *Trop de zèle*, he figured, there must be equally efficient ways to make a point, although he couldn't think of a single one as good as a decisive explosion.

Nancy was obsessed by the baby; she nursed it almost constantly.

"Doesn't he ever stop drinking?" Barker asked.

"He's not drinking. He's eating," Nancy told him. "And he's on the small side, so he has to eat a lot of little meals instead of two or three big ones. His stomach is so tiny, Jake; just think, it's no bigger than a walnut." This idea was captivating; what she said made sense, too. Still, it bugged him the way she fussed over the infant. He was always on the tit, gurgling and guggling while on Nancy's face was the sort of dumb bliss Barker associated with ballet dancers. At the same time as Barker begrudged her the time she spent with Guy, he realized his feelings had a high jealousy content. This was his curse: the clarity with which he saw his failings coupled with his failure to do anything about them.

"What would you like me to do?" Nancy said. Her voice told him that whatever he answered, it would be the wrong thing.

"I don't know," he said, "but you're going to spoil him if you keep picking him up every time he makes the slightest noise and sticking him back on the spigot."

"Spigot!" Nancy said. "Your humor's losing something, Jake."

"I'm sorry, Nancy," he said automatically.

"Hey," she said, looking up at him from eyes that had been gazing at the fuzzy skull of their child, "I believe you just might be jealous. Are you, Jake? Are you by any chance jealous?"

"Me?"

"No, the other Jacob in the room. Yes you, you resent the time I spend with the baby. Look at him, Jake, isn't he the

31

cutest baby you ever saw, look at his little fat cheeks. Don't you just want to hold him close to you forever?"

There were moments when Barker wanted to lock eyes with Guy and try to listen to his thoughts—if a baby could be said to have thoughts. He wanted to wrench him from his mother's embrace, pulling off the tight little mouth now clamped around his mother's nipple and bruising his eyes with masculine kisses. But he couldn't move, for he was paralyzed by reticence in front of her. Why, why? Why couldn't he act like a normal person?

"It's nothing extraordinary," Nancy said. "New fathers often feel that way."

"Fuck new fathers," Barker said. "You're not talking to new fathers, you're talking to me, Jake Barker, your husband."

"You know," she said, "it's not a good idea to fight in front of the baby. Even if he can't understand, he can tell by your voice that you're angry."

"And you're not?"

"Oh please, Jake, isn't it time for your meeting? I wish you'd go now, everything's getting upset." As she said this, the baby gathered itself into a kind of knot, then straightened abruptly and threw up into Nancy's lap. "See what I mean?" she said.

"Aw, shit," Barker said.

Banished, he threw on his parka and left the apartment (they had recently moved to larger quarters, the third floor of a big old house owned by a pair of shrinks) and ventured into the chilly Cambridge night. He walked at a fast clip toward the Lutheran Church, where a group of agitated Harvard students and a scattering of Harvard faculty were, at this moment, assembling to plan their participation in a statewide rally for the purpose of lighting a fire for peace under Lyndon Johnson's ass. Barker had become politicized largely as a reaction to Nancy's excessive maternity. He's up, she's down; she's harp, he's cymbals; she's silent, he screams.

Just as you know that the next time you put your toe through the hole in the sheet it's goodbye sheet, Barker knew that he and Nancy could not live together much longer without doing damage to one or both of them.

It was after a brilliant, funny, eye-opening lecture on a winter day in 1968—the day after the antiwar meeting in the basement of the Lutheran Church—that a small group of students gathered around the lectern on the stage where Barker was cooling down (for whenever he lectured he perspired like a stuck pig). Each of a half-dozen boys and girls clamored for his attention. One wanted an extension on a paper—"my mother's getting married tomorrow." That was a new one and Barker granted it, on the grounds not of veracity but of novelty. Another wanted a clarification of the term "cognition." Yet another asked Barker when his office hours were, and when Barker said, "I wrote them down on the blackboard first thing, classes one, two, and three. Where were you?" the boy acted hurt. "I was right here," the boy said. Barker wanted to pull his long, shaggy hair. "I didn't mean literally," Barker said.

"Oh," said the kid. "But when are they? You're my adviser."

Not for the first time, Barker wondered about Harvard's famous admissions standards. Where were they when this boy came up for consideration? Had he actually got above four hundred on his verbal SAT? What the hell. If he were at South Dakota U., would things be better? Barker sighed and gave the boy the information he needed.

He disposed of students four and five in short order. Number six, a tall girl with long glossy—or was it greasy?—hair, wearing jeans and an army jacket far too big for her, held back, looked frequently down at her chest, then back over at him. The others drifted off and she, too, started to leave, when Barker said, "You in the army boots, did you want to speak to me?"

"Um, well, I guess so." Her color was grayish: she was not a washer.

33

"Why don't you walk me over to my office? I've got someone coming in half an hour. We can talk on the way."

He asked her name. She said, "Patty. Patricia."

"Patty what?"

"Patty Weissman."

"Freshman?"

Patty ducked her head and nodded.

"Well, Patty Freshman, what is it you wanted to ask me about?" She was so poignantly young, it made him feel middle-aged. She looked more high school than college. The skin on her face was as tight as a bathing cap; her eyes were huge, at least compared to her nose, a little snubby thing, and her slit of a mouth. He would have liked to take a gander at her eighteen-year-old breasts, but that was obviously out of the question. The breasts were in the promised land.

"I'm very interested in psychology," she told him. "I mean, like it makes you understand why certain people act the way they do."

"It's certainly supposed to," he said.

"Well, I was wondering what was involved in concentrating in psychology. I mean, like, how many labs and was I the sort of person who should go into it. I did okay in science back in high school, but your lectures are, well—they're different. It's something I could see myself doing seriously." Patty's thin little mouth moved vigorously as she spoke, drawing back to reveal dead-white teeth.

"Where are you from, Patty?"

"Stamford, Connecticut," she said precisely. "My dad's in real estate."

"That's very interesting," Barker said. They had reached the door to his office. He took out a brass key, inserted and turned it in the lock, threw open the door, and gestured for her to go in first. He flicked on the ceiling light—it threw a naked glare—and dropped his papers on the desk. He avoided looking at Patty. Why? Riffles of heavy emotion seemed to rise from her body as steam off a pond in chill morning air. But it wasn't quite emotion, it was closer to pure sensation. Barker entertained an impulse to grab her skinny shoulders (for, unbidden, Patty had shed her jacket and stood before him in a gigantic man's shirt that could not disguise an emaciated torso), spin her round, and shove her back through the door. He dismissed the impulse.

"Sit down, Patty," he said, sweeping some journals off his guest chair. "We have ten minutes to talk."

"Thanks," she said, and sat down, crouching over her bony knees as if she had cramps.

Barker stared, making an honest attempt to read Patty: was she really an innocent or did she know what she was doing to him? He sat down and crossed his legs, praying that she had not noticed that his penis was acting up again. Damn thing never followed his instructions.

Patty asked him a couple of questions that revealed she had his discipline somewhat confused with psychiatry on the one hand and physics on the other. He explained—quite patiently, he thought—just where she was wrong. He mentioned his work.

"Do you mean girls and boys are different as soon as they're born? Girls are smarter?"

"That's what we're doing our best to find out," he said. "Look, Patty"—and here the words emerged on their own, without any help from him—"if you're really interested, why don't you visit the lab and see what we're up to." He did not expect her to refuse this invitation; she came and hung around for over an hour two days later.

She paid a second visit the following week. Her presence there made Barker's fingers nimbler, his insights more startling; the Barker machine revved up and threatened to take off. He began to obsess about Patty. When he went home at night, he looked at Nancy and saw Patty's face superimposed on his wife's, like a papier mâché mask. "Would you like to go get a cup of coffee and talk some more?" he said to Patty on her third visit as he shrugged into his coat and prepared to leave the lab for the afternoon.

"Oh, that would be very nice," she said.

"Omar's all right with you?"

Patty nodded prettily and lowered her eyes.

Omar's was so hot Barker's glasses steamed up and he had to take them off and wipe them with his handkerchief. They sat down at a table smaller than the top of a garbage can. He felt conspicuous: the teacher taking refreshment in public with his student. But it was done all the time; it was a sight so commonplace in Cambridge that hardly anyone noticed. Still, Barker told himself, he was not without a conscience. He was married, a father, and the fact that he and his wife got along about as well as two toddlers fighting over the same shovel was irrelevant. Patty was very quiet. She ordered tea and drank it dark and straight.

"Would you like a piece of pastry or something?" Barker said. "They're quite good, especially the ones with strawberry filling."

She made a face. "Oh, no thank you, I'm fine."

"Well, you won't mind if I have one, will you? I'm famished; I think I forgot to eat lunch."

"You must be the absent-minded professor I heard about."

He winced at her joke. "You might say so," he said. "Then again, I usually remember the important things."

Barker felt the twin engines—sex and power—surge along buried pathways and come out on his face with an intensity most girls were unable to resist. He was too smart and too careful to beam his look on the wrong girls, girls who would surely refuse him. Barker rarely suffered rejection.

It was hard work; he talked, Patty listened. She asked some questions that indicated she had begun to understand what he was working on. He was delighted that she was concentrating on his face. Her large eyes had fastened themselves on his own. And all the time he talked about left side of brain, right side, about awareness, recognition, and so on. Soon Barker was obliged to keep swallowing the lust that flooded his system. At that moment he didn't give a hoot about the left side of anyone's brain, he wanted only to devour this girl. He told her she was one of the smartest students he'd seen in seven years of teaching. "You have a grasp far beyond your years," he told her, mimicking the Von Stampler style. "You have the makings of a brilliant psychologist. You think laterally. That's extremely rare in someone as young as you are."

Patty lapped it up, a kitten at a saucer of sweet cream. It almost made him feel guilty, the ease with which he fed her.

By the time they left Omar's, she had agreed to meet him the next afternoon on Acacia Street, where they would get into his car and drive twelve miles to a Best Western motel.

She said very little during the forty-minute journey. Barker registered under a fake name—it tickled him to write "Mr. and Mrs. William James" in the book—and they took possession of the damp room. It was one of those places where he had to drag an enormous, thick curtain across the entire wall because the wall was made of glass and anyone on the outside of it could have seen everything going on inside. And as soon as Barker drew the curtain, the room was thrown into a murky dusk. They stood blinking at one another.

"Aren't you going to take off your things?" Barker asked Patty, for he read confusion on her face. A major problem with females: so rarely clear-cut, you could never tell for sure what was bothering them; you had to keep analyzing and guessing all the time. "Something the matter?" he said.

"It's cold in here," Patty said, but in so low a voice Barker had to strain to hear her. She did an exaggerated shiver, then wrapped her arms around her middle.

"Let's see if we can turn up the heat," he said. He fiddled with the thermostat, saw that it was locked at sixty-seven degrees, and pretended to adjust it. When he turned around, Patty, still in her hideous jacket, was sitting in an armchair and looking up at him dully.

"I'm not sure . . . ," she said, but her face said otherwise. Her face told Barker that she had already caved in—if indeed she had had much strength to begin with. Her mouth might as well have said it outright: you have chosen me from among scores of women; I will let you do whatever it is you do with women.

"Would you like to talk about it? You have every right to change your mind, Patty. I don't want us to do this if I have to persuade you. It's got to be something both of us want in the same loving way." He was afraid that if he began to undress he would frighten her off. Maybe it was the room that checked her: it was a dump, with every single thing in it somehow secured, the floral and seascape prints nailed to the wall, the topheavy lamp bolted to the table, the chairs chained to the floor. Who would want to steal any of this junk? The suspense was killing him. It occurred to Barker that Patty might be a cocktease. He sat down in the only other chair. Upholstered in a durable gray man-made fabric shot with silver thread, it stank of cigarette smoke.

"It's just that . . . ," she said. The girl was mastering the art of the unfinished sentence.

"What, Patty? It's just that what?"

"You'll laugh."

"I promise I won't."

"Promise?"

"I just did."

"Okay," she said. She closed her eyes and said softly, "My mother said I shouldn't go out with any of my professors."

"And you always do what your mother tells you."

"I try."

"Well, I'll tell you what, Patty. We won't go out together. Going to bed isn't exactly going out, now, is it? It's making love, something altogether different from going to a movie or walking by the river or meeting friends for a beer. But look, honey, if we don't make up our minds soon, we'll have to pack our bags and start off for home."

38

"Bags?"

"Just a figure of speech." Impatience made Barker's head pound and the skin on the back of his neck prickle as if brushed with burrs. He was just about to abandon hope, when Patty jumped up and cried, "But I want to!" She began to undress so quickly that her limbs were a blur. Then she stood there buck naked, smiling at him in a shy sort of way, as if he were a doctor about to listen to her heartbeat.

"Oh my God," he said.

"What's the matter?" Patty asked, frowning.

"Are you sick, Patty, do you have a serious disease—I mean condition?" Patty was so thin she made Nancy seem obese. Where most people had a little something between bone and skin—a layer of fat, a layer of meat—Patty had nothing, zip. Her skin covered pelvis, knee, shoulder like soft grayish paper on a knobby gift. She was a walking corpse, risen from a pile of the dead. He wanted to weep: the breasts he had longed to see were flat as any man's. He shut his eyes against the sight and got into bed.

"What do you mean?" Patty said. "I'm fine. I had a physical just before I left for college. The doctor said I was in perfect health."

"Did he by any chance suggest that you put on a few pounds?"

"Heavens no," Patty said.

What to do? His lust, in the face of this horror, had gone limp. What to do? "Why don't you climb into bed and have a little fun? Make this old man happy."

"Old," she said. "You couldn't be more than thirty-three. That's not old."

"Twenty-eight," Barker told her, as she opened the covers and slid into bed beside him. "But let it pass."

He closed his eyes and prayed, and soon he felt the limpness being replaced by energy. He worked very hard. All the while he was pinching her cold little clitoris and stroking her chest—for he could not give this place a happier name—the image of Buchenwald inmates when the Allies discovered them, no more than a day or two away from death, kept intruding itself between him and Patty. And when she responded with vigorous pelvic labor, her bones hurt him, leaving him bruised on both hips.

After it was over and he lay on his back, exhausted, Patty started to talk about her roommate and about how they both ran six miles a day, rain or shine, and about what grade did he think she'd get in his course, while he thought about Nancy and how she had given all her love to their baby and had none left over for him.

It wasn't meant to work that way, was it? Didn't it go: the more love you have to give, the more you have in reserve? But he was forced to smile; this wraith was what he deserved for betraying his marriage vows. It might be a sign from God to cut it out, but then again, it might just be a reminder to Barker to be more prudent next time.

Chapter Four

◆

IT WAS a conversation with his new girlfriend, Anita Andrews, that made Jacob Barker, age thirty-eight, decide to write a book. Not that he didn't feel secure at Harvard. Barker had been spared the fate of some of his colleagues, that of being dumped after they had achieved the rank of assistant professor. This, in spite of the fact that they had published like crazy, most of it monographs on areas of research so arcane one needed a gloss to understand them. Off they went to places like Oklahoma, Kansas, Louisiana, often with less knowledge of small-town life than a kid watching "Leave It to Beaver." The dry truth of these towns was crushing to some of these men, who lost the will to hustle and settled down in ranch homes near the campus and read two-day-old *New York Times* while their wives contributed to potluck suppers and grew skilled in the art of passing gossip without getting tackled. Barker stayed put, partly through his own brilliance and partly through the power wielded by his mentor, Otto Von Stampler, retired but still a potent force in the department he helped found. "Keep this man," he said in a voice grown croaky. "Keep him, he's very good. No, he's better than good.

41

One of these days, you will see, he will do something so spectacular that sparks from his achievement will shower down upon you and light up this entire institution. Keep this man, don't banish him with the others." The tenure-granting committee was not altogether sold on Barker; although his classes were invariably oversubscribed, there were things about him that had begun to trouble a few people on the committee, like his yelling at a student for asking a "stupid" question and his growing standoffishness with junior faculty and graduate students. Although the Psychology Department was in no sense a team, Barker was nonetheless known as "not a team player." But they bent under Von Stampler's weight and Barker was awarded an associate professorship. Thus, Publish or Perish meant little to him. Still, the book idea seemed a good one.

In 1978 Barker was now, as previously, said to have "promise." At what precise moment "promise" fades and becomes "achievement" he could not say, but thinking about it made him uneasy. He knew men of fifty whom people regarded as still in the "promising" stage, but he couldn't go along with that; if you hadn't done it at fifty, you probably weren't going to do it at all.

"If I was a mathematician like you," Barker said to Bennie, over a lunch to celebrate his appointment, "my best days would be over. You guys seem to peak at seventeen and a half. I guess you could say I'm lucky to be in a relatively soft field."

"Soft," Bennie echoed. "Try puréed." He held a tongue sandwich in both hands and looked at it quizzically. He bit into it, chewed, and swallowed. "When is Boston going to get a decent deli? This stuff tastes like bus transfers."

Barker felt expansive. He could relax now about tenure; coincidentally, he and Nancy had at last decided to call it quits. Relieved to think of the liberty that awaited, Barker was willing to give her whatever she wanted—pictures they had bought together, the six-foot couch, the designer sheets on sale, the butcher-block table and thirteen-inch color television set, the curtains, the pots and pans, and all the LPs, except Glenn Gould doing the Goldberg Variations and Schwarzkopf's *Der Rosenkavalier.*

From time to time Barker suffered pangs about his son Guy. The boy was ten years old and overweight—a fatso whose right hand seemed to be on a nonstop journey between food supply and mouth. Guy went to the Locke School, the only decent public elementary school in Cambridge. The boy wasn't doing well in school—his teachers complained about his faulty concentration, his inability to make friends. The principal suggested a counselor, a notion that sent Nancy into a snit. She blamed the school, Guy's teachers, and Barker himself, accusing him of "distance. You're a distant father." Barker sidestepped the potential argument. "Why don't you take him to a counselor the way the lady at Locke suggested?"

"He doesn't need that kind of help," Nancy said. "He needs a couple of teachers who understand him and a father who cares."

"What's to understand?" Barker said. "Guy hates school and doesn't like the other kids. Big deal."

"For a psychologist, you're amazingly dense," Nancy said. She was folding laundry she had dumped in a large mound on their bed. Barker stood by the window, looking down into the street where a woman was trying to back her station wagon into a parking space too small for it; he wondered how long it would take before she gave up. "You know I'm not that kind of psychologist," he said, watching his breath mist the inside of the window, demonstrating that he was a pulsing organism, something life with Nancy made him doubt from time to time. They argued about everything, from what kind of paper towels to buy to what to do about Guy. Large/small, concrete/abstract, trivial/momentous—the number and variety of the things about which they differed, sometimes with a shrug, often on the edge of violence, astonished him. They ought to have separated years before; Barker credited inertia and bad judgment for their not having done so. Or was it possible—a two-hundred-watt light bulb went on inside his head—was it possible they stayed together for the sole purpose of making each other miserable? Small wonder Guy was a fuck-up at age ten. His parents' woes had gotten to him. Poor kid, poor fish. It was time to change his water.

There were two women in Harvard's Psychology Department, two out of sixteen members. Anita Andrews, an assistant professor, was one of them. Anita told Barker that when she was interviewed for the job, the head of the department, a slippery number named Bruce Factor, had informed her that one of her recommenders had written that she had an "attractive personality," something she insisted would never in a million years be said about a male candidate. Barker thought she was being oversensitive about this, but it wasn't worth an argument. He liked her too much to argue—besides, she really did have an attractive personality. Unlike Nancy, she didn't make a federal case out of everything, nor did she bring every topic back to herself; and when she had something to say she said it straight, the way she thought it, without injecting an editor between thought and speech. In a word, she was natural. After the angst-ridden Nancy, Barker found this trait intoxicating.

Anita first caught Barker's eye because of the way she looked: she was his type—tall and thin, rangy like a cowgirl, with light brown hair pulled back in a ponytail and held in place by a wide rubber band. She wore long solid-colored skirts and cowl-neck sweaters at work, and high, incredibly sexy leather boots. She called these clothes her "Harvard disguise," and as soon as she got home she changed into tight bell-bottoms and sandals—leftover hippie clothes. She looked twenty-seven or -eight tops, but was actually thirty-four. Anita had been married briefly when she and her husband were fellow students and antiwar activists at Berkeley. "Tommy wasn't the reliable type; he fucked everything on two legs. Also, he was a baby. His favorite word was 'gimme.' Do we have to talk about him?"

"Just tell me what he does now," Barker said. He was fascinated by her former life.

"He's a CPA. He makes scads of money at it, but he tells everybody he's a screenwriter."

"And do they believe him?" Barker said.

"Some do, I guess, and some don't."

It was hard to get her to talk about herself; she preferred to talk about his work. She asked moderately intelligent questions. "Jake," she said, "your work could be—pardon the expression—seminal."

"But suppose I discover that boys are smarter than girls?" Barker said.

"You won't," Anita said. Her interest in his work made him happy; moreover, it dovetailed with her own, for her area was adult gender roles, the family, nature versus nurture, that sort of political thing. Her mission, she said, was to destroy the notion of penis envy, a subject about which, alas, she had little sense of humor. But he forgave her this—the girl was entitled to one or two blind spots. And as a matter of fact, he was prepared to agree with her on this point; even he thought Freud's theory to be somewhat completely off-the-wall.

For a girl to whom sexual politics was almost as important as sex, Anita was surprisingly nice to him. She was so warm and responsive, in fact, that Barker began to wonder why he had spent so much time and energy seducing his students. Still, it was strange and wonderful how these several forbidden encounters inflamed him, the chance he took each time, feeding the fire that raced through his body. He knew how risky it was to bite the forbidden peach, the taboo cherry, but he just couldn't help himself—they were luscious, he was hungry. He was hooked.

Barker would search in his mirror for clues, try to see himself with their sweet young eyes: a sturdy beard and, above that, a face scarred by the rigors of intellectual exercise, lines born of thought, study, and conjecture. He looked the part of the brilliant teacher. But there was something else, too, an invitation to a girl to couple. He would almost blush. He'd think, Jesus, it's as obvious as my front teeth. It was the gestalt of his face, the "look," an amalgam of authority, hope, and animal longing. It was male mastery, appetite informing tissue. He radiated sexuality, that was the long and the short of it. What's more, it complemented a look—vulnerable, biddable, without any sort of armor—he could recognize instantly in his potential "victim." Whenever he saw one of these girls, their eyes met and they held a silent conversation, confirming the mutual truth. The other ones—those females uninterested in what he had to offer—he avoided. The coming of Anita into his life was a blessing; besides, she made love like the best of his girls. Maybe, at this late hour, he was finally losing his addiction to forbidden fruit.

Barker had moved out of his and Nancy's apartment and was again living as a bachelor. He admitted to himself—though not to anyone else—that this new life took more adjustment than he could have foretold: all those chores—putting a new roll of toilet paper on the back of the john, within reach, before he used up the old one, making sure he had a clean shirt for work and a couple of clean sheets every couple of weeks, buying replacements for light bulbs and garbage bags. He opened the icebox one day and found half a loaf of bread that had grown lime-colored fuzz. He smiled ruefully, thinking how dependent he had become on Nancy, and reminded himself to thank her one of these days.

Barker hated to eat alone; the silence of his empty apartment—three rooms overlooking Cambridge Common, sublet from a friend of Bennie's on sabbatical—depressed him. He turned the lights on at night and left them on (except in the bedroom), ate out at a neighborhood bar and grill that featured a weekly Mexican night, and brought Anita home as often as he could.

Anita lived in a house she had bought jointly with some

friends in Watertown, near where Barker had lived as a graduate student. They had divided the house vertically, so that Anita had three floors and so did they. When Barker lay next to her in bed, he could hear them on the other side of the wall.

"Why does she have to vacuum on Sunday morning?" Barker asked.

"Who says it's Jeannie?" Anita said. "Actually, I think it's Carl. She has a bad back or something so he does the heavy work."

"You don't say," Barker said. He had never in his life worked a vacuum cleaner and wondered if it was fun. He decided only the first few times. After that, like all mindless tasks, it would get boring. His own place was cleaned by Kate, a girl he had rented from Harvard Student Agencies. He rarely saw Kate; she left him notes in a prep-school hand, telling him that he was running out of Mr. Clean or paper towels or please to vote for Jimmy Carter. "Come on, let's do it again," Barker said, grabbing Anita around the waist and pulling her smack up against him. She seemed to like his nakedness—a joyous contrast to Nancy, who acted as if his penis was an open switchblade. "You're awesome," Anita murmured, teasing him, her eyes closed and her hand busy between his legs.

Barker began to think about what life with Anita might be like on a permanent basis, and they circled the subject on tiptoe. Barker and Nancy were still legally married, but the final papers would be issued within the month, freeing him to try it a second time. Bennie was skeptical, as usual—what else could he expect? Still, Bennie's skepticism was a useful antidote to Barker's zeal. "It seems to me I've said this before: why buy a cow, et cetera?"

"Anita wants children," Barker explained.

"There's that," Bennie said. "I like Anita. Why don't you two come to dinner next Sunday? I just have to check with Patsy but I'm sure it's okay." Barker almost hoped it wouldn't be okay with Patsy, Bennie's wife, for she was one of the people who made him distinctly uneasy. The way she looked at him—

as if he were Count Dracula with blood dripping off his fangs—was enough to make Barker regret being in the same room with her. As far as he was concerned, Bennie's wife was a witch—she could see through his clothes and flesh to his shrunken heart; she sensed his unhealthy appetites; she knew that he was beginning to coast on his early reputation.

As it turned out, the evening at chez Goodrich was not as painful as Barker feared it would be. Patsy was cordial to Anita, Bennie had some good new jokes, and Anita was at her charming best. The meal was fair, considering that Patsy was an unwilling cook. But on the way back, Barker admitted that he was feeling shaky about his career. "I used to be the golden boy," he said. "Now I feel more like tin. A lot of people have never heard of me." He drove over the Cottage Farm Bridge toward Cambridge, glad he didn't have to look her in the eye.

"Then why don't you write a book?" Anita said. "Don't tell me you've never thought of it. You've published more than enough articles to make a book—all you need is a little judicious padding and some new documentation. And voilà, a book that will make you rich and famous."

Barker had, in fact, thought of it many times. But for some buried reason, the thought frightened him more than the idea of root canal work without Novocain. "I'm a lousy writer," he said.

"I can help you."

"That's a generous offer," Barker said. "Help in what way?"

"You know, with a blue pencil. I'm a good editor," she said modestly. "No, really, I edited the literary magazine at college. Even wrote for it when we needed filler. I can beautify your prose, knock out some of the more egregious academic language—like the ubiquitous passive voice: 'It is understood that,' 'It was shown to be . . .' "

"What would be in it for you?" Barker said.

"I beg your pardon?" Anita was suddenly very angry. He had said the unforgivable; he had questioned the purity of her offer. Barker could hear fury as the timbre of her voice altered. "Are you serious, Jake? Do you really think I think that way?"

His blood froze, his stomach, with Patsy's undercooked duck resting heavily against its walls, lurched upwards. Sweat gathered in his armpits and began to slide down his flanks. Desperate to undo the damage, Barker tried to move his question into a pinker spot: she shouldn't neglect her own work; helping him with his book would be not only painful but, in the long run, thankless; she should be doing everything she could to enhance her own career, not his.

"I want to do this because I admire you," Anita said. "Is that such an alien notion? You're so suspicious of people, Jake. Some of us just *like* doing favors for our friends. Not *every*one has ulterior motives."

"I know that," he said. But he didn't believe it. Not even this open, fair-minded, sweet creature sitting beside him was untainted—not because she had shown herself to be calculating but because it was inherent in man's nature to preserve and advance himself, and if this meant that others collapsed along the way, so be it. A bleak reading of human nature, but realistic, justified. Barker felt himself to be, above all, realistic, justified.

When they kissed goodnight in her front hall (Anita having begged off anything more prolonged), Barker couldn't help thinking that the worm had entered their apple and was starting to eat its way through crisp flesh. He was so distracted that he ran a red light and missed his street. Once inside his apartment, he undressed in the bathroom, avoiding his face in the mirror, and leaving his clothes in a heap on the floor. He longed for sleep but was wide awake. Nothing had happened, really, he had inflicted no more than a nick; her skin wasn't broken, no blood had bubbled up, and yet Barker felt guilt and dread creeping along his neck. Cursed with an astonishing talent for saying the wrong thing, Barker felt like banging his head against the wall, screaming. Instead, he poured himself a stiff vodka and sat in the only chair he had rescued from his marriage. "Anita, my only love," he said, "I'm sorry. Please forgive me. I'm a brute, but you can change me." He swallowed some vodka, which turned to fire as it proceeded downward. He would try to be a wiser, better person; he would try not to shout so often at stupid secretaries and lazy graduate students. He would work harder, believe in himself again, write the book, find the answers. Barker fell asleep in his chair.

The next day Anita looked as fresh as an Ivory soap commercial, pouring herself a cup of coffee from the department's Mr. Coffee, a piece of equipment that turned Barker's stomach—no one ever washed its surface or flushed it with vinegar, so that the brew it produced was permanently stuck in the bitter/sour range. She spooned in some nondairy creamer, dropped a dime in the Chock Full O'Nuts can, and smiled at Barker as he tracked her. "Feeling better?" he asked.

"What?" For a moment a frown creased her face. "Oh, you mean about last night? I wasn't in the greatest mood after that weird dinner. I'm not perfect, Jake, but I'm sure I don't have to tell you that." She was wearing her ultimate Harvard costume: a dark tweed skirt, a cotton blouse, a wool cardigan with wooden buttons—straight out of the fifties, except the skirt was shorter and instead of loafers she wore boots with heels.

"Keep reminding me," he told her. "You know, I think I'd like to take you around to meet Otto Von Stampler next time I visit the old boy."

"The dread Von S.?" Anita said. "I'd like to meet him—I think."

Barker visited his mentor every three weeks or so. Whenever he skipped a visit, Verna Von Stampler phoned him and made him feel guilty as hell. Get one of these things going with old folks and you can't stop until they drop dead—or you do. From time to time Barker brought with him a friend or colleague. This seemed to rouse Von Stampler from a nostalgic stupor and he once again became the almost mesmerizing presence he had been in classroom and on lecture platform.

Barker's visits refreshed his oxygen supply and prodded a memory now approaching the upper seventies.

"Should I bring him something, an offering of some sort?" Anita said. "I feel like I'm about to pay a call on God. . . ."

This surprised Barker, who felt like the child of a famous artist or powerful statesman who forgets that his father is the object of both curiosity and veneration. Famous? At home he's famous for his displays of temper, for his lack of sensitivity, for his peculiar taste (which he sticks on all the members of his household, such as only well-done lamb or pineapple juice for breakfast), and for his stinginess. "God?" Barker said, and laughed. "Okay, if that's the way you feel. Crystallized ginger would be right, I think. Oh, and by the way, don't wear your bell-bottoms. He's down on hippies."

"Hippies?" Anita repeated. "That's hysterical."

"You mean hilarious," Barker said.

"I do? Okay, Doctor Pedant, it's hilarious. *I'm* hysterical. I mean here's this brilliant, almost legendary psychologist and he's worried about hippies? Doesn't he know that it was us so-called hippies who lanced the wound and released the poison? Who does he think bagged the war?"

"I'm not so sure he was that set against the war—at least not until the last year or so. In the Von Stampler view, the world is making a swift descent into hell; the natural order of things has been turned on its ear. Von S. was one of SDS's principal targets. You must have heard about how one of his students made him eat a banana in front of his class? It's hard to be objective when you're called a monkey in public by a nine-teen-year-old."

"Well, I didn't hear about it and I wouldn't have eaten it if I'd been him," Anita said. "Now I'm not sure I want to meet him. What does he think people like me are up to?"

"Drugs, *Liebchen*; drugs, booze, and anal sex."

Barker swelled with optimism when he was with Anita. When alone, the fear returned to him like an intermittent toothache. Would that there were a dentist capable of removing this pain by removing the moral decay that caused it. Sometimes, as he sat by himself in his borrowed living room, he felt a dread force threatening to enter and destroy him. Sometimes he heard guns going off, sensed rivers overflowing; sprang aside as taxicabs drove straight at him, watched in horror as the mole became malignant. He was afraid that doors were about to slam shut in his face, that the knife would slip, slicing into his wrist, and that those few whom he loved would turn suddenly and say no. He was scared much of the time. Marijuana took the edge off, whiskey soothed, sex helped a little, but these eventually wore off and Barker was back where he started, with fear crawling over his skin and fluttering like a dead soul near the ceiling. He knew this fear so intimately he had a German name for it: *Genosse*—pal.

Barker and Anita walked from his place to Von Stampler's house on a Saturday afternoon in February. An inch or two of cold gray slush lay over the sidewalk; where they stepped in it they left prints behind. A northeaster with teeth went to work on their faces and Anita's nose turned pink. "Why do we live in this vile climate?" he said. He had neglected to wear boots and wet ice was starting to leak through his shoes; his socks were like wicks.

"We live here because the life of the mind flourishes in adversity," Anita said. "You'd hate it where the sun shines all day, every day; you'd go crazy from the monotony."

"Maybe," he said, "but I'd sure like to try it for a while. What's New Mexico like? Or Arizona? I think I'd like Arizona."

"They have seasons. They have snow in winter and flowers in the spring. In California it's like endless summer. I know you, Jake, you'd go crazy in California."

"Maybe," he said again, unaccountably tasting melancholy. And then, out of nowhere, she said, "You make me feel good, Jake, you know that?" just when his mood had shifted into reverse. Obliquely touched, he thanked her while his heart was bounced around and slammed up against the back of his throat and his knees felt as if they were about to give way.

Von Stampler had a cold that had burrowed into his chest. He was tucked into a tapestry armchair, with a cashmere blanket over his lap and tight around his legs. He looked fragile, older than seventy-seven. He smiled as they entered and Barker noticed for the first time—it must have happened since his last visit—that his teeth were of an ivory evenness that could only have been achieved by human fingers. Menthol fumes rose off him as mist off a bog. He hadn't shaved in a couple of days and hairs stuck straight out of his chin like white thorns. He excused himself for not getting up to greet them, shook hands with Anita, and touched the couch at his left, indicating where she should sit.

Anita said, "I brought you some ginger."

"Thank you, my dear," Von Stampler said, and put it down on the table next to him. "I've heard a great deal about you," he continued in an accent Barker could only think was laid on for the occasion. Why, he could actually see the old guy's blood hurry along vein and artery to revive him. "Your fame precedes you." Anita looked at Barker, who shrugged noncommittally.

"How very nice," she said, sitting. Von Stampler leaned toward her, inquiring about her research; Barker was amused at how deftly she avoided saying anything tendentious—a rather neat trick, given the potentially explosive nature of the work that daily occupied her. For she was, as she told Barker, determined to straighten things out, to separate myth from fact, to liberate women as much from their self-made, self-tied bonds as from bedroom and kitchen. But today she soft-pedaled the rhetoric. Good girl, she knew how to behave, like a kid who says "shit" and "fuck" at home and "thank you, ma'am" at school.

Left out of the conversation, Barker ranged around the Von Stampler drawing room, which was walled with books lined up by category on oaken shelves. There was almost everything in this cafeteria of the mind, from first editions of Hemingway and Evelyn Waugh and row after row of psychology texts to table-sized four-color art books. Von Stampler had spent a small fortune on books, but then, what else did his heart desire? Dozens of photographs held upright by sterling silver frames stood on every available surface. Barker could identify every subject in each picture, having been present many times when Von S. took a visitor on a tour of what he called his "Rogues' Gallery," supplying biography and characterization—as well as his connection to them—in excruciating detail. Erik Erikson was much in evidence, as well as the faces and/or figures of Harry Stack Sullivan, Wolfgang Köhler, Arthur Jensen, Henry A. Murray, Lyndon Johnson, Jerome Wiesner, and, for some unexplained reason, Red Skelton. In each picture Von Stampler's bearded visage was seen gazing on his companions with pleasure and, in some cases, idolatry.

The noise that startled them could have been nothing other than a large silver tray bouncing on the pantry tiles. "I believe Verna is preparing hot chocolate for us," Von Stampler said with a frown.

"I think I better go see if I can help," Barker said.

"So kind of you, dear boy," Von S. said, making goo-goo eyes at Anita. Relieved to get away, Barker set off for the kitchen, where he found the professor's wife pouring liquid chocolate from a saucepan into a huge silver pitcher.

"Ah, it's you," she said. "Could you pick that up for me; my back is out." Verna was wearing a heavy blue caftan; her silver hair was pulled back tightly and secured with a kind of African bone thing. For an old lady, she wasn't half bad—she hadn't gained much weight, she still had her cheeks, and her wrinkles somehow worked for, rather than against, her intelligent resignation. "Otto's driving me nuts," she said as she transferred Dutch butter cookies from a tin box to a silver plate. "It is the first and only cold in the history of the world."

Barker lifted four porcelain cups and saucers down from a shelf.

"So. You have a new girlfriend? And Nancy?"

"I'm in the terminal stages of being bled dry by the legal profession," Barker told her. "I never realized it was so expensive to get a divorce. If people only knew, they wouldn't get married so casually."

"You have my sympathy," Verna said offhandedly. "Will you carry this in for me please? Did I tell you my back is out?"

"Yes, you did," Barker said, but not loudly enough for her to hear him. He picked up the tray and carried it into the drawing room, where it was obvious something awful had happened. Barker could tell by the way Anita sat, with her knees tightly together and her chin lowered, and the way Von S. picked at his blanket. And they weren't looking at each other.

Verna busied herself with the tray of sweets. Von S. began to tell Barker about the three honorary degrees he was slated to receive in June, though not from Harvard. "But one of these days," he said. "A prophet is without honor, *und so weiter*."

"Don't be greedy, Otto," his wife said. "You already have so many hoods you could make six or seven quilts out of them."

"A most peculiar idea," Von Stampler told her. "What do you know about quilts—or about honorary degrees, for that matter?" He coughed in a disgusting way. Barker could hear the fluid moving around in his pipes. Then he spat into a large blue handkerchief. Anita kept staring at her knees.

"Grumpus," Verna said when he was through spitting. "You're driving me nuts."

Barker was desperate to escape. He looked at his watch and calculated that they had been there forty minutes. In another eight or ten it would be okay to begin making verbal moves toward the front door, in another fifteen to actually leave. He then concentrated on responding in a suitable manner. Peer but not quite peer, student but no longer student, disciple whose mentor was well over the hill, Barker was exquisitely conscious of the gulf between this ancient cough-box and himself.

55

As soon as they were beyond hearing distance, Anita exploded. "Do you know what that old goat did as soon as you were out of the room?"

"Don't tell me, let me guess." He couldn't tell whether Anita was angry or amused. Across her face there flickered a regular Whitman's Sampler of emotions. "He came on to you?"

"You've got it, sonny," she said. "He put his hand on my thigh and started advancing toward my crotch. It felt slithery, like a snake. I was so startled I thought maybe it was inadvertent. Hah! The old goat knew exactly what he was doing."

"And what did you do?" Also startled, Barker could not help but admire the strength of the libido in the broken-down old chassis of his former teacher.

"Well, if you really want to know, I sat there like a fool, without saying or doing anything for maybe thirty seconds. Too long, as it turned out—he interpreted my silence as an invitation to proceed."

"And?" Barker found himself riveted.

"He asked me if I liked to do it doggie style."

Barker laughed.

"It's funny, Jake, but not all *that* funny. Your famous Von S. is just a dirty old man who thinks he can get away with it because of his age or eminence or something. And you know something? He's right. He *does* get away with it."

"Aren't you being a little hard on him?"

"Just as hard as you are soft," she said. "But you men have to stick together. You know that. Us girls know that. It's the way things operate."

"I guess you could say our visit was a bust."

"That's where you're wrong," Anita said. "I wouldn't have missed it for the world." Barker figured the incident would be all over Cambridge within a couple of hours.

Chapter Five

OVER the next several years, Jacob Barker was loved by the
supremely desirable, full-breasted Anita, the living image of
his most inward longings. She was perfection walking about on
two nearly perfect legs; it was almost too good to be true. Each
time a doubt about his beloved threw a shadow of gloom across
his mind, she would do something that demonstrated not only
her love for him but her innate kindness, her generosity of
spirit. For instance, one day, on taking his hand in hers, she
nearly burst into tears. "Your skin is so rough," she said,
"doesn't it hurt?" And she went right out to the drugstore
where she bought him a tube of sticky white cream. "This is for
your dishpan hands," she said, which he knew was a joke
because he never washed a dish or stuck his hands into a
panful of soapy water if he could possibly help it. His knuckles
were raw and cracked—no wonder they hurt. The cream
worked, softening the skin and healing the cracks; it also left
grease circles on his papers.

Occasionally Anita changed the sheets on Barker's bed,
even though she hadn't actually moved in with him. She
reorganized his bureau drawers, and saw to it that he bought

orange juice and whole wheat toast for his breakfast. This she did by going to the grocery store with him and breathing down his neck by the bread shelves until he picked up the health-giving loaf.

And there was an added benefit he had no reason or right to expect: she was almost childishly eager to help him with his manuscript, persuading him to let her take his prose—which she said was "clotted"—and apply the blood-thinner that ran out of her Sheaffer fountain pen. Barker had an IBM Selectric in his office and so did Anita, but she preferred to work in longhand, telling him there was a direct path from her brain to her fingers that did not track properly over a keyboard.

Barker's manuscript had the kind of muscle that struck him as potentially dramatic, both to himself and to those women who believed they had located a holy cause. He had discovered, for example, that four-month-old baby girls were more accomplished in some visual areas than boys of the same age. Barker's tendency to say "So what?" was only scientific skepticism. So he said it again, "So what?" What could it ultimately mean? Did it mean that girls were going to be better than boys—and, by extension, women better than men—at doing those things that required the use of eyes rather than fingers? That was nonsense, there was absolutely no evidence, past or present, to persuade him to believe such a thing. If it were true, wouldn't there be many more female painters, architects, graphic designers, and so on? And there just weren't—these areas were totally dominated by males. So what did it mean—and what did it matter? But, as a scientist, meaning wasn't his province, at least not in the way datum was. Let others draw meaning and inference—his work was in the laboratory, and now, in finishing this book.

Anita was elated by Barker's findings, by what he had discovered in the children drawn to his lab by advertisements in two local papers: "We need your infants—aged two to four months—for painless visual research. Five dollars an hour

58

plus carfare." More mothers applied than Barker and an assistant could handle; they had to turn several dozen away on the phone.

Barker was aware that Anita was doing more than simply correcting his grammar, changing passive to active voice, getting rid of jargon, and clarifying his voice. She was putting a political spin on some of his data, something not unheard-of in scientific circles. In fact, unless the stuff had the purity of abstraction—like the numbers Bennie worked with or theoretical physics—most of what his colleagues found out, like the work of sociologists and anthropologists, could be (and often was) forged into weapons and transformed into public policy.

"Jensen does it, so do Herrnstein and the two Wilsons," Anita said, making a face that suggested she had a mouthful of dirt. "Let's get realistic here, Jake. You want this book to do well, don't you?"

"Of course I do," he said. "Do what you will."

Bennie had a friend who worked for a publisher in Boston. (Bennie knew people in professions that Barker had barely heard of—like color consultants and holistic healers.) Bennie thought this person might be interested in Barker's book, but first, he said, Barker should get himself a literary agent.

"How do I do that?"

"You go to a cocktail party," Bennie said, "and meet him there."

"You've got to be kidding," Barker said.

"Only half," Bennie told him. "If you don't live in New York, a worldly party's as likely a place as any to meet an agent. You ought to come with me on Saturday." He named a couple called Payne who lived on Beacon Hill, an ancient Boston family. They had, Bennie said, "shitloads of money" and were vaguely literary.

"But I wasn't invited," Barker said.

"Yes you were—I'm inviting you."

When he told Anita about the party, she assumed he would take her with him. "I can't, honey," he said. "One uninvited guest is enough."

"People bring their girlfriends. You could take me."

"Bennie said it wasn't a good idea," Barker lied easily. He wasn't sure, himself, why he didn't want Anita with him. Did he think he might pick up something juicier, sweeter than even the sweet Anita? Or was he incapable of sustained harmony with a woman? As this thought occurred to Barker, fear crisscrossed his chest, but only for a second. Sustained harmony might just be the world's most boring state—better to thrive on change.

But Anita got very angry—much angrier than Barker felt she had a right to be; she wasn't his wife, after all. They didn't even share the same living quarters. She seemed determined to make an issue of this stupid party thing.

"Please try to understand, Anita. These people live on Beacon Hill; they aren't your Cambridge, take-out pizza crowd."

"Beacon Hill! Oh my God, I have to sit down—I feel faint."

"Come off it, Anita. I don't see why you're carrying on like this. It's just a fucking cocktail party."

"I'm not carrying on, as you put it. I'm not hysterical and I'm not raving. And by the way, if it's just a fucking cocktail party, then what does it matter if one uninvited guest brings along another? You just don't want me to come with you."

"That's crazy, Anita, now you *are* raving. There's nothing I'd rather do than take you with me. I just can't this time."

Anita looked baffled for a moment. Then she said, "Well, bad cess to you, too, Jake Barker. Go to your fancy cocktail party. I hope you have a good time. Make sure they know what a marvelous writer you are. . . ."

60

Inside the Payne's townhouse near the crest of Beacon Hill, Barker met not one but two literary agents, as different one from the other as a trout and a duck. The Payne living room was tastefully done up in velvet and taffeta, grays and dusty rose. The carpet underfoot was thick and springy. Waitresses in black dresses and below-the-waist white aprons passed trays of hors d'oeuvres so delicate they put Barker in mind of tissue samples on slides—rounds of melba toast covered by a slice of cucumber with a dot of something pink on top.

Their hostess was a middle-aged anorexic; the tendons in her lengthy neck stood out like badly buried wires. She wore a severe black dress, a double rope of pearls, and gold shell earrings. Barker immediately sized her up as not interested in his wares. Just as well, these inbred types were tricky. There were several dozen guests, most of whom he had never seen before, one or two of whom he recognized from having seen their picture in *Time* or *Newsweek* or *People,* and one he actually knew—a psychologist who had recently published a book about male impotence. This fellow he avoided speaking to.

Bennie introduced him to a pale, intense youth with large, round, intelligent, somewhat needy eyes behind granny-type glasses. Regulation over-the-collar hair, thin and neatly brushed. "This is Martin Savory," Bennie said, but Barker thought he'd heard wrong. Savory, or whatever his name was, told Barker he was a graduate of Yale, where he said he had been a member of the tennis team, the aesthete's sport. Barker said that was nice. Savory was just starting out as an agent. "I've already got three clients on the Harvard faculty. One of them's sending me a completed manuscript next week. I have high hopes for it; it's a novel about space travel." Again, Barker approved. Savory told him that to supplement his income he worked as a picture framer—"something I can always fall back on if the agent thing doesn't work out. Tell me about your book." The young man seemed to have a vague understanding of what Barker told him, for he nodded vigorously and asked a couple of questions that showed he had ventured, however briefly, onto Barker's turf. "Looks like you're on to something the women's movement would be smart to pay attention to," he said. He handed Barker his card. On the upper right it read *Custom Framing*. On the upper left, *Author Representation*. His name was Martin Savory after all, and Barker was tempted to let the man represent him on the basis of his name alone.

"How many books have you sold?" Barker said.

"Not that many," Savory told him. "But I'm just about to cut a deal with an independent producer in L.A. I'm very excited about it. It's about a television anchorwoman with ESP."

It struck Barker as odd that two literary agents had landed on this rarefied planet, its atmosphere so thin you needed a canister of oxygen to breathe comfortably. The other alien was Mimi Caballero, a woman whose New York accent was as thick as a bagel. As unlikely as it seemed for Mimi and Martin to be guests of Celia Payne and her grayish husband (an investment specialist with a two-hundred-year-old bank), Barker reminded himself that Boston was, in fact, a cosmopolitan town, although it might be difficult to convince all the young people who trooped off to New York by the boxcar-load in search of fame and fortune.

"Is it sexy?" Mimi asked. "It sounds sexy to me." She had the voice of a baritone and bright orange hair. She was nudging fifty and was the size of a troll, coming up to Barker's armpit.

"I'm afraid not," Barker said, looking down at her scalp. "It's about the things I've found testing infants in the laboratory. Even taking Freud's theories about infantile sexuality into account, I doubt you could make anything very sexy out of my material. That would be stretching things beyond credibility." He heard himself babbling, but wanted to please this small person who had about her an air of knowing her way through difficult publishing mazes.

62

"Then you must come up with a selling title, young man," she said. "Here's my card."

Not only were there no females at the party who responded to Barker's signals, but he found himself regretting that Anita wasn't with him. He could have kicked himself for not bringing her. He poked around until he found the master bedroom, sat down on the Paynes' king-size satin puff, and used their telephone to call Anita. There was no answer at her end. He sighed and said, "Shit! I ought to have my head examined." The closet in the bedroom was covered with mirror. The man he saw looking out at him from it was a handsome enough fellow, but his expression was sad; Barker was sad because he did not know how to do the things that came to others so easily.

Barker liked Martin better than Mimi. But when Martin called him the next day, Barker put him off by saying he still had a lot of work to do on his manuscript. "I'll get back to you when I think it's ready to be submitted." Then he called Mimi in New York and had a chat with her, promising to send an outline and three chapters. Business was business, and as Bennie had advised him, "It doesn't matter who you like as a person, when it comes to publishing a book you've got to look out for numero uno. I know what I'm talking about."

Barker yearned for outside validation; he also needed the money because Nancy was applying thumbscrews. Suddenly, new projects, urgent problems—all requiring big bucks—had made their appearance. Nancy's rent had taken an unexpected (although perfectly legal) leap. Guy's shrink (for Nancy had finally conceded this point) had cranked up his therapy schedule, for it appeared Guy had begun to "act out" in ways that made life hell for his mother, his teachers, and his classmates. And his pediatrician had put Guy on a special diet in order to bring his weight down. When Barker looked at the numbers, he figured the diet must be high in quail meat and saffron. Twice, Nancy had got her lawyer to write Barker letters which were downright scary and sent him posthaste to the checkbook. He paid up, every fucking cent of child support she asked for, without complaint. There was almost nothing left for Barker to have fun with. He was reminded of his graduate school days—scrimp, scrimp, scrimp. He couldn't take Anita to a good restaurant without allowing her to pay her share—this killed him. They rarely went to the theater—not that either of them was that crazy about live drama, but he would have liked the option. He couldn't buy a new car—he was still driving around a 1972 Volkswagen eight years after buying it—or purchase a gold pin with a ruby eye for Anita.

These hardships were unfair. Barker nearly wept. A man of his stature, a Harvard professor, author of dozens of articles on a subject that seemed daily to increase in both intrinsic and extrinsic interest. A man of his importance reduced to humiliation by a woman whose only motive was revenge. The book would change all that.

Anita gave up what little free time she had in order to work on Barker's manuscript. She convinced him to put his statistical tables into an appendix: "Nobody reads those things; they make most people feel stupid." In this case, she claimed, a picture was far more daunting than the words that described it. "Girls slowed their turning response markedly," Barker had written. Anita changed this to "Girls can concentrate on an image on the screen longer than boys." A small difference, but a significant one. She went through his manuscript with an eye Barker praised as "wicked."

"I'm very impressed," he said. Barker meant what he said. She was a whiz with the blue pencil.

"I know that," she said, somewhat frostily. When the manuscript was as good as he and she could make it, Barker had it retyped (it cost nearly three hundred dollars, an amount that made tears gather in his eyes) and sent it off, via registered mail, to Mimi Caballero.

Almost immediately after mailing his still-untitled opus, the tension that had been building up over months of labor hit

Barker like an attack of the flu. In fact, there was no difference in the symptoms. He took to his bed, aching in each joint, even the ones in his toes. When he rolled his eyes they hurt cruelly. He could only eat jellied soup, for his digestion was on the blink, and he lay in his bed feeling as if his own body belonged to an ailing stranger, a man he had never met who spent days watching bad television—game shows and the dramatic equivalent of peanut butter and Marshmallow Fluff.

Barker's favorite program was "The Mary Tyler Moore Show," for it confirmed his deepest beliefs about the way the sexes worked together—and against each other. Mary was this bubblehead one was meant to think was a liberated lass, but no such thing: she was *Mary*, while he remained *Mister* Grant. That difference would never change, not if she worked for him for twenty-five years. Little simp, her voice trembled constantly on the edge of a good cry. And then there was that extra frisson: was Mister Grant flirting with Mary? Was Mary flirting with him? The producers certainly wanted you to entertain this notion, for it was the subtext of their every encounter. Slip it to her, you imbecile, Barker told Ed Asner, you know you're dying to get into her panties. Plus ça change; the game was immutable. Men and women would remain with their feet trapped in the same slots until the human race expired. He had to hand it to Mary Tyler Moore, she knew which side her bread was buttered on. . . . Here, Barker paused to consider this image: if you buttered your bread on the wrong side, all you had to do was turn it over and it would be the right side. So what was the "wrong" side of a slice of bread? In any case, Mary's bread was buttered on the money side. Mary Tyler Money. Waves threatened the boat, but she turned the boat to meet them head-on so it wouldn't overturn. Clever girl.

Barker flipped off the television set and lay in the dark. He felt as if precious things had been removed from him—ideas, happiness, love. His eyes brimmed and tears fell back into his ears. They were surprisingly cold. Why were his tears cold? "Anita," he whispered into the gloom, "where are you?" For

65

she had taken off for two weeks with Penny Graff, a girl, for crissake, and the two of them were tramping around on the outer Cape, getting mud on their ankles, staring at the sea, and for all he knew, tickling each other's back at night. Was Anita bisexual? This thought hit him hard and he sat bolt upright in bed, and groaned as pain dispersed itself in several directions—arms, legs, head, stomach. He flopped back again with a second groan. He considered her refusal to move in with him—or let him move in with her. He thought about her angularities, her obsessive feminism. (Try to tell a joke that poked fun at women and she hit the ceiling; she was worse than a Polack reacting to a Polish joke.) He remembered instances where she had turned away from his ardor as if in pain.

"Fuck," he said, "I'm fucking in love with a fucking lesbian."

Barker eased himself out of bed, put a Joni Mitchell record on the stereo, sat down in his armchair, and began to work up next semester's syllabus inside his head, a feat of memory and control that dazzled even himself. He felt better.

After spring break, as the Harvard campus once again bustled with boys and girls filling their heads with fact, theory, and speculation in order to arm themselves for battle in the real world, Barker felt himself to be standing on somewhat firmer ground. For one thing, his labor in the lab continued to bring forth interesting results; he had accidentally discovered that during testing male babies fussed more and were more restless than their female counterparts. When he asked Anita what she made of this she said, "It's obvious. Boys aren't as organized as girls, they can't get their act together as well. Just look at the way we consistently outperform you guys in school."

"Not after the fourth grade, you don't," Barker said.

"That's because of cultural conditioning. Their teachers

66

treat them differently. We've got to reeducate teachers into giving girls an even break. You'd think, most of them being women, they would behave themselves. Or at least be more aware of what they're doing."

"Well, it's one explanation," Barker said. "But I'm not sure we're not jumping the gun here."

"Just an idea," Anita said. "Just another idea floating in space waiting to be grabbed and tested." She had a nasty-looking zit on the side of her nose, which acted as a magnet for his eyes. Also, her fingernails were dirty.

She saw him looking. "You think this is dirt, don't you?" she asked. "Well, it isn't. I've been staining a bookcase."

"I believe you," Barker said. "You want to go to a movie tonight?"

"Maybe," she said. "Ask me at four."

"What happens between now and four?"

"I'll be making up my mind," Anita said, walking out of the lab and closing the door behind her.

"Suit yourself," Barker said.

Barker took off to meet his class, a seminar for seniors doing honors work and bright juniors majoring in psychology. This class demanded more from him than his lecture courses; the kids who took it were sharper and asked harder questions. He was obliged to really listen up. From time to time he sprung a quiz they were not expecting, mainly on the readings he had assigned, such as "The Visual Habituation of Three-, Five-, and Seven-Month-Old Infants." The students bitched about these spot quizzes, and Barker knew that to test them in this simpleminded way was to test their memories rather than their reasoning power. But he had to fill up the time somehow and he had to keep them on their toes, and how better to kill two birds with one stone? He marched into the room and said, "Take out paper and pencils, we're having a test."

There was a girl in this class, Elaine Ferrier, about whom

Barker often thought after the bell signaled the end of class. He had not slept with a student for almost a year, a record of sorts, and he was beginning to miss it. Elaine was what his mother would have called "pretty as a picture." She had high pink cheekbones, a symmetrical mouth which, unlike most of her mates, she colored with bright lipstick, and smooth brown hair cut in an old-fashioned style—straight, with bangs that ended less than half an inch above her gray eyes, not that windblown look some of his students favored, which made Barker think they had just crawled out of a wind tunnel. While her classmates wore jeans and mud-colored shirts borrowed from their fathers or boyfriends, Elaine wore cotton skirts that hit her legs just below the knees and nice, tight turtlenecks in strong colors. By her singular appearance Barker felt Elaine was telling him something—precisely what that was and whether it was worth bothering about were matters still deliciously in the future. When she looked at him from her end of the conference table, it was with the briefest glance, the sort of look you give the person who tears your ticket in half at the movies. Whenever he called on her (he called on people in the same spirit he quizzed them—to keep them on the qui vive), forcing her to look at him, she pulled this little trick of looking just to the left of his face, as if at something affixed to the wall behind his head.

Elaine's friend, George Goldstein, always sat to her right and the two of them passed notes back and forth. Barker would have given his incisors to read these notes. Goldstein was an eye-roller, one of those infuriating kids who responds to what they don't like hearing by an elaborate turn of the eyes toward the ceiling. Sometimes, watching the byplay between Elaine and George, Barker would stumble over his words and start to sweat.

Six weeks or so after Barker sent Mimi Caballero his manuscript, she called him at work. "I've just been offered an advance for your book by Lothar and Bright," she said. "It's a fairly hefty advance—forty-five thousand, in two installments—with an almost guaranteed reprint sale. It should keep you in piccalilli for the next six months." He could hear her shuffling through some papers. "I think we should accept."

"Do we have any other offers?"

"One or two," she said. "But none as sweet as this one." Mimi did not elaborate. It was quite obvious this was a pro forma call. She wasn't asking—she was telling him.

"I don't know anything about publishing," he said. "Go ahead and do what you think best for the book."

"And for you, Jacob sweetie. Without their authors, publishers would be forced into another line of work."

"Please," Barker said. "Proceed with the negotiations."

"I was hoping you'd say that," Mimi said. "They want a few changes. That's why they're paying you the advance in two stages. Half on signing, the other half when you hand over an acceptable revised manuscript. Not to worry, my pet, they all want changes; it reassures them that they aren't merely printers, but bona fide"—she pronounced it *fee-day*—"publishers. I told them you'd be delighted."

Nervy broad. "What sort of changes?" Barker asked. "I mean, how extensive?" The idea of having to go back to work on something he thought finished made him slightly ill.

"I wouldn't know, sweetie," Mimi said. "That's for you to negotiate with your editor. Her name is Paula Marks, by the way, and she's a hot ticket. I told her you'd be calling her. Fortunately—although I didn't plan it this way—Lothar and Bright are right up there in Boston. You won't have to do any traveling on that cattle car they call the shuttle."

"You mean I won't be taken to lunch at the Four Seasons."

"Don't be greedy, Jake. From what I hear, there are some pretty classy eating places in Boston—so long as you order the fish. I ate at one myself, the weekend we met at that dreadfully dull party. It was in a new hotel, I can't remember its name. No matter, just give Paula a call—unless, of course, you want to take back your manuscript and try to market it yourself. . . ."

"No, that's fine," Barker said. He admired the way Mimi did business—part wisdom, part intuition, part bullying; in her business, no doubt, an unbeatable combination. Before Mimi rang off she said, "And oh, by the way, you'd better start thinking title. Paula hates the one you have now."

"I haven't got one," he said.

"That's right, sweetie, it's just a working title. Something about gender. I suggest you change that to sex. Nobody's sure what gender means."

Barker waited a day and a half—best not to seem overeager— to call Paula Marks at Lothar and Bright. She had the deep, uninflected voice of a jaded, middle-aged female. She was businesslike on the telephone, while he waited in vain for her to tell him that she liked his book or was excited by its prospects or anything, in fact, that he could chew on after he hung up. But it didn't happen—their conversation was solely about where and when they were to meet. Barker hung up vaguely depressed.

"Bitch!" he said. Clearly Ms. Marks was one of those No people who could make life hell for you if you let them. Their instincts were negative, death-drawn, and they got positive pleasure from making you feel lousy. Maybe Marks was a hot ticket, but to what exactly did her ticket give him entry?

Barker put on his best tweed jacket, polka-dot tie, and flannels before going into the city to meet his editor for lunch. Checking the mirror, he knew that his clothes gave off a strong smell of older generation; men not much younger than he wore all sorts of odd pieces: tieless shirts in loud checks, jackets of blended stuff with strange lapels. Pointy black shoes, thin strips of leather around their waists; a touch of the zoot suit. Anything to keep from looking like one's father. Screw that. Barker liked the tweed/flannel combo; he felt organized, in control, in this conventional costume. Before leaving the apartment, he swallowed a slug of vodka, neat.

Ms. Marks was already at the restaurant when Barker swung open the front door, had checked her coat, and stood waiting by the maître d's lectern. She held a slim leather briefcase in her left hand; her right she thrust at him—having identified him by his professorial duds, no doubt. Her greeting was more enthusiastic than anything she had said to him over the phone. This rankled. She was nowhere near middle age and not yet, Barker guessed, thirty years old, which would put her in the wunderkind class. Marks's handshake was surprisingly firm and short-lived. The restaurant was handsomely done up by a decorator who favored chrome, frosted glass, and 1930s posters from the Cunard line. The tables were separated by a lot of expensive Boston footage; this was no hash house, this was top drawer. She might not tell him what he wanted to hear, but her choice of restaurant indicated definite respect for the product—or would she call it "property"?

When they sat down, not across from one another, but he to her right, Barker examined Paula Marks. She was tiny—he guessed size six, tops—and gravely handsome, like an American Puritan girl painted by a literalist. She had pale yellow hair and wore granny glasses like those of Martin Savory, the agent he had sent packing. As for her sexual voltage, it was almost nonexistent. Paula Marks gave off a light so dim she was no better than a single candle burning in an enormous house.

Marks ordered the schrod. Barker never ate hot fish at lunch. Hot fish was something adults ordered for you when they took you out to a restaurant as a child. Barker ordered the steak tartare. Marks asked him several questions about his work, revealing, to his relief, that she had read his manuscript with care and understanding. This was somewhat off-putting, because if she'd read it so carefully why the fuck didn't she tell him she thought it was great? He wanted desperately to ask her whether she loved his book.

71

Instead, he said, "Is Marks your married name?"

"I'm single," she said, looking at him as if he had just blown smoke at her face. "And if I were married I still wouldn't take my husband's name."

"I never understood that name business," Barker said. "One way or another you assume a man's name, either your father's or your husband's, so what difference does it make?"

"Plenty." She stabbed three green beans with her fork and inserted them into her tight little mouth.

"Is there a boyfriend in the picture?" This time Marks's eyes widened and she presented him with a fake smile. "You certainly are direct," she said. "It so happens that my boyfriend is a girlfriend. We share an apartment in the South End."

"Ah," said Barker, profoundly shocked, not because she was gay but because he hadn't realized it. He had nothing against gays except regret that so much potentially good sex was unavailable. That didn't make sense, did it? And yet the regret was there. On the other hand, Marks didn't seem in the least regretful, he'd say proud was more like it. Pity.

"And what does your girlfriend do?" he asked.

"Judith designs software for Texas Instruments," Marks told him. "Is there something else you'd like to know?"

"Actually, no," he said, looking at the moist raw tenderloin on his plate. It put him in mind of what Guy used to call "throw-up." Yes, there was a good deal more he would like to know; his imagination grew great wings and took off, flapping wildly. What did girls do to each other that could be half as good as a man and woman coming together in sexual unity? A little rubbing here, a nudge there, the introduction of tongue, teeth, whatever. How sad and skimpy it seemed. So badly did Barker want to ask Paula what she did with Judith that he was afraid the words would emerge by themselves. So he ate more steak, although he was no longer hungry, and followed it with a breadstick. Then, with enormous effort, he summoned the bird back to its perch and sternly told it to stay put, for crissake. Barker was sweating again.

72

It wasn't until the waiter removed their plates and brought coffee (she urged him to have some dessert; he declined) that Marks dove into her briefcase and brought out a long, lined yellow pad, the kind used by lawyers.

"About your manuscript," Paula Marks said. "Your prose is adequate. As a matter of fact, it's surprisingly readable—for a scientist, that is. Most of you people can't write your way out of a paper bag."

"So you like the book?" His heart bounced.

"We're publishing it, aren't we?"

"Well, I guess that means you like it." He wanted to stuff a handkerchief into his mouth to keep himself from going on in this humiliating way. What was wrong with him? Why couldn't he just accept her as a tight-ass, who would rather have her tits put through the wringer than offer somebody a compliment and leave it at that?

"We think it should do fairly well. It's a timely book. Given the right push, the proper timing, a decent advertising budget, and some good luck, we might sell fifty thousand copies."

"You mean you people count on luck to sell books?"

"Partly," Marks said. "The market's pretty soft these days. If your book was fiction, we probably wouldn't have bought it."

"How could it be fiction?" Barker said.

"It couldn't," she mysteriously answered. Paula looked down at her pad, which was covered with handwriting so small he couldn't decipher it. "We'll save the real work for the next time—in my office. Right now I just want you to think about the following questions." She looked up at him through her glasses. Her eyes were like marbles—he couldn't read them either. "Maybe you'd like to take notes?"

"I didn't bring any paper with me," he said. "I didn't think I was going to need it. But in any case, I've got a crackerjack memory."

She shrugged and began to read to him. He hated her for uncovering his book's structural weaknesses so acutely. At the same time, he couldn't help admiring her skill. Were he to take her objections seriously, untie all the knots she had discovered, fill in all the spaces, it would take him six, maybe eight months. "I'm not going to sugarcoat the pill," she said, pausing briefly. "One of my strong suits is candor. I'm known for my directness."

The coffee and sparkling water had worked their way south. Barker excused himself and went to the men's room. Once there he lingered, reluctant to return to the table. Instead of giving his homework the A he expected, she had given him, what, a B or even a B-minus. If she had found so many things wrong with his book, why had she bought it in the first place? Why the forty-five thousand dollar advance? He couldn't figure it out. All he knew was that he felt like crying. It occurred to Barker that she might be trying to punish him because he was a male.

"Tell me something, Paula," he said as they left the restaurant. "If you think my book's such a loser, why did you take it on?"

"A loser?" she said. "Did I say that?"

"Not exactly," he said. "I'm just judging by your reaction."

"My reaction to what?" She switched her briefcase from one hand to the other. "I'm this way with all my authors. I don't believe in overstimulation; it backfires."

When he got back to his office, Barker called Mimi Caballero to complain.

"Paula is one of the sharpest young editors in the business," Mimi told him. "She's also known for her candor."

"So she informed me," Barker said. "I think I'd prefer a touch of tact—"

Mimi interrupted him. "This isn't a domestic drama, Jacob sweetie. This is business. Tact has nothing to do with it. Paula Marks is going to help you make a better book. Now be a good fellow, will you, and stop complaining. I got you a hell of a lot of money for a book that still needs a hell of a lot of work."

So his book was going to be published. Still ticked off at Mimi for putting him in the hands of a humorless lesbian, Barker began to cheer up somewhat when a book club—not the Book of the Month or the Literary Guild, but a smaller, more intellectual outfit, took the book as half of its dual selection for the following October.

Crisp, cool Paula Marks phoned Barker with this news and said, "Now we'll have to come up with a really good title. This is getting silly."

Barker said, "How about *Jaws*?"

"I'm afraid that's already been taken."

"I was joking," Barker said through his teeth.

"In any case—" Marks began.

He cut her off. "I'll get back to you. I'll send you a list." He hung up before she could give him an argument and went down the corridor to Anita's office. "They need a title," he told her. "The Furrowed Brow Book Club's taken my book. Isn't that nice?" Anita looked up from a pile of student papers on her desk and smiled. "We don't have much time," he added.

"Would you like me to help?" she said.

"If you wouldn't mind, I'd really appreciate it."

Something unpleasant but swift passed across Anita's face, sending a tremor of uneasiness through Barker. It was as if she were a doctor telling him, "Let's do a biopsy—just to be on the safe side." Anita said, "How about at lunch? I've got to finish grading these papers before noon."

Barker thanked her again and went back to his office, where he took out a pad and began to jot down combinations of words that might work together as a title. Fifteen minutes later he had twenty-seven, none of which seemed sufficiently amazing. How come he could write a whole book and then get stuck on something three or four words long?

Chapter Six

SOMEBODY said you were divorced from President Roosevelt's grandniece," Elaine Ferrier told Jacob Barker, surprising him. People actually made up stories about you behind your back? What people? Elaine sat in his office—door conspicuously open—twiddling twenty-year-old hairs as fine as silk, and looking past Barker's right temple.

"Somebody was incorrect," he said, trying to engage her eyes; twisty little thing, why was he bothering with her? He couldn't do it; he couldn't get her to look at him. "I *am* divorced. But my former wife is an ordinary citizen. Her family is unremarkable."

"That's funny," she said. "I wonder why they said that."

"Folks need a dash of drama in their dreary lives," Barker said. "And since you've asked me a rather personal question, now I'm going to ask you one. About George Goldstein—are you and he, by any chance, engaged?"

"Engaged! Nobody I know gets engaged. We both live in Blythe House, in North Quad. George is my best friend. We do almost everything together. He's giving me lessons in Judaism. It seems"—and here she flicked her eyes toward him for the briefest of milliseconds—"it seems I'm woefully ignorant."

Barker recrossed his legs. The fair Elaine was his meat, his lamb chop, his cornish game hen. Barker hadn't felt like this—the thrill of arousal cruising nerve and hormonal pathways—in a long time. As for Anita, ever since she came back from her vacation with Penny she had been skittish. On the surface their relationship was much as it had been—they saw each other at work, ate Chinese food together, went to the movies and to bed, listened to music, smoked a little dope, saw friends—but underneath he could tell, she'd had enough. Why? What had he done? Anita was fickle, a word dredged up from another time. Fickle. Women couldn't maintain a serious interest in a man even as long as a man could maintain an erection.

Barker focused on this succulent girl, sitting not three feet away from him, on a late winter afternoon in 1981. "Well," he said, trying to sound businesslike, "and what has brought you here to my bunker? You're not my advisee, are you?"

"No, I'm not," she said. "But I wanted to talk to you about graduate schools because my adviser"—here she named someone Barker had heard of but didn't know—"is in the German Department. He doesn't seem to want to help me on this."

"You mean you don't want to ask me any more questions about my former wife?" Enough, he told himself, don't do this.

But apparently he had not crossed over into the danger zone, for she said, "I'm really interested in marriage. I mean, like why people get married at all. Isn't it an awful drag?"

"I imagine some people get married because their parents did. A kind of mindless decision. Others take the plunge because they have the mistaken notion that love will last longer for them than for anyone else. Then, I suppose, there's a third group who feels the need to legitimize whatever children they have—an obsolete notion, if you ask me. Could you marry a Jew?"

"That's a funny question," Elaine said. "Of course, if we decided that was what we really wanted. Why not, what's the big deal about marrying a Jew?"

"I suggest you ask your folks," Barker said, "even though I don't know them."

The look she gave him told him to bag this topic—it was getting too personal. She said, "The reason I came to see you is I need your advice about applying to graduate school."

"Here?" Barker said.

"Yes. Is there something the matter with right now? I can come back . . ."

"No no. I didn't mean that. I meant, do you want to apply to Here University—as in 'I assume you teach here?' "

"That's funny," she said. "I was thinking about here, Stanford, Berkeley, Chicago, Michigan."

"And you're right, too," Barker said. "Think from the top."

"Are you teasing me?" Elaine said. "I feel like you're trying to make me feel stupid."

Barker approved of the cut of her jib. This odd image said perfectly what he felt about Elaine Ferrier. A girl like Elaine was a sailboat. She was holding her own in an honorable, not to say adorable, way. He wanted to leap across his desk, pounce, rip off her clothes. His forehead exploded with sweat, the back of his throat tightened. He coughed. "No, I'm not teasing you, Elaine, I'm just trying to get you to relax a little. I'm not a monster, I'm perfectly harmless. Think of me as a coach who only wants you to give your personal best."

A sigh escaped her pretty mouth. "I know that," she said. "Well, what do you think I ought to do?"

"I think we should talk about it some more. This isn't something I want to give you an instant response to." He looked at his watch. "Oops," he said, "I should have been at the lab five minutes ago. Look, how about meeting me later at the Bristol for coffee? We can talk there." His pulse was making a mess of his voice. Did he imagine it, or was she looking at him with scorn and loathing? It was bullshit, this games-playing, this verbal foreplay. The girl was an A student doing B work, this they were both aware of. She had missed several classes in a row—without bothering to come up with an excuse—not too smart there. She'd failed a quiz, too, which, in its way, was reassuring, as it simply meant that she hadn't done the reading at all, not that she didn't know how to answer the questions. She was lazy . . . or something. Barker wasn't sure what the trouble was. Maybe she was too busy getting porked by her smart-ass boyfriend George (for he didn't believe for one second that they were just friends). What a pity. Yet it was her laziness (or something) that had brought her here to him.

"I'd like to ask you a question that may embarrass you," Barker said. She looked at the floor and said, "What is it?"

He figured she figured he was about to come on to her. But he fooled her. "Would you mind telling me why you want to go to graduate school? Somehow I don't have the feeling that you're entirely committed to the sort of grind it requires. Graduate school is no picnic. You have to really want to teach or go into the sort of research that's probably never going to make you a rich woman."

"I'm not that interested in making money," Elaine said seriously. "I don't know, over the last couple of weeks I seem to have gotten a second wind or something. I know I've been lazy, but like, I got turned on again to psychology. I want to do something important in the field. And I don't care if I never own a Porsche."

"Well, good for you," he said. He could tell she had given her problem some minimal thought. Girls like Elaine dropped like flies once they entered graduate programs.

Still keeping her eyes to herself, Elaine told him that she would meet him later, stood up, and left quickly. Barker's face broke out in relief and happiness. He still had it, that iron power over girls, the seductive art that would fall into desuetude if he did not exercise it from time to time. And if Elaine's right was to make practical use of the knowledge of how things

79

worked, then it was only fair—his right—to take what was offered, wasn't that so? Elaine offered, Barker accepted. As for that look of scorn and loathing, surely he must have imagined it, for wasn't she as anxious to make this bargain as he was? The bottom line was she needed a letter from him to the Dean of Admissions of the Graduate School of Blank University, a pure, almost abstract example of tit for tat.

Within the Bristol Coffeehouse, thick with smoke and under-oxygenated air, Barker returned to a question that had bothered him on and off for years.

"Do you think Jews are smarter than Gentiles?" he asked. "What does your George say?"

"George is prejudiced," she said. "The reason I probably would never marry someone like George is that he's a chauvinist. Not a male chauvinist, but a Jewish one. He looks down on me." She thereupon looked down on herself, no doubt aware of her double entendre.

"Then he's exceedingly silly," Barker said, delighted to be clued in to his rival's silliness.

The Bristol was packed from front door to back wall with students. Barker was aware—and not for the first time—of a new phenomenon: girls together having a good time. Attractive girls, not dogs, girls who could have been sitting with boys. In the old days (Old days? Was he that old?) you only saw unattractive females with each other, and those so self-conscious you wanted to order them to sit up straight and for crissake do something about their appearance. Girls with fat stomachs, lousy complexions, stringy hair, big flat noses, receding chins, low hairlines, mustaches, short little necks . . . *Basta!* he told himself. All around him, inside the Bristol, were women together, acting as if they were enjoying each other's company. Barker would have gladly held any one of them in his arms and caressed her with the utmost pleasure. What was happening? Maybe this place had turned into a gay hangout and they were all lesbians. This thought cheered him briefly.

"I never knew any Jews before I came to Harvard," Elaine was saying. "There was this hardware store in town, run by Mr. Heyman, but his kids were grown up and there just weren't any others. Is that possible?"

"Little pockets of lily-white middle America," Barker said, "entirely possible. What does your father do?"

"He's a lawyer. A small-town lawyer," Elaine said. "You didn't ask me what my mother does." She looked at him reproachfully. "She teaches little kids how to play the piano. Most of them don't want to learn. She went to Wheaton."

"I assume George is educating you in all sorts of ways."

"George is mucho smart," she said. He could sense her pulling away. His insistence on drawing George into this was putting her on guard. It was obvious she didn't want to talk about George, so why was he doing this?

"George writes clean and crisp papers," he said. "He's a thoughtful fellow. Somewhat glib perhaps, but thoughtful. I shouldn't be discussing another student with you. . . ."

"No," Elaine said, "I don't think you should." She reached into her backpack. "I've brought along some catalogs," she told him. "I was wondering if you could take a look at them and tell me what you think."

Incredible. "I'm acquainted with most of the better schools," he said. "I know their graduate faculties and course offerings pretty well. I don't need to look at catalogs."

"Okay," she said, ignoring the implied criticism. "That makes it easier, I guess."

Barker didn't like the espresso he had ordered; it tasted as if there were dirt in the bottom of his cup. But he sipped at it like a man while he gave Elaine a rundown on several institutions, including faculties, housing, climate, athletic facilities, cultural amenities, food service, transportation in and out of the place, etc. It was remarkable how much he knew about Berkeley, about Chicago. But then again, not so remarkable when you took into account his prodigious memory. Sometimes he thought he was in the wrong racket. Put him at the twenty-one table in Vegas and he would never have to work another day in his life. Trouble was, he enjoyed working. It was the only thing—apart from fucking—that made him feel alive. He could not suppress a shuddering sigh for the melancholy in his life. A tear formed in each eye but dried up before it had a chance to fall. . . .

For one moment, Barker tried to see himself as she saw him. Shifting sand. An old (forty-one was old), slightly myopic, still trim, bearded teacher with glasses. The sexual attraction was mainly in his glance now, for he was past his prime and had bought a seat on the train doing the long, slow descent into the void.

Never mind; Elaine appeared to be succumbing. "And what do you think my chances are of getting into graduate school here?" At this, she smiled, acknowledging his joke about Harvard. Her teeth were lovely, straight, as befitted the daughter of a small-town lawyer, the color of young ivory, slightly opalescent. "I'd say you have a pretty fair chance," Barker told her. "But you can't fail any more quizzes—you understand that?" She nodded. "You're up against some fairly heavy competition."

"Oh, I know, I've been terrible. I can do the work. . . ."

"I know you can, Elaine."

Barker upped the sex/power amperage; Elaine's face colored in response. Satisfied, he began to praise her work, her style of thinking ("imagistic"), her approach ("skeptical but optimistic"). She devoured it, a child with a container of french fries all her own. "You've made me feel so much better, Professor Barker," she said. "I was beginning to get a little down." She wrapped a strand of hair around her forefinger, then released it. Then she did it again. His own fingers ached to join hers. He moved his leg against hers; she jumped away as if stabbed.

"You're much too young to be depressed," Barker said,

telling himself to take it easy. He almost said "too beautiful," but stopped himself in the nick of time. These young tricks wanted you to like them for themselves, not realizing that their beauty was as much themselves as their brains were.

"Lots of people my age are depressed," Elaine said, with a trace of indignation. "Someone killed herself on my corridor last week."

"How did she do it?" The details of this sad tale might distract her.

"She OD'd on Valium and some other stuff. I suppose if you're going to do it, that's the least gross for the person who finds you. Think if she'd cut her wrists. . . ."

Or, like Hemingway, shot off the top of her head, Barker added silently. Then he thought of the man who had recently thrown himself from the fifteenth floor of the Yale Club, falling in a three-piece suit toward Vanderbilt Avenue, his arms and legs spread, afloat on a sea of air.

Elaine was on a roll, anxious to talk about the swallower of pills. She told Barker that she had been one of those people who never had any fun. "Nina was a wonk. She studied night and day. She even took books into the bathroom with her. She made Junior Phi Bete in molecular biology—I don't even know what molecular biology is."

"She wasn't pretty," Barker said.

"No," said Elaine, "she was gorgeous. Nina was the most beautiful girl I ever saw. *You'd* think so, too."

"You're a romantic," Barker told her. "You think death is beautiful."

"I do *not*," Elaine said. "I think Nina was beautiful. There's a difference."

"Well," Barker said. They had run into a cul de sac. How to retreat without sounding heartless? "Drink up," he said, pointing to her lemonade, a glass of what looked like plain water with two fuzzy lemon quarters drowning in it. The ice was long gone. "I definitely think you should give Harvard your best shot," he went on. "After all, you've got me behind you."

"Oh," she said, looking startled and unhappy. He had said the wrong thing, come on too strong. But his blood was on the boil: he was sure that if he did not have Elaine soon, he would fall sick and die, poisoned by his own desire.

It took Barker three weeks of steady labor to erase Elaine's hesitation. He bought her coffee. He wrote a flattering note on one of her papers: "You've exceeded my expectations for you—well done!" He asked her to stay behind after class and gave her a copy of Elizabeth Bishop's *The Complete Poems*. "This is for me?" she said. "I think you'll enjoy them," he said. "Keep it," he added, when she told him she would return it the following week. Then she turned her eyes to his and in that moment he knew he had her fast as a fish impaled through the lower lip. The poetry had done it. Barker congratulated himself: it was just a matter of locating their softest place and going for it. After Elaine left the classroom, Barker howled with happiness.

"Where are we going?" Elaine said as she settled into the front seat of his Rabbit. She was wearing a denim skirt and a man's jacket, super-lovely, her hair emitting fumes of expensive shampoo—more like perfume than soap. "We're going to the North Shore," he said. "You'll like it. We can look at the Atlantic Ocean, it comes right up to the edge of town."

She was quiet on the trip, he figured a small attack of cold feet. He couldn't blame her, really; she'd have to have a soul of granite not to be nervous. Barker tried to fill the silence by talking about his work, peering sideways at her as he drove toward the town where he had booked a room in a motel over the telephone, for Mr. and Mrs. Mills, looking at her to make sure she was still there, as if she were an abstraction—Desire—that might evaporate at any moment. But no, there she was, with her squeaky-clean hair and fresh pink cheeks, her mouth molded as exquisitely as a Botticelli nymph's. He wondered what she was thinking about and then reminded himself that it didn't matter, didn't matter—so long as she did not disappear.

"Let's find a place to eat," he said, parking the car at a meter on the main drag. Barker was perfectly willing to wait, now that he knew that at the end of the waiting came Joy. They found a bar that served food—he needed a drink or two, and he wanted Elaine to have one. She asked for a whiskey sour; he quickly downed a scotch on the rocks and ordered a second. The alcohol fed into his arteries, setting his nerves to rest— for he was too nervous. This blazing beauty was to be his prize in less than an hour. He would, by invading that hidden orifice, travel deep into her being, win something of ineffable worth: one could not buy this, one could not hope to hold it except for a moment or two, yet it was as amazing as life itself.

Barker watched Elaine's mood shift several times during the sandwich meal—tuna for her, roast beef for him. Was she doing some heavy thinking? Second thoughts? Third? Despite what anyone said—liberated females, guys in the locker room, smutty kids—sex was not something you did lightly or without thought; unless, of course, you were a psychopath who went around raping people. No, it was *not* like eating or leafing through a magazine or staring at a peacock. It was sui generis; it was the ultimate experience.

"I'm glad you came with me today; you make me feel optimistic."

"Really?" she said. "Are you anti-nuke? I am. I'm a member of Clamshell Alliance. My father's having a fit. It's hard to be optimistic when you think how easy it would be for someone to push the wrong button."

"I don't think it works that way," Barker said. "They have fail-safe systems. Would you like some dessert or something?"

"No, I'm fine." In fact, she looked anything but fine; she looked as if she were on the way to changing her mind.

"I know you're fine," he said. "But are we finished here?"

She nodded and got up. Barker helped her back into her jacket and when his hand touched the hem of her hair he nearly cried out with excitement. "I'll pay up and we'll be on our way," he said. "It's just around the corner."

"Oh," Elaine said. Barker wasn't sure what she meant by this.

"I don't want you to feel in any way compromised," he said once they were outside. "This is supposed to make us both happy." He felt, abruptly, protective toward her, as if he wasn't who he was—a rake, a cad—but an older brother or uncle. The idea of incest inflamed him further and he thrust his hands into his pockets to keep from grabbing her right there on the sidewalk.

"I don't feel compromised," Elaine said. "I think you have a peculiar idea about women. I think you think their brains don't function as well as a man's. I know what I'm doing."

"You've never called me by my first name," he said. "It's Jake. . . ."

"It's hard to," Elaine said.

"Call me Jake," he said. "Please." Were the two fast drinks making him say things he wouldn't, sober?

"I'll try," she said.

Elaine stayed outside while Barker went into the office to get the key from the room clerk, a kid about sixteen years old wearing a mustard-colored jacket that looked as if it were made of painted cardboard. "It's room twelve, my lucky number," he told Elaine, making it up; he didn't have a lucky number. He opened the door and gestured for her to enter.

"This is the first time I've ever done anything like this," she said to him over her shoulder.

"Me too," Barker said, fibbing smoothly. "Do you think we're crazy?"

"I hope not," she said, heading for the bathroom. Women always went to the bathroom before making love; whether they used a diaphragm or not, off they went. What were they doing in there that took so long? Barker stripped, placing his clothes

86

in a neat pile on a chair, and got into the bed. The sheets were cold, chilling his limbs. He looked at the ceiling, which resembled stucco with flecks of sparkly stuff. He closed his eyes, trying to relax, but all his systems tingled and his eyes twitched. Finally, Elaine came out. She was naked from the waist up, had removed her bra but was still wearing a half-slip; the roundness of her breasts drew from Barker a gasp of admiration. On the small side, her breasts were identical twins, with dark brown aureoles the size of fifty-cent pieces. Her nipples were flattened on top, as if sliced with a scalpel. Each rib pressed against the skin enfolding it, bending in gentle arcs over and near her heart.

"You're very beautiful," he said. "Please take off your slip. I want to see the rest of you."

"I will in a second." Elaine came over to the bed and sat with her back toward him, working the slip and panties down over her hips. Then she joined him under the covers.

"Cold. They feel like they've been stored in an icebox."

"Never mind the sheets," he said. "I'll keep you warm."

Elaine lay rigid beside him on her back, her eyes squeezed shut, her forehead pleated. "Are you okay?" he said, not really caring, but eager to make her relax, for she was stiff as a corpse. As his hand crept toward her belly, she made a sound like a groan. "Are you sure you're all right?" he said, beginning to curse his luck. Twelve must be his unlucky number. The hand kept going and landed.

"What's this?" he said, pulling back sharply.

"It's my scar," Elaine said.

"Scar from what?"

"From surgery," she said softly. He lifted the covers, forcing himself to look at it: a great purple welt stretching from belly button into the delta of black pubic hair, bunching the two halves of her abdomen together so that it resembled a seamed turban squash. The sight of it wilted his penis. He fell back and closed his eyes.

"What's wrong?"

87

"Your scar surprised me." Surprise merely skimmed the surface. Beneath it lay horror. Why hadn't she warned him? Barker tried to imagine what it would be like to have a scar like Elaine's, lying awake at night and running your hand over it, creeping along its fleshy intaglio with your fingers. She should have warned him.

"What do you think?" she said. "You think you can see it through my clothes? You think it's something I want to talk about? You think I like it any better than you do?"

"What was wrong with you?"

"They had to take out my uterus. If you don't mind, I'd rather not talk about it."

"I don't mind," Barker said. How could he have guessed such a thing? Elaine was wounded, maimed. The split in her belly made bile rise into the back of his mouth. He tried to feel pity for her but was unable to take it that far; he felt too sorry for himself. She had cheated and tricked him. She could have told him. . . .

"Are we going to do it?" Elaine asked.

"Well, if you'd like. Trouble is, I seem to be having some difficulty at this point in time." For the first time in his whole life, he could not get it up, and impotence was as dire as death. There was no point in living if he couldn't get it up.

"I've got a joint," she said.

"Good idea," Barker said weakly.

Together they smoked the joint down so far he singed his fingertips. Somewhat numbed, he tried again. Obligingly, she slid down in the bed and fastened her mouth around the top of his prick, working her tongue over it in a way that suggested she and George were sophisticates. He should have been happy, but when at last he arrived in the secret garden, his desire and delight had all but evaporated, gone, gonzo, taken to the hills, or wherever such things go. It was done quickly, she seeming to be no more in the grip of joy than he was.

On the trip back, a much-subdued Elaine asked Barker if he would be willing to write a letter for her to the graduate admissions people at Stanford. Barker smiled. "I'd be more than happy to," he said. Stanford would put a good three thousand miles between them.

A week or so later Barker began to ask himself some difficult questions, such as why he persisted in messing around with students when there was so much pussy elsewhere. What, in fact, was the difference between a Harvard girl and one from, say, Wellesley? Maybe the Wellesley product was not quite as smart as the other, but what did that matter when speech was hardly the language of the bed? *Niente.* The adage "Never dip your pen in the company inkwell" seemed to make a lot of sense, so why did he keep on doing it? Barker realized that were someone to ask him, he would not be able to offer a respectable answer to account for his behavior except that he couldn't help it. Sex wasn't enough: it had to be sex with someone who—if the two of them got caught at it—would break the most bones, cause the most pain.

Chapter Seven

As Barker's book began its nine-month journey toward birth through the production canal—copyediting, styling, the imprinting of characters on the naked page, design, jacket copy, the obtaining of fulsome blurbs by people who owed him one—the author found himself forced to face an angst that sapped his strength and shot his concentration all to hell.

Fortunately, his friend Bennie was in the neighborhood and not, for a change, bent over with his nose in the trough; Bennie put it in this crude way himself, Barker figured, so that others would be less likely to do so behind his back. Bennie spent a good deal of time lecturing all over the United States for astronomical fees, flying off to China or the Soviet Union to meet with fellow laborers in the vineyard, there to confer over negative numbers, and to Washington, D.C., to consult in a panel configuration on financial grants for those still scrambling up the shaky ladder toward fame, responsibility, and chronic headache. These, Bennie insisted, were the perks due him after a lifetime of steady, plodding work. He was sanguine about his future.

"My best work," he told Barker, "is behind me." They stood beneath adjacent showerheads in Harvard's athletic facility, a mammoth, multi-use structure where the two played squash from time to time. Bennie's chest was invisible behind a dense thicket of black hairs. Bennie spun a cake of white soap in his armpit.

"How can you tell?" Barker shouted. Looking down, he realized it was not quite so easy to see his member as it had once been . . . when? Last year? Last month? His abdomen bulged ominously. These inches had an insidious way of creeping up on a person, even though one watched one's diet carefully and exercised several times a week.

"Because I haven't had an original thought—I mean one that lifted me out of my chair—since the year they almost impeached Nixon. Now *that* was a vintage year for my gray matter." Bennie closed his eyes, lifted his chin, and let the water sock him in the face.

There were two other men taking showers at the same time. One had a wide purple scar slicing his flesh from hip to knee. The other, a man who looked to be in his early thirties, was completely bald—not a hair in sight, not on chest, arm, leg, or surrounding the sacred phallus. He put Barker in mind of a large rubber doll lathering his scalp, as if preparing himself for brain surgery. Barker shut his eyes briefly—the sight made him queasy. He was certain it all had to do with him— the scar, the polished head, the drying up of imagination, the threat of extinction. The sliver of soap popped out of his palm and landed on the cement beneath him. He dove after it, cursing lightly. Telling Bennie he was going to get dressed, he padded out to his locker and felt a vicious tingling between the two final toes on his right foot. When he bent over to look, he saw three tiny bubbles. "Shit," he said aloud, "it's the filthy athlete's foot again. Filthy Harvard. Might as well go to the Y. Save a bundle, too."

Barker dressed slowly, reminding himself to stop at a drug-store and buy a tube of Tinactin and trying to think of something to cheer himself up, something to chase the blues away. But if he knew not whence they came, how could he possibly send them back? Well, there was one piece of good news: he had at last found a title for his book, a title everyone— including his tight-ass editor—liked.

"*Cleopatra's Nose*," he had told Paula Marks over the phone, wishing he could see her expression.

"It's sort of catchy," she said, "but what does it refer to? What does it mean?"

"Frankly," Barker said, "I found it in *Bartlett's*. It goes, 'Cleopatra's nose, had it been shorter, the whole face of the world would have been changed.' It's Pascal."

"I know that," Paula maddeningly said. "But I don't see what it has to do with your book."

He had to explain to this brainy woman? "It has to do with how you see Woman. And I suppose a long nose is more attractive than a stubby one. It gives the woman dignity rather than cuteness. As for the actual saying, it focuses on the power of what you see—the image." Barker felt himself making verbal knots.

"I'm not sure I follow you," Paula said.

"Well," Barker said, "I think the title works in any case."

"I'll give it a conditional pass," she said. "I'll try it out at our editorial meeting tomorrow morning and let you know."

"Should we bag it and look for another?" Barker asked with a sinking heart.

"I wouldn't go that far," Paula said. "I just hope people won't think it's a book about cosmetic surgery."

"Oh hell," he said, hanging up.

Barker called his agent. Mimi was crazy about it. "Jacob Barker," she said, "you're a bleeding genius. It's a blockbuster title." She flattered him by telling him how literate he was. She had, he decided, very peculiar ideas of what people like him did when they weren't fucking, eating, going to the movies, or talking shop.

As for Anita, whom he called afterward about the title, she sounded less interested than Dr. Minor, his dentist, who was invariably interested in Barker's work and, in fact, exhausted him with questions even as he poked around in his crumbling molars.

One arm in his sleeve, Barker stood without moving, as if caught in a paralyzing draft, and when Bennie said something close to his ear, he jumped. "Whoa," Bennie said. "Nerves. Why don't we go get a beer?"

"What did you say?" Barker asked. He began to shake somewhere deep in neural tissue.

"I said I was thinking about that title of yours. I like it. It speaks to me. Not that I'm absolutely certain what it means, but it's arresting; people are going to remember it when they get inside a bookstore. Hey, Jake, why are you looking so down? You think Ronnie Reagan's going to change your life? Forget it. One skunk down in Washington is just like any other skunk. They're all after the same sleazy things."

"Maybe Ronnie smells worse," Barker said. He sat down on the narrow bench in an attempt to calm himself. Heat rose to his forehead and peppered his brow with sweat.

"It's all megasmell, what difference does it make who's sitting in the Oval Office? My advice to you is to ignore it and go about your business." They left the building together. Barker had beaten Bennie fifteen–thirteen and felt pretty good about that, but his right calf hurt as if a clamp were attached to it. He found himself limping. Bennie appeared not to notice. "What's up with you and Anita?" he asked.

"We've decided to cool it for a while. See how we both feel. She seems to be preoccupied with other, more urgent matters. I think she's bucking for dean."

"Your girlfriend, Anita Andrews, a dean? At Harvard? I didn't know you had any lady deans. Jesus, think of the harm she could do."

"Oh, come on, Anita's harmless enough. What can she do?

What can any dean do, for that matter? Most of them are just overgrown camp counselors, counting the linen and seeing that nobody hangs himself at 3:00 A.M."

"I don't know, Jake, there's a streak of toughness in that lady I don't think you appreciate."

"I don't like my ladies to have that kind of streak," Barker said, wondering if this conversation was about to get serious and did he want that. "If they have any kind of streak—and I sense you to mean part of their character structure—it should be kindness. Maybe you're right, maybe that's why Anita and I aren't going to make it. Funny though, last year I thought she was the best lady I'd ever met. She made other women seem hard as nails. Pretty beast, I wonder what happened to her."

They climbed into Barker's Rabbit and sped off toward M.I.T., where Bennie had a date with an academic committee. "If I don't show my face once in a while, they'll take away my desk, my chair, and my blackboard and sell them. Besides, the place is getting overrun with right-wing political theorists who compose diabolical theories on computers. I've got to try to put a stop to it, although it's probably too late. Military Institute of Technology."

"Mouse Institute of Technology," Barker said. "Anita thinks she's got a good shot at first-ever Dean of Women's Affairs. It seems the ladies are clamoring for representation."

"We've got a couple already," Bennie said. Barker brought the car to a smooth stop as a freight train crossed slowly in front of them on Massachusetts Avenue. He began to count the cars. "Some of our lady deans spend most of their time investigating claims brought by overwrought girls bent on nailing their teachers," Bennie said.

"Nailing? What for?" Worms crawled over the skin on the back of Barker's neck. He took a deep breath.

"For what's politely called harassment. You know, *an A for a lay*. It's a nasty bit of business. You know what I'm talking about." The gate's striped arm rose to the accompaniment of a buzzing noise.

"I've heard rumors," Barker said. An artery sucked blood from his brain. For a moment he thought he was going to pass out. His fingers tightened around the steering wheel.

"It's a genu-wine problem," Bennie said. Barker wondered if Bennie had ever indulged, but decided against asking. When his friend fell silent, Barker distracted himself with thinking back. Every damn one of the girls he'd had sex with had asked for it—of this he was absolutely sure. Asked for it, either explicitly or covertly, by muted signals, and now they were busy finding ways to make the men pay for what was indisputably a two-way transaction. Barker was about to open his mouth and start to dismember current feminist theory when two cars half a block up the street hit each other head on. From the passenger side of one of them, a red late-model two-door Honda, a teenaged girl emerged, stood briefly, and collapsed on the street. The driver of this car was obscured by the windshield, which had buckled as if made of sheet metal. "We ought to stop and help," Barker said. The head of the girl on the ground started to bleed. Barker's pulse quickened and made a loud sound in his ears.

"No need, here comes a cop car. *That* was quick." Barker executed an abrupt maneuver to avoid getting back-ended by the ambulance.

"That's the third bad accident I've seen in the last ten days," Barker said, trying to steady his foot on the gas pedal. "What do you think it means?"

"Means?" Bennie said. "I don't get you. If you're thinking it has something to do with you, that's a sure sign you're working too hard. Your porch lights are beginning to flicker. You don't have both oars in the water, your elevator's not going up to the top floor."

"And I'm not playing with a full deck. Very funny," Barker said. Nevertheless he did think it had something to do with him, he was certain of it; danger moved toward him like a wind-driven radioactive cloud. Soon it would stop over his house and rain destruction, the poison from the sky meeting the poison beneath his skin.

The two men didn't talk about it, but Barker was sure from the crease across his brow and the way his lower lip was trapped between his teeth that Bennie was trying to erase from his memory the sight of the girl in the car. It was only after Bennie had said goodbye, got out of the car, and shut the door, that Barker realized he had failed to inquire what had happened to the poor bastards whose students were determined to nail and crucify them.

Barker loved Bennie. Bennie was the one constant in his life, while others—especially women—swam past him, fish in the middle of a fast-moving stream. Bennie was a rock, a boulder. Barker could never tell him this, of course, it would embarrass the man, perhaps even frighten him off. Barker knew he couldn't count on most folks, excuses by the score would materialize, wild and improbable excuses in order not to have to accede to a perfectly reasonable request: in-laws arriving, exams to correct, sick dog to take to the vet, dentist appointment, the attic to clean, a grandchild to sit for, a closet pole to install, a fire to put out, a barbecue to build for the wife. Anything, just get me out of this. Barker despised the meanness around him.

There was a heaviness in the atmosphere above Cambridge; clouds, roiling and swollen with rain, held on to it like tubs with blocked drains. Barker felt as if his brains were pressing against his skull. Did the tissues there actually swell? What would happen if they swelled to a size larger than their container?

Thus preoccupied, half expecting his head to crack and split, Barker climbed the stairs to his office on the second floor.

"Not feeling too well, are you, Professor Barker?" Emily Compton asked as he tried to slip past her desk. "It's that dreadful Asian flu going around. Best not fight it."

"I can't go home," Barker said impatiently. "I've got to see my publisher this afternoon."

"Well then," said Emily, apparently unimpressed by his reference to a publisher, "just remember to drink plenty of grapefruit juice. Do you have enough aspirin?"

"I've got aspirin, thanks, Emmy." Barker closed the door of his office and sifted through his mail. Two invitations to speak; one invitation to contribute an article to a journal known for its practice of turning down the work of world-class psychologists via printed rejection forms; three letters from colleagues that would require him to write long, complicated answers; a request from a former student (male, uninspired, thirty pounds overweight) for a letter of recommendation to graduate school; a letter from a textbook editor seeking his imprimatur on the newest book in his field; and two invitations to buy time-share condos in backwater Florida. Barker sighed, unable, or so it felt, to draw enough oxygen into his lungs in order to breathe freely. He shoved the mail to one side, aware that he looked forward to dealing with none of it. In fact, it was all a pain in the ass. He got up and went down to the cul de sac in the basement where four squat vending machines purred, one of them always broken; they took turns. He bought himself a tuna sandwich on a soft roll, the mashed fish oozing from between bread jaws onto its plastic wrap. When he tried to extract a Diet Pepsi from the drink machine, it balked and threw back his two quarters and a nickel. Cursing, Barker took the sandwich to his desk and, realizing only when he sat down that he'd forgotten to pick up a napkin, got fish smell all over his fingers; even after he washed them, they continued to stink. These same fingers he then employed to write a letter— for he made up his mind that he would not give in to inertia— to one of his correspondents, picked at random. It turned out, alas, to be one of the complicated letters, requiring him to organize his thoughts, compose a diagram, and to speculate. But when he had finished the letter to Phil Jones in Australia, he was pleased with the result, so pleased (for it contained the germ of an idea about the possible effects of protein intake on spatial performance) that he asked Emily to make a copy of the letter for him to file. It happened every time, didn't it; there was nothing like a spot of work to make a fellow feel happy to go on living.

Soon after this the clouds' seams burst apart, releasing millions of gallons of acid rain across the body of New England. Barker set off for Lothar and Bright in a good mood, indifferent to the fact that he was getting soaked and trying out, in his head, various methods to test the idea conveyed in his letter to Jones in Queensland. He still had it, didn't he, the thing that Bennie had kissed goodbye, the spark that lights the fire of imagination?

Inside the conspicuously decorated waiting room of Lothar and Bright—an ancient room in a brand-new building, rather like a period room in an antiquarian museum—Barker was loath to sit down; his trousers were wet and all the chairs were covered in satin. What exactly was the effect they were trying to produce? Tradition rampant? Backlist gravity? Sound investment policies? Lothar and Bright books stood in rows behind glass-covered, floor-to-ceiling bookcases. You had, Barker saw, to ask for a key in order to get to one. His appointment was for three. At three-fifteen the receptionist informed him from behind her cage that "Miss Cheng will be with you in a moment."

"My appointment with her was for fifteen minutes ago." Barker looked severely at his watch.

The receptionist could have cared less—as she surely would have put it. She eyed him as if he were a courier who spoke no English and might be carrying a shiv. Where did they find these people? Had they no sense of public relations? For a moment Barker considered departure, but as he was making up his mind to give her five more minutes, a small, dazzlingly beautiful Chinese girl, whose medium-length black hair had the gloss of polished marble, and whose body—slim and seemingly boneless—had been composed by a master hand, came into the room and spoke to him.

"I'm Susan Cheng," she said in a rippling waterfall voice, holding out her hand for him to shake. "I work with Tom Shachter in Advertising and Promotion. I've been assigned to your book."

"You have?" Barker said. "But you're hardly out of high school." Wrong. Wrong thing to say. She looked surprised, then displeased. "I've been here for two years," she said. "I'm a graduate of the Radcliffe Publishing Procedures course. Would you like to see my credentials?" Her skin was warm mother-of-pearl, pale and opalescent. On neither skin nor clothes could Barker detect a single wrinkle.

"I'm sorry," he said. And he was; he wanted this girl to like him, the softness at his heart's core melted and oozed outwards. Disinterest changed to desire.

"We can go up to my office," she said. He could hardly talk, for the lava had begun to spread warmly to the back of his throat, thickening his tongue. He nodded, and followed her. Under her turtleneck shirt (quality stuff, probably a mixture of silk and something soft and supple) he could see the knobs on her backbone, a soft rope that disappeared down into the divine crevice.

"Mr. Barker?" She had said something he could not hear because of the racket his heart was making. No longer did he try to analyze the devastating effect created by a pretty female; it was as much a fact of his life as his mega-IQ. While other men seemed able to take women or leave them, Barker was cursed and could not. He could leave Paula, his editor, but only because she was gay and threw off menacing pheromones. He had never been able to leave a straight female without gasping for breath.

99

They rounded a corner and entered Ms. Cheng's office, whose one small, impeccably clean window gave out on another office building opposite and a very thin slice of Boston Common. She indicated a chair for him to sit in; he sat, she sat. She swiveled to face him and, drawing her dark blue skirt self-consciously over her knees, said, "We were wondering if you would have the time to go on an author tour." On the wall over her desk was a bulletin board to which were pinned pieces of paper, photographs of Chinese folk—her family, no doubt, and close buddies—ads she probably had had a part in composing, a book jacket in an early stage (no type, just the picture), a tan dog with long floppy ears, several babies looking amused. On the wall opposite the desk was the poster of a blue and gray fan-tailed bird with Chinese writing beneath it. Susan Cheng's desk was awash in papers; this disorder was a surprise to Barker, who thought all Asians were compulsively neat.

She waited while Barker summoned his answer. "Sure," he said. "What exactly does it involve, and how much time will it take?" Why hadn't she yet said anything nice about his book? What was wrong with these people? Had they taken a blood oath, chanting by candlelight, not, under any circumstances and under pain of death, to permit their authors to hear a single word of praise?

"It should take three weeks or so," Susan Cheng said. "You visit eight or nine key cities around the country, appear on local TV to plug the book, and get interviewed by the local press. It's exhausting, but we've found it sells books as well as anything else—including advertising." Susan Cheng flipped her thick black veil of hair back over her right earlobe. The little ear itself, that curling shell of flesh, stunned Barker; he wanted to grab it between his teeth, maybe draw a drop or two of her blood.

"Well, yes," he said, "I think I can manage that. Of course, I'll have to know far enough in advance to make arrangements for someone else to meet with my classes while I'm away." The idea of appearing on TV screens all over America did not exactly turn him off. He would have to buy a suit—or at the very least a new jacket and several red ties. Barker had often appeared on Boston television; whenever a story broke that needed some commentary by an expert—the high math scores chalked up by little girls, for instance—they called either on Jacob Barker or on a corpulent young woman who invariably wore overalls in front of the camera. Sometimes they had them appear together; she didn't use deodorant—Barker figured this lapse to be a political statement of some kind. "Can I call you Susan?"

"What?"

"I asked if you would mind if I called you by your first name—since we're going to be working together for a while— at least so long as my book is viable."

"It's up to you," she said.

Barker knew full well what was happening; he was no stranger to the symptoms nor to the fact that once they started up, goodbye sense, goodbye sanity. He was falling for this almond blossom, this tea leaf, this freshwater pearl. Forty-two years old and smitten like a kid whose hormones have just recently begun to interfere with his thought processes. It was humiliating. And this person whose knee he had only to stretch his arm to caress, this child barely out of her teens, talking schedules and coming on like a big-deal executive, this girl looked at him as if he were a used-car salesman.

Susan tried to pin him down. "*Cleopatra's Nose* will be out mid-September. That doesn't give us all that much time. I'll need a list of people you would like us to send bound galleys to. Also people who should get copies of the book before publication." And still another list: those folks who might want to review *Nose* (her name for his baby). She was escorting him along strange byways.

"I always thought the cream rose naturally to the top," Barker said. "That is, if a book is good enough, people will buy it. Or am I wrong? I can see by your face that I'm wrong."

Now Susan Cheng smiled for the first time. "How we wish that were true," she said, lapsing into a verbal style no doubt filched from one of her Brahmin bosses. The phone on Susan's desk rang and she picked it up without apology. While she talked into it (it was quite rude of her, Barker thought, she might have told the person on the other end that she was busy), Barker got up and pinched a dead spider off a plant hanging from the window frame and dropped the corpse in the waste-basket. Silently he said, "Get off the phone, girl."

"Sorry," she said, hanging up.

Barker nodded coolly. His blood was on the boil.

"You're not married," he said.

"No, I'm not," she said. "What about Chicago? It's a big book town. Do you know anyone there you think might want to review *Nose* for the *Tribune* or the *Sun-Times*?"

With lightning speed Barker ticked off seven midwestern names inside his head, discarded five—he and they could have been on far better terms—and gave the remaining two to Susan Cheng, who wrote them down on a legal-size yellow pad. Her handwriting was tiny, the letters as perfectly formed as her ebony eyes. She was made of the finest stuff—ebony, alabaster, porcelain, silk. He had never made love to an Oriental girl; the very idea set his epidermis tingling. He closed his eyes and leaned back. Susan kept right on going as if Barker were not three feet away from her and about to expire with lust. Perhaps she was accustomed to making men faint; perhaps she had planned it. If that were true, it meant that her beauty was a mask for a wicked heart and he should proceed with the greatest caution.

"Fool," he said to himself, having escaped to the men's room to cool off. "What sort of person are you?" he continued. "Concentrate on your book, idiot, that's what you're here for. This girl means nothing to you; you've known her less than an hour."

"What say?"

"I beg your pardon." Barker turned to a middle-aged man in an expensive-looking dark brown suit, striped blue and white shirt, and yellow foulard tie. The man was standing over the next sink lathering his hands.

"I thought you said something to me."

"Ah, no," Barker said. "I was thinking out loud. Sorry. It's a bad but harmless habit of mine." His head began to hurt.

"No problem," the man said. "We all have our little kinks, eh?" He shook his wet hands over the basin and tugged two paper towels from the dispenser on the wall. He frowned. "Feels like cardboard," he said to Barker, "smells like glue. I keep telling them to purchase better-quality paper goods, but pennies, it seems, are more important than a man's comfort. I don't think I've seen you before?"

"No," Barker said, wondering if this man were about to come on to him. "I'm one of their authors."

"Oh really," the man said, backing off. He seemed to be deciding whether or not to shake hands with Barker. "What's the title of your book?"

"It's called *Cleopatra's Nose*," Barker said, liking the sound of it more and more.

"Oh," the man said, "so you're the one!"

"So I'm the one what?" Barker asked.

"The snake-in-the-grass. The fellow who thinks women ought to have the vote." Here he guffawed, presumably to let Barker know that he knew women already had the vote.

This was his publisher? Barker cringed. "By the way," he said. "I'm Jacob Barker. You are . . . ?"

"The name's Vogel, Arthur Vogel. Means bird in German. I'm treasurer of this outfit. Been here for fourteen years and before that at John Hancock. Every book the editorial board wants to buy has to get past Art Vogel first. When Art Vogel says it's gonna bomb, they turn it down. I've got an uncanny feel for this game; my wife thinks it's more like an illness. You can call me Art." This time the still-clammy paw was extended

103

and was taken briefly by Barker, now thoroughly rattled. Snake-in-the-grass? Damn Anita. He should never have allowed her to get her mitts on his book. "I stand by what I wrote," he said, aware as soon as these words were out of his mouth that they made him sound like a horse's ass.

But apparently Vogel was used to writers who acted like horses' asses, for he said, "I'm really delighted to hear that. Wouldn't do at all to have one of our authors produce a work he refused to stand by and then palm it off on Lothar and Bright."

Barker bowed out, shaken. He got lost on the way back to Susan's office and had to ask for directions. When he found it at last, he also found a note tacked to the door, addressed to him, saying she was sorry, an emergency had come up in production; she would be back, she wrote, in fifteen minutes. Like most people who leave such notes, Ms. Cheng had neglected to indicate what time it had been penned. So it could be as long as half an hour (since most people also misjudged how long things take, erring on the too-short side) and as little as seven or eight minutes. "Story of my life," Barker growled. What sort of emergency did they have in publishing houses that obliged a person to abort an important meeting with an important author? Although it practically killed him, Barker decided not to wait.

Chapter Eight

By the time Barker climbed out of the subway tunnel and up into the hub of Harvard Square it was too late to go back to work, so he set off for his apartment, picking up a copy of the *Harvard Crimson* on the way. This newspaper was written and edited entirely by undergraduates, many of whom would never experience the joys of searching for employment but would go directly to desks at the *Posts*—Washington and New York—*Ms.* magazine, *Mother Jones*, the *Berkshire Eagle*, the *Middletown News*, and so on. Barker admired the style of these youthful journalists and editors—they had picked up the niceties of the craft without ever having taken a single journalism course, for Harvard's educational philosophy excluded from the curriculum all hands-on courses, trusting, rather, that if a young man or woman had a solid enough background in the arts and humanities and a smattering of science and technology, he (or she, but preferably he) could pick up such skills as journalism, acting, performing on musical instruments, dancing, writing fiction, and sculpting in a relative jiffy along the way. Barker believed this to be an extremely foolish notion, but there was no route by which he could make known his views—and in any case they hardly kept him up at night. So it was all the more remarkable that the *Crimson* came out at all, let alone five times a week, with relatively few typos and only an occasional error of fact.

Barker opened the front door to his apartment, entered its dusk and sourish smell, and immediately turned on every light. He went into the kitchen and poured himself a hefty drink, noticing that the soda was flat and the ice shrunken. He sat down on the living room couch and opened the paper, sipping at his drink from time to time until it began to shut him off from everything he could not see or feel at the moment. Even Susan Cheng ended up in a past now sealed off from the prying eyes of recent memory.

The first thing Barker read was a story about a Harvard-owned apartment house on a street in Cambridge whose name he did not recognize. If you believed the article, the tenants of this establishment were completely bent out of shape about their living conditions. "Roaches big as lima beans," one tenant was reported to have said. "Plumbing hasn't worked since 1979," a second claimed. "Ceiling leaks like a watering can," a third complained. Then, too, someone, a teenaged girl, had got herself raped on the roof, though what this child was doing on the roof at 3:30 A.M. the story did not say. The tenants had formed an association, hired a lawyer, and were threatening to sue the university unless a specified number of improvements were made by such and such a date. The writer of the article was squarely on the tenants' side—several loaded adjectives here and there and the general tone of the piece made this perfectly clear. Sympathy for victims was a hallmark of the *Crimson*. Ah, youth . . . too soon would this inspiring spirit fade, along with the blush on their youthful skin. As this corporeal image occurred to Barker, the porcelain face of Susan Cheng swam briefly through the mist inside his head.

Barker sighed, swallowed down to one half inch of booze, and turned the tabloid over. What was this? A picture of a woman who looked just like Anita Andrews. He re-angled the paper and saw that it was, in fact, his former girlfriend wearing, for crissake, a suit with mannish lapels and a blouse buttoned clear up to her chin. As far as Barker could tell, she was sitting in an office that looked to be in newly renovated Harvard administrative headquarters, with a great expanse of window behind her and in the distance the statue of the founder, John Harvard, dressed in bronze knickers and cape, sitting solidly staring at something only the model for the statue could see. Anita was identified as Dean of Women's Affairs, the first ever. Accompanying the picture and caption was a short biography, omitting her hippie period and brief marriage. Her duties were, in her very own words, to "act as a clearinghouse for a range of gender-related projects and grievances. Everything, that is, from unequal athletic facilities to charges of sexual harassment on the part of Harvard faculty members. We intend to put a stop to this loathsome practice once and for all."

"Judas Priest," Barker said, "the harpies are coming." He smiled ruefully. Something for the ladies to do in their spare time. How fortunate he was to have escaped from the embrace of a woman so angry, so burdened with political agenda that she had become nothing more than a walking advertisement for revenge.

Their romance—some would have called it a "relationship," a word that caused Barker's skin to prickle—had lapsed like membership in a club you find you're no longer patronizing the way you once did, and it isn't until you get a dues notice that you realize you have no further use for the dining room (food tastes like cardboard and library paste) or the private facilities (gloomy and airless, lax service). Barker and his ladylove, Anita Andrews, had simply lapsed, the spaces between their meetings (not counting those at work) had grown larger, intimacies revealed were less tantalizing, promises made vaguer. The clasp of hand and hand had lost its muscle. Barker's recollection of the heat once generated by their love affair made his temperature flare even now, even as he decided she was a bitch. For a sweet moment it had been the real thing, there was no denying it; Barker was not one to rewrite history in so blatant a fashion. And he was prepared to blame its dissolution on himself as much as on her sexual restlessness, for the fact was that he, too, was restless. He decided then and there to be a mensch. He would call her soon and tell her just this: "It was as much my fault as yours. Our tree was not meant to bear fruit."

Barker opened a can of Campbell's tomato soup (wondering by what means the folks at Campbell's had managed to achieve absolute dominion over the soup-buying public), rummaged around until he found a box of saltines, saw that grubs had taken up residence within the wax paper wrap, tossed the box into the garbage can, and found at last an end of French bread as hard as a lemon. Most of the cheese in the fridge had turned either green or gray; a chunk of mild cheddar had some interesting grayish fluff growing on it. Desperately sorry for himself, he heated the soup, poured it into a bowl, and ate it standing at the kitchen counter, uncertain if he would ever again find himself inside the cage of a marriage. Was it worth it for the meals he would be fed? He was beginning to think it might be.

Barker had just put the soup pot in the sink to soak overnight when the phone rang.

"Dad?"

"Is that you, Guy?"

"Who else would it be? How many people call you Dad?"

The call surprised Barker, for his son, now fourteen years old, rarely spoke to him. Guy was enrolled in the Preiss School, an institution for children with a range of problems so various Barker could not help admiring its extraordinary ability to pinpoint obstacles. Eating disorders, dyslexia, emotional retardation, muscular-skills deficiencies, social misalignment—these and a host of less manifest problems were grist for the Preiss School's educational mill. The kids on the cover of the school's brochure looked perfectly okay, but then who but a total loser puts a spaz in its brochure? Guy boarded at the Preiss School from Monday to Friday and came home to his mother's house on weekends, a forty-five-minute trip by commuter rail. Barker was well versed as to the particulars of Guy's life, though he saw the boy—by mutual consent—only three or four times a year. Guy was unbelievably skittish and Barker quite believed that his mother had been feeding him hate-your-father pills over a long period of time; the stuff had built up in his system like antibodies. Not without grumbling did Barker pay his son's astronomical bills, term bills, shrink bills, and bills for all those incidentals teenaged boys seemed to accumulate like zits. Barker decided they must be injecting Guy with growth hormones, for he appeared to need a new pair of footwear every three months or so—sneakers mainly, items which had cost Barker fifteen dollars when he was Guy's age and now cost fifty.

It was hard for Barker to muster a great deal of warm feeling for his son.

"Where are you, Guy?"

"I'm here, at school. Can you meet me for breakfast tomorrow, Dad? There's something I have to talk to you about."

"You want me to come out there?" Barker said. He didn't know how to talk to Guy, it had been so long. What do you do? Do you say what you're thinking or do you say what you think he wants to hear? Barker began to sweat.

"No, I'll come in to Cambridge. Can you make it?" Barker realized with a start that since he had last spoken with Guy, the boy's voice had, thank God, changed. At one point, he had thought that Guy's voice would never deepen at all and suggested to Nancy that he be enrolled in a music academy and trained as a castrato.

"I have a nine o'clock class," Barker said. "But I can meet you at seven-thirty."

"Can't you cancel your class or something?"

The boy was forcing him to say no, a trick widespread among Barker's acquaintances. He had it in mind to ask a writer friend of his to work up a piece about the power game involved in getting your friends to say no to you (and thereby gaining the moral upper hand). In any case, Guy was doing it to him now.

"No," he said firmly. "That's absurd, you know I can't cancel my class."

"Okay, okay," Guy said in his new voice, "I was just asking. It doesn't hurt to ask. I'll look up the train schedule." There was a pause. "Okay, here's a train that gets into North Station at seven. Shit, that means I'll have to get up at five-thirty."

The words "suit yourself" formed themselves, ready to go into orbit. Barker stopped them. "You wanted to meet me," he said.

Guy made a noise Barker heard as assent. He told Guy to meet him at Pearl's, where "they have great blueberry muffins. Best in the Square." Guy said nothing. "Hey, pal," Barker said, "is there something you'd like to tell me right now? Are you in trouble?"

"It can wait till tomorrow, Dad, thanks anyway." And Guy hung up, leaving his father unaccountably nervous.

When Guy walked into Pearl's the next morning at seven thirty-two—Barker having arrived ten minutes early and stationed himself at a table from which it was impossible to miss anyone entering by the front door—Barker gasped. His son, the plump, moon-faced boy, had turned into a slim and lovely youth whose erstwhile piggy eyes had widened and become intelligent, whose feral hair was now domesticated, and whose demeanor was startlingly attractive; the girls must be falling at this fellow's feet in a way that might even become routine. Guy was wearing jeans and a denim jacket under which was a faded blue oxford shirt. Good independent touch, that shirt; other boys his age sported tee shirts embossed with unintelligible pictograph and message.

Guy sat down opposite his father. His posture was admirable—back straight, shoulders even but relaxed. "I got you a muffin," Barker said, "but I didn't know whether you drink coffee."

"I don't eat those things anymore, Dad," Guy said. "I've lost nearly fifty pounds. Didn't you notice?" Guy's fingers were long and thin. He wore a watch with a red face and no numerals.

"Sure I noticed," Barker said. "You didn't give me a chance to say anything. As a matter of fact, I hardly recognized you when you came in. How did you do it?"

"They have this overeaters' table at school. You keep track, and they keep track. It works, I guess. And I've gone out for the tennis team. Do you mind if I get some coffee?"

"Mind? Of course not. Here"—Barker dug into his pocket and came up with a couple of ones and some change—"get yourself some breakfast."

Guy looked dubious. "Are you trying to make me fat again?"

"No, no no no," Barker said. "I meant something on your diet. What do you have for breakfast anyway?"

"Special K, that kind of stuff. Sometimes a hard-boiled egg."

"You must be hungry all the time," Barker said.

"I'm almost never hungry anymore," Guy said, getting up. "I almost never think about eating."

"Oh," said Barker. Had Guy been brainwashed or was he lying? Pearl's was filling up with breakfast eaters, mostly solos. Nearby were a pair of men who looked like they were on their way to the big city (dark suits, attaché cases); a few college kids, the rich kind, those with extra cash to spend on eggs and bacon here while their parents were paying Harvard for uneaten eggs and bacon back at the dorm; the usual elderly folk concentrating on bowls of oatmeal and Cream of Wheat; two hyperactive females in their thirties talking to one another simultaneously with their noses only inches apart; several men

111

in tweedy jackets whom Barker figured to be retired and/or widowed Harvard professors.

Guy came back and sat down again, placing his thick mug squarely in front of him and cupping it loosely with his palms. The kid was withholding like crazy.

Barker bit into his muffin. It crumbled all over his fingers, making a mess. Guy looked away. Barker sympathized; he could never bear to watch his own father eating, something about the way he had ferociously chewed. . . . Barker swallowed and said, "You've got something heavy on your mind. Now's as good a time as any to come out with it."

Guy looked at him warily.

"You know," Barker said, unexpectedly finding himself eager to break through his son's reticence, "it's kind of a waste of your time to come in all this way and then clam up on me."

"Take it easy, man," Guy said. "I'm trying."

"When was the last time you asked me to meet you?" Barker said. "I think you were about nine years old."

"What did I want then?" Guy said.

"You wanted me to take you to the circus."

"Oh yeah, I remember. You couldn't make it. So what else is new?"

"I couldn't make it, Guy, because I had to be in Paris for a conference."

"Big deal," Guy said. "Big effing deal."

At this, Barker's adrenaline surged. He tightened both hands into fists but kept them safely under the table. "Listen up, pal," he said. "I know you think I'm a lousy father, but that doesn't mean I'm going to sit here and take this shit from you. If you've got something to tell me—something that isn't just let's get Dad in the balls—go ahead, that's what I came here for. Otherwise, I've got plenty to do. *Comprende?*" Barker had said it exactly right. Guy's eyes closed briefly; the admirable posture melted.

"I'm sorry, Dad," Guy improbably said. And just as improbably, Guy's apology made Barker's chest go warm and soft; the back of his throat closed up. "Are you sure you don't want something to eat?"

"I'm sure." The thing that needed a voice lay between them on the table, opening and closing its mouth like a perch dying on the floor of the boat. If Barker read Guy's frown correctly the boy was hosting a struggle between the forces of speech and silence. Although he felt it was generally improvident to spend time visiting the past, and although he practiced retrospection only as a last resort, Barker tried now to recall what it was like to be almost fifteen, confronting a father to whom he could not, for an entire arsenal of reasons, open up; the main reason being that father was the ENEMY, ready to shoot him down with one eye closed and forefinger arced over the trigger. History, he realized, was repeating itself with all the banality of young love or the oedipal tangle.

"Guy," he finally said, "I hope you're going to tell me what's making you miserable."

"What are you talking about? How can you tell?"

"Trust me," Barker managed to say without smiling. "It's the business of fathers to read their children's minds."

Guy made a sound suggesting that all the air was being pulled from his body. "I guess I know that," he said in a whisper.

"Would it make it any easier for you if I asked you questions—you know, like a lawyer, only I'd be deliberately leading the witness?"

"Well yeah, Dad, it probably would. That's an okay idea. . . ." He tried to smile.

"Does it have to do with breaking the law?" Barker guessed.

"Fuck, Dad, what do you think I am?"

"Okay, okay, just asking. Does it have to do with your schoolwork?"

"Not exactly. No, it doesn't."

"All right then, does it have to do with drugs?"

"Un-unh. Not really."

"What do you mean, not really?"

113

"Christ, man, everybody does drugs. I mean marijuana, for crissake, it's all over the place, even the teachers do it, you can smell it, the teachers' lounge reeks of grass. I shouldn't have said not really. Drugs have nothing to do with this thing."

"Right. So it's not the law, not your schoolwork, not drugs—what's left? I believe the only thing left is sex. Is it sex?" Guy's ear lobes turned crimson. He nodded.

"*Ah zo,*" Barker said, feebly attempting to lighten things. He could not suppress, however, a sigh of pleasure that Guy appeared to be his father's son, after all. "You've knocked up your girlfriend, What's-her-name? You're aware, of course, that it's a relatively easy business to get an abortion these days—unless the lass is Catholic. It's not like when I was young and the girl had to get herself to Sweden or Mexico or Union City, New Jersey, one of those places. And poor people who couldn't afford the trip—Jesus, some of them actually died of asepsis. . . ."

"Dad, please," Guy said. "I didn't say anyone's pregnant. It's more complicated than that . . ."

Brakes screeched; Barker shifted to neutral. "Explain," he said. Someone behind him dropped a plate; it rotated, bounced off a hard surface, then hit the floor with a crackling noise. A man said, "Shit," a woman laughed. The manager, a fat Lebanese who operated the cash register, looked over and shrugged with disgust. Barker did not turn around.

"I want to," Guy said. Barker noticed that most of Guy's coffee was still in its mug. "But I'm not sure how."

"Start at the beginning," Barker said. "You met this girl. . . ."

"No, Dad."

"What do you mean, 'No, Dad'?"

"I mean there isn't any girl."

"Woman then. I keep forgetting. Although it's my under-standing that it's all right to call someone under twenty-one a girl. All the rest are women. They don't appreciate 'girl' any-more. It's just like people of color don't want to be called

114

Negro, they want to be called Black. You can't exactly blame them, but the negative connotations—black heart, black deed, and so on—you'd think they'd want to stay away from that word. I think if I were black I'd prefer the word 'colored'—though why they have to be singled out at all is beyond me. But I'm getting off the point. . . ." Barker knew he was babbling but couldn't stop.

Guy did it for him. "No!" It came out as a lingering howl. For a second or two the echo of this syllable went careering around Pearl's, bouncing off wall and ceiling. Heads lifted, trying to locate the source of the sound. Guy held his head still upon its long and graceful neck, standing his ground; it must have taken all his strength not to duck or blush or cover his face. After the moment passed, the diners went back to their waffles and oatmeal, English muffins and hot chocolate, their scrambled eggs, home fries, and half grapefruits, *Boston Globe*s and *New York Times*es, their economics and child-development textbooks. Barker felt awful.

"I think," Barker began, "I think," he repeated, "I know what you're trying to tell me. You think you're gay because you prefer the company of boys. That's it, isn't it?" When he saw that Guy wasn't protesting, he went quickly on. "Now look, what you're feeling is perfectly normal for a kid your age. It's the norm. I remember when I was fifteen" (and here Barker made another unexpected visit to the past) "I experimented like crazy. I fucked anything on two legs. There was this boy George, I can't remember his last name, who lived in our apartment house. We were on the fifteenth floor and he was one floor below, we used to meet in his apartment after school because his mother was a working gal, and we, well . . . we screwed on many a winter afternoon. Obviously . . ."—here Barker paused for emphasis—"my tastes have changed and narrowed significantly. I tell you it's perfectly standard, what you're going through."

"I wish you'd let me talk," Guy said in a soft voice.

"Of course I'll let you talk. What do you mean?"

"Man, you're doing all the talking. And you're telling me things that happened almost fifty years ago. Things that have nothing to do with me."

"Hold on there," Barker said. "I'm still on the sunny side of fifty."

"I know that," Guy said, appearing not to notice his inconsistency.

"I'm only telling you about me to demonstrate how normal it is for teenagers to experiment. I want to be sure you understand this. Freud called it polymorph-perversity." As soon as this was out of his mouth Barker regretted it, for Guy was looking at him the way he used to, as if he were getting ready to spit. "I'm sorry," Barker said. "Forget the big word. It just means that all of us have bisexual natures. I'm sure it's true, Guy. It doesn't mean you're a freak. Ninety-nine percent of boys like you get over it—I did."

"But you liked girls, too."

This had to be the understatement of the postindustrial era. Barker had had his first girl at the age of eight, another third-grader named Beverly Small. Funny how her name—long hidden in memory's muck—now came crawling to the surface. Instantly she stood there with her blue cotton panties clinging to white baby thighs (sneaky little thing, she was as eager as he was). Barker shook his head. "Yes, I liked girls, too," he said. "What exactly are you trying to tell me?"

"If you'd stop talking at me for a sec, I'd tell you. I don't like girls, too, Dad; I only like guys. . . ." He seemed baffled by the repetition of his own name. "I only like boys. Girls have *never* interested me. Girls make me feel weird." Guy rubbed his cheek with the heel of his hand.

"Weird? What does that mean?"

"I get a funny feeling in my stomach, sort of like I was on one of those rides in the amusement park that turn you upside down."

"And you never tried . . . that is, you've never been physically close to a girl?"

116

"Sure I've been physically close. I sit next to them in class, don't I?"

"That's not what I mean," Barker said.

Guy pulled a grayish handkerchief from his pocket and blew his nose into it. An ancient, shuffling Hispanic began collecting dishes, piling them into a plastic tub set high on wheels. He approached their table and swerved off when he saw there was nothing to gather up. Guy stared at him. Barker stared at Guy.

"What's the matter, man, can't you swallow it?" Guy tipped his chair so far back Barker was scared it was going to fall over with Guy still on it. The idea that Guy might be homosexual— for what else had the kid been trying to tell him from the moment he sat down—was so abhorrent that Barker felt he had to disprove it. "Listen, son," Barker said. "I don't want you to worry about it."

"I'm not worried about it, man. Not the way you think I am. I'm not like the other guys at school—all they talk about is tits and whether they got any last night. They fuck their girlfriends in the boathouse and after dances behind the tennis courts— there's a bunch of trees there. Some guys even bring girls into their rooms. . . ."

"Aren't their rooms off-limits to girls?" Barker asked.

"Jesus, Dad. You still don't get the point, do you?"

"Apparently not. Why don't you enlighten me?"

"A couple of them grabbed me and sat on my chest and made me listen while they told me what they did. They know I didn't want to hear. They called me a faggot. You know what that's like? It's like one of your black people being called nigger. It doesn't tickle, Dad. There are other things they do, but I don't want to talk about it. The reason I had to see you right away was to get your permission to quit school."

"You're kidding! You want to leave school because of a few things some stupid kids said to you?"

"I don't want to quit all school, just this one. I want to go somewhere else. I need your permission—yours and Mom's."

117

Barker tried to cover the bitterness of Guy's surprise. He would have felt better had he found out his father was not really his parent, his mother was a whore, and his book's publication had been indefinitely postponed. Barker's denial was not properly installed: gusts of the truth blew through the cracks. Guy had said "they fuck girls" in the same tone he might have said "they eat their own shit for breakfast." The boy was a pansy, a fruit, a fairy, a faggot, and chances were he would *not* outgrow this adolescent homosexuality; it seemed to be the real thing. And so he would become one of those men whose entire lives were a reflection of the matter of where they stuck it—as if anyone truly cared which of two holes it went in. All that fuss about where they stuck it—it did appear to matter so much to them. It colored their lives; it informed their choice of job, food, books, furniture, and pictures, their recreation—just about everything. It appeared to matter more, even, than their intelligence, talents, or genes. It was a puzzler; Barker did not begin to understand.

Guy said something Barker caught only the tail end of; he hoped it wasn't something crucial. "Would you like to see someone about this?" he asked his son.

"See someone? You mean a shrink? Man, I'm up to my eyeballs in shrinks," Guy said, reasonably enough. "All I want right now is to get out of my fucking school. I'm serious, Dad."

Barker sighed.

"Well?" Overwrought, Guy upset his mug. Coffee spread across the tabletop. Guy looked at his father helplessly. Barker pulled some paper napkins out of the dispenser and laid them over the puddle.

"I'll talk to your mother," Barker said. "I can't make a decision like this alone—it's in the divorce agreement."

"Oh, shit," Guy said. "I've already tried to talk to Mom. It's no good. She says"—Guy did a fair imitation of his mother's voice, inflection, vocabulary—"she spent six months searching for the appropriate school for me, and she sees nothing remotely plausible about my objection to Preiss. She's not going to budge. I know it."

"I'm surprised," Barker said, and he was. "Nancy's always given you just about everything you asked for. Let's face it, Guy, she spoiled you. . . ."

"Dad, why are you telling me this? It isn't helping."

"Poor kid," Barker said, half to himself. "I'll do what I can. But I can't promise anything. Nancy and I . . . well, the way the scenario generally goes is I take one side of an issue, she takes the opposite, just so we can't agree. And I suppose I do the same. Childish, isn't it?" This moment of self-revelation was so unexpected that Barker grinned and nearly laughed. Guy misunderstood.

"It's not funny, Dad. I don't know what I'll do if I have to stay there. And I don't want to hear about your troubles with Mom."

"Fair enough," Barker said. This meeting with Guy had brought him a passel of surprises; Barker was replete with surprise, not the least of which was discovering this pocket of tenderness toward his son. Its softness astonished him. Barker got up, the force of his emotion weakening his knees; he held on to the back of his chair to steady himself. "This is the last of the great cafeterias," he said, "and I've heard the owner is selling for one point one million. There are going to be a lot of unhappy people around here."

Guy said, "When are you going to call Mom?"

"Today, I'll do it today. Can't do it this morning. I've got a class in five minutes and then there's the usual Wednesday department meeting, which goes right through lunch. But I'll do it this afternoon, soon as I'm free. Don't look so skeptical, Guy. I said I'd call Nancy and I will."

Jacob Barker dialed Nancy's number at work. It was a number he had to look up each time—funny how he could never remember it. Nancy was now working in the employee-relations department of a phenomenally successful computer firm, making use of her anthropology background and training in psychology. It was her task to persuade the company's workers not to ask for too many benefits, too much free time, a dental plan, or a shorter work week, and to convince them that to let a union in through the front door would, in the long run, hurt them rather than do them good. She made three times the money Barker did and lived in a huge Victorian house near Bedford with her boyfriend, an ex-Marine named Tony Callisi, who was seven years her junior and who earned his living, as far as Barker could make out, by performing such seasonally oriented chores as fireplace-wood vending, swimming-pool cleaning, and apple picking. Nancy claimed that she and Tony were quite perfectly happy unwed and had no plans to marry.

As soon as he heard her voice saying hello, Barker took a deep breath and began: "I had breakfast with Guy today."

"Not really? You went all the way to Beverly to eat your boiled egg?"

"How about we eschew sarcasm for the length of this conversation? This is serious. Guy's very unhappy."

"I know all about it, Jake, it's just adolescent acting-out. Forget it."

Barker tightened his jaw. "He doesn't want to quit school for good, Nancy, he just wants to leave Preiss and go somewhere else. By the way, he looks wonderful. He's lost a lot of weight."

"Am I hearing you correctly? Are you the man to whom parenting meant less than putting out a Roach Motel? What's going on, Jake? What's on your agenda today?"

The urge to whack the ball back at her as hard as he could was so great Barker had to stop and count, holding on to his temper as to a struggling puppy. "If you mean by 'agenda' an ulterior motive—there is none."

"I find that hard to believe," Nancy said. Hard as rivets, with a chunk of basalt for a heart, she was impossible to deal with.

"Could we not talk about me or about you," he pleaded, "and just concentrate on our son?"

"Are you drunk again, Jake?"

For a minute, for one minute out of your sorry life, be a saint, he told himself. Act as if she's a normal person. "Has Guy told you why he wants to leave Preiss?" he asked.

"You mean he thinks he's gay? That screen? Don't you realize, Jake, it's what he's manufactured because he hasn't learned how to have normal relationships with other adolescent boys? He's got to pin it on something, he's displacing. He's no more gay than you are. Listen, I spent months looking for the appropriate school for your son, I spent hours listening to boring history classes and talking to idiotic headmasters. I'm not taking him out on a whim."

"You don't honestly believe he's making it up?"

"Yes, Jake, I do. I'm going to be tough for once. As I told him, he's got to balance the positive with the negative. He's actually learning something at Preiss—for the first time. At this rate, he might actually get into a decent college. Do you have any idea what his grades were like before he went to Preiss? No, I don't suppose you do." Barker heard a click. "Excuse me a minute, Jake, I'm going to put you on hold."

"Don't put me on hold," he shouted, but he was too late, she already had. For a two full minutes—he clocked her—he remained floating in limbo along with fellow hold-victims, and would have hung up but for the memory of Guy's pain.

"Sorry about that," Nancy said, when she came back on the line. Barker swallowed an impulse to chew her out for her rudeness and said, "Guy's grades may be up, but his mood is in the cellar. If something doesn't change for him pretty quick, the grades are going to follow the mood."

"May I ask you something, Jake?" Nancy's voice cut thin pink trails along his flesh. "Since when, if you'll pardon my French, since when did you give a flying fuck about Guy's grades or his moods or his friends or anything except the matter of his allowance and support money? Since when?"

Could he say, "Since I had breakfast with him," and get away with it? He could not; who, especially his ex-wife, would believe such an unbelievable statement? Like many a truthful revelation, it was surrounded and disguised by the incredible, the mysterious, even the divinely touched. Barker could not bring himself to say this to Nancy, so accustomed to his not caring, not giving a hoot. "Nancy," he began, walking on the balls of his feet, ever so lightly, "it's Guy's life I'm talking about. Will you reconsider?"

"Probably not," she said. "I don't think he knows what he wants, he's acting out, like I said before. It would be tragic to take him out now, just when he's beginning to find out he has a real brain. No, I don't think so." Barker heard a click, and before she had a chance to do it, he said, "Don't put me on hold again."

"Okay," she said, "but I'll have to hang up. Why don't you call me tonight, at home? I'll be there after six-thirty." And she was gone.

"Shit," he said. He found his shirt was soaked with sweat.

Barker's phone rang. It was Guy, calling to see if his father had spoken to his mother. "What did she say?" Guy asked. "Well, pal," Barker said, "we started to talk about it, but she was too busy to give it the attention it needs. I'll call her again. Try to be optimistic; I'm sure we can work something out." All of it was true, except the last part—he was sure Nancy was as fixed to her position as if her feet were nailed to the floor.

Chapter Nine

SUSAN'S face appeared, faded, reappeared behind Barker's eyelids. So, for a while, did Guy's, skewed by the force of pain. That Guy liked boys more than girls struck Barker as the sort of ironic punishment no father deserved. But then, how many people managed to get what they deserved? Bad things happened to good people almost as often as good things to bad. He figured that fathers minded homosexuality in their sons more than mothers did; mothers, however kind and generous, find secret solace in the fact that their gay sons are unlikely to prefer another woman over themselves. Small comfort. Barker blamed himself. The firm masculine hand had been missing at the domestic helm, and that's what had done it. Barker was aware of a convincing body of evidence to the contrary, chiefly of the genetic variety, but he nevertheless believed himself responsible: a boy needed Dad around the house and Barker was a bust as Dad. God only knew what sort of games Nancy and Guy had engaged in over the years. It made him tremble to think of the possibilities.

Barker sat in his office staring unhappily at a pile of student papers waiting to be read and corrected. Should he pass them along to eager-beaver Len, his teaching assistant? There was entirely too much of that sort of thing going on all the time: professor strides into lecture hall, delivers lecture, leaves room as bell rings, gives papers and exams to overworked T. A., manages to get through an entire semester without once holding a conversation with an undergraduate. Some of his colleagues even boasted about it. Not for Barker this slothful practice. If you agreed to teach, you taught, and if that meant grading papers, answering stupid questions, and being available, well, he considered these activities to go with the territory. He gave himself a small pat on the back but it didn't help his mood much. Goddamn Guy, why did he have to go and turn into a faggot! Goddamn Nancy, why did she have to be so hard-nosed?

Barker's mind moved a notch to the right on the conscious/unconscious continuum, and he began a daydream about one of his prettiest sophomores, Kathleen Peters. This girl often raised her hand in class to ask questions whose answers, Barker could tell by the eye-rolls around her, were obvious to most of the rest of the class. Yet each time that slim arm went up in its mock salute, so did her teenaged breasts beneath a tight, bright turtleneck, momentarily choking off Barker's supply of oxygen. He composed a hotel room, putting into it a double bed with freshly laundered white cotton sheets, surrounded by a tastefully muted color scheme, new furniture, a thick rug, a couple of standard New England land- or seascapes, a large clean window giving out on something leafy. Barker had just about completed this mise en scène when he heard a gentle tap-tapping on the other side of his office door.

"Professor Barker?"

"Come in," he said, furious as the curtain came crashing down on his tableau. He watched as first the hand and then the head of Kathleen Peters herself entered the room, sent no doubt, by a minor official of the Divine to cheer him up.

"Ms. Peters," Barker said, trying not to let lust mangle the words. "What can I do for you?"

124

Kathleen was wearing jeans so tight Barker could tell the exact place where her thighs began that wondrous division. Into this most sexy of garments was tucked a navy blue turtleneck shirt. The body was A-plus but the face was unremarkable: the nose looked as if many noses had been tried out and this one stuck on by default. It didn't rise smoothly out of her flesh the way Susan Cheng's did. Her mouth was on the thin side, her blue eyes a tad too close to her nose, and her skin showed the ravages of an epidermal invasion. She had two earrings in one earlobe, three in the other, little rings and tiny beaded studs. Her hair was long and untamed. But the bod, oh, the absolute Twentieth-Century-Western perfection of it. Kathleen deserved a ten for everything below the neck, a six and a half for everything above. That averaged out to a little over an eight; not bad.

Kathleen had said something while he calculated, something he had missed. He asked her to repeat it.

"I asked if you'd read my paper yet." Her eyes went straight to the pile on his desk.

"Not yet," he said. "They're next on the agenda."

"I was—ah—wondering if I can have it back?"

"But I haven't read it yet."

"I wish you wouldn't," Kathleen told him. "I'd like to work on it some more. I think I can make it better."

"That's the most unusual request I've ever had from a student. Do you mind if I sit down. I'm feeling faint."

Kathleen's cheeks colored at Barker's sarcasm. He realized that if he weren't careful he might miss an astonishing opportunity.

"Please," he began. "I guess I was so surprised I didn't know how to respond. Forgive me."

Kathleen unhooked her backpack and dumped it on Barker's desk. Then, uninvited, she sat down in Barker's extra chair. He cleared his throat. Her bad manners startled him. She was either innocent, stupid, or brazen. Females—you never could tell where they were coming from. How was it possible that he didn't have the slightest idea what Kathleen was up to, sitting down as if she owned the place, looking at him with a smile playing around on her unremarkable features. He looked her full in the face and saw there nothing helpful.

Barker was aware of a stale smell and remembered that he had left a pair of dirty socks in the bottom drawer of his filing cabinet again. It was possible, however, that he misread the odor and it was raw sex coming off Kathleen, radiating from her youthful torso like steam from a stewpot. Barker just never got enough sex. Never, never enough; the need buoyed but crushed him. Oh yes, he knew what was said: sleeping with your student was nothing more than an abusive display of power. He didn't believe this. If all he was interested in was power, there were plenty of other ways to wield it. A man did not have to engage in intercourse in order to throw his weight around. Look at Kissinger (who had done it with bombs), Idi Amin (poleaxes and thumbscrews), Sam Goldwyn (pink slips and money), Henry Luce (words), and so on. The big-time villains of history, all they needed to do was to flick an eyelid and thousands disappeared from the face of the earth. They didn't bother with bedding their victims first.

"Kathleen—may I call you Kathleen—would you mind telling me about this paper of yours? Or is that really why you came to see me?"

"It's Kathy," she said crisply. "Why else would I come to see you? And I already told you about my paper. I want to improve it. I need a three-point-seven average to graduate with honors. If I get at least a Cum, Daddy's going to buy me a Porsche Targa." She paused. "You think I'm crass?"

"I didn't say that," Barker said, stunned. No doubt she was heading straight from the shores of the Charles River into mergers and acquisitions at Lehman Brothers or some such place. "And what will Daddy buy you if you get a Summa—an oceangoing yacht?"

Kathy smiled at him. Beneath the smile was a warning.

126

Barker retreated. He riffled through the stack of papers until he found hers. She had written about the effect of the mother's voice on infant test performance—a safe and tired subject. He ran his eyes down the first page, caught two statistical errors, a sentence without a verb, and a passage rendered illegible by erasures. Small wonder she wanted it back.

"What made you think this could be improved?" Barker asked. He waved it at her.

"I wrote it in too much of a hurry," Kathy said. "When I thought about it after I handed it in, I realized—" Here she stopped abruptly. "Hey, do I have to explain everything? Can I have it back or not?"

Barker decided he didn't especially like this girl, who seemed to have more than her share of unattractive habits. "It's very unusual," he told her. "I'd have to lower your grade for being late—so it would probably come out to the same thing."

"Are you putting me on?" she said. "You mean, if I go back and revise my paper you'll take points off my grade?"

Barker shrugged. At the same time, Kathy shifted in her chair, spreading her legs an inch or two; someone not clued in to the delicate choreography of their dance would not have noticed; to Barker, however, it was a signal carrying the utmost significance, a signal as direct and loud as if she'd come over, sat down on his lap, and thrust her tongue into his ear.

Barker forced himself to stare at his hands. "Look, Kathy," he said. "I'm going to give this back to you—by the way, I suggest you check out your stats—and then, when you return it, we ought to have a chat about how to get it right the first time. Okay?"

"What's my deadline?" Kathy asked, starting to get up.

"How about next Tuesday? That's five days with the weekend in between. That should give you enough time—if you don't party all weekend."

It wasn't until she had been gone for more than an hour that

Barker began to feel the first twinges of regret, deciding—and this was a first—that he was not going to honor his side of the bargain. Kathy was too disagreeable to bother with. The two-tiered payoff was interesting, but it disgusted him to have to be party to it. Barker felt he owed himself a minimum of moral prudence.

Barker pulled open the bottom drawer of the filing cabinet, found the socks, stiff with dried sweat, and dropped them in the wastebasket. Then he opened the window, and stood looking out over the landscape—dead leaves and yellowed grass beneath a sky of blueness unbroken except for a gull strayed from Boston Harbor adrift on a current of fall air, its wings in a curve like the embrace of a woman just before she locks her arms around your neck. Barker blinked, struck by the absolute consistency of his thought processes; give them half a chance and they returned to physical passion as inevitably as a Midas to his money or a hungry infant to its mother.

The weekend took a long time. Barker hated Sundays—no mail, the threat of creeping sloth. For him not to *have* to shave only meant yet another choice—whether or not to shave. The newspaper, bloated with advertisements for vacuum cleaner bags and dog food in twenty-pound sacks, made a mess; people called you while you were in the shower and sometimes showed up at the door without calling first. He ate too much or too little, and whatever discipline he managed to impose on his work weekdays, even Saturdays, was shot to hell. Where did it go? What happened to it?

Barker tried to reach his son by phone but was told that Guy was at an "away soccer game." This surprised him, for he hadn't even known that Guy played soccer, let alone had made the traveling team. Barker then phoned Bennie, who invited him for dinner. "Patsy says its potluck. I call it leftover meatloaf." Even though cold meatloaf ranked low on Barker's

128

scale of favorite foods, he was so grateful for the invitation he almost wept.

By Tuesday Barker's agitation had tossed his scruples out the window. When at three o'clock Kathy knocked again on his office door (less timidly this time; it sounded, in fact, as if she had knuckles of brass), he had a hard time disguising his pleasure.

She was wearing the same crotch-jamming jeans (or else an identical pair) and a black top. She handed him her paper without a word. He dropped it on his desk and asked her to sit down. She did so, positioning her legs as before. Barker tried not to stare. "Well?" she said, and Barker noticed a kind of nasal twang as she spoke that indicated either a genetic or a social milieu somewhat beneath what he would have selected on the open market. He smiled at his own snobbishness.

"What's so funny?"

"Nothing, Kathy, I was just thinking of something." Barker noticed that she was chewing gum.

At that moment she extruded the wad of gum on the tip of her tongue, then held it between thumb and forefinger, turning to look for a wastebasket. Her right buttock, cuddled by the jeans, seemed to wink at Barker. Kathy was exactly the kind of person he disliked most; she appeared to have little or no idea what sort of impression she made on other people. There was also in her the suggestion that had she known she wouldn't have cared whether the impression was good or bad. Kathy, and people like her, breezed along through life sans the usual gut-wrenching anxieties: Does he like me? Am I doing what they want? Am I wearing the right clothes? Have I come on the right night? Did I say the wrong thing? Does my smile seem fake? Will they answer me? Nothing seemed to touch these people—except their own needs.

"Are you gonna read it?"

"Read what?"

"My paper. The one I just gave you."

"You mean while you're here? Absolutely not. I never read anyone's work while they're in the same room. Saves me a lot of grief."

"Oh," she said. "Then I guess I'll get going."

"I thought we were going to have a little talk about your work habits. . . ."

"You mean getting it right the first time? Okay, if you want, but I have to be at practice in half an hour."

"Practice? What is it that you practice at?"

"Soccer," she said. "I'm on the varsity team. Coach gets bent out of shape if anyone's late for practice."

"My son, Guy, plays soccer."

"Oh yeah?" Kathleen said. "He here?"

"He's still in high school," Barker told her. "Maybe in a few years."

"Professors can, like, get their sons and daughters into Harvard without even trying."

"That's not the way I heard it," Barker said. "It's not that easy."

"I'll bet," Kathy said.

Barker wanted to strangle her.

"Well, if we can't talk now, how about some other time? I hate to see a smart girl like you missing out on the good things in life because of a few reformable habits."

"You know," she told him, abruptly unbuckling her armor and stepping out of it, "this may sound stupid, and tell me if it's no good for you, but I could, like, meet you sometime over the weekend?"

"Why not?" he said. This leopard, Jake Barker, would never change his spots.

Barker told Kathy he'd like to buy her a drink in a hotel in Boston.

"No funny business," she said. "I'm not into sleeping with my teachers."

"And I'm not in the habit of sleeping with my students. I

just thought we might both enjoy a little urban glitter. How about it?"

"Okay," Kathy said, "but I don't want you to get the wrong idea. I'm not about to go to bed with you."

"I'm shocked, Kathy, I truly am. You make it sound as if you've had a lot of experience."

"Listen, Professor Barker, it wouldn't be the first time someone like you came on to me; though I have to admit, they didn't have your bedroom eyes—just kidding."

The hotel was both expensive and sufficiently vast to be impersonal; Barker was fairly certain they wouldn't run into any of his colleagues—why would they go to a hotel when they lived here already? Kathy wore a skirt and a rather pretty, blue, woolly sweater—as if she'd known that her usual costume wouldn't do. This confirmed for Barker that she was smart, the kind of kiddo who knew how to keep her head above water when everyone around her was sinking. A modern girl, a true girl of the eighties.

"The bar seems to be this way," he said to her as they entered the dust-colored lobby.

Kathy followed him. The bar was empty, save for two middle-aged women at a table on the other side of the room. Barker enjoyed prolonging the foreplay, with his meal within reach but not yet fully cooked. He drank one whiskey and soda down to the ice cubes before Kathy had consumed half her beer. He ordered a second.

"Where do you plan to drive in your little roadster?"

"Roadster?" she said.

"Your Porsche," he said.

"I don't have it yet."

"But you're counting on it."

"Why do you keep bringing up my car? It's a long way off."

"Two years? I guess that is a long way off for someone of your tender years."

"What's that supposed to mean?"

"Why don't you finish up that brew? Then we can go up-stairs."

"I told you," Kathy said. "I'm not into that."

"You can't really be surprised that I reserved a room for us."

"I am surprised," she said. He stared at her. When she was sitting down like this, he could see very little of her splendid body and a good deal of her face. Amazing the way these two pieces of Kathy were mismatched.

"You know what they call you, don't you?" Kathy asked.

"What do they call me?"

"Professor Romeo. Isn't that a hoot?"

With this, Kathy drove the knife directly into Barker's left ventricle. She smiled at him as if pleased by her cleverness. Barker felt the blood drain from his head. "A hoot," he said finally. "You just made that up, didn't you?"

"No, I didn't. Honestly, I heard it from a couple of people. That's how you're known. Maybe I shouldn't have told you. . . ."

"I'm glad you did, Kathleen."

"I don't think you believe me about—you know."

"Well, frankly, Kathleen, I don't. Or else why would you have come with me? If you really mean what you're saying, then you've sent me some distinctly odd signals. Mixed messages. A girl doesn't go this far unless she intends to go still further." Barker would have liked to put this in a slightly more acidic form but felt that if he did he might kill any chance for a yes. It occurred to him, with a shock, that he might be losing the famous Barker touch. He began to sweat.

Kathleen looked down into her lap. Something about the way she sat with her shoulders curved over her body, her head down, was reassuring: she hadn't yet made up her mind either way. He plunged: "I think I can help you get that little auto of yours."

"What do you mean?"

"I think you know what I mean. Look, Kathy, we're both adults."

"I'm only twenty," she said, interrupting.

"But you're mature. I wouldn't bother with you if you were a child—that's not my style. As I said, we're both adults. We both know what we both want." He let this sink in. "Besides, girl, I'm a grand lover; I don't think you'll regret a moment of it."

Kathy sighed deeply. When she looked at him he could see her eyes magnified by tears. "This isn't what I want. . . ."

"You can't know what you want until you've tried it. And there's no getting without first giving. No free lunches to be found anywhere. You might say life is a series of bargains. . . . Come on, Kathy, let me show you." He fixed her with his powerful eyes, using them to lift her to her feet. As if in a trance, she stood and followed him and stood at a discreet distance while he collected the room key. They rode up in the elevator in silence, and when they stood outside room 1203, he said softly, "I promise you this will be extremely pleasant for both of us." Kathy ducked her head.

It was amazing how closely the room resembled the room of his fantasy: neutral and classy, everything was done up in rose and gray, the pictures visual clichés—an Audubon print of a cranelike bird and a square-rigger breasting North Atlantic seas. "Man at the desk didn't raise an eyebrow," Barker said. "No one gives a damn these days whether you book a room for two hours or two weeks." He wanted to distract her so she would relax.

"What did they do in your day?" Kathy asked.

Yet another thrust of the knife. He was going to emerge from this like Swiss cheese. "Well, you see, in my day they had house detectives patrolling the halls with six-shooters, and if they suspected that two of their patrons weren't married and had just come in for a little fun, why they'd kick in the door and haul both sinners off to the slammer. Just when exactly do you think my day was?"

133

"I don't know," Kathy said. "The thirties?"

"Now *that* qualifies as a hoot. How old would you say I am?"

"Fifty?"

"Even if that were true," Barker said, "my day, as you call it, would be more like the forties than the thirties. How did you manage to get into Harvard?"

"It wasn't so hard," Kathy told him. She looked at him shyly now, her resistance totaled.

"You're a very clever girl, I can see that." While they talked each of them had been shedding clothes. Now Kathleen stood ten feet away from him. Her torso was one of nature's triumphs—a body put together perfectly; her breasts the sort that appeared half-full of whatever it was that filled breasts. Their upper surfaces descended gently, the skin like pale silk. Her bellybutton was a smooth dimple, as if scooped out by a demitasse spoon. Her pubic hair was a lush, black isosceles triangle. Barker found himself gaping at her.

"What are you looking at?" Kathy said. "You've seen plenty of naked women."

"Ah, but not like you, Kathleen, never one like you. You have a marvelous body."

"I'm too fat," she announced.

"Where? Where are you fat?"

"Here," Kathy said as she placed her right hand over her perfect right hip.

"Why do all you girls think you're fat? Even you skinny ones?"

"You really think I'm skinny?" Barker saw Kathy's teeth for the first time as she grinned at him. He had almost forgotten that bit of magic: tell a female she's thin and she's yours for life.

"Where are you going?" he said.

"I'm going to pull the curtains," she said. "I don't like doing it in the light."

"I don't care, myself. Sunlight, starlight—it's all wonderful. Come here, you."

134

They came at the bed from opposite sides, meeting in the middle. Each time he did this he was struck by the astonishing variety in the human body. He touched Kathy's shoulder (her eyes were closed, naturally; they all shut their eyes, as if they feared they would be blinded by the act), which had an oddly shaped bone in it. Her breasts seemed soft and hard at the same time. Her stomach was flat as any boy's; it went hollow as she turned onto her back. The hip she said was fat had a layer of flesh over it no thicker than a good flannel shirt. As his fingers made their way into her, his prick responded with a terrific thrust of energy. He sighed against the tension that sent waves along nerve, muscle, vein, bone, tissue. All systems were set for lift-off.

Kathy responded with a spurt of moisture. "Glorious girl," he said, kissing her above the collarbone, opening his mouth.

"Hey," she said. "Don't do that—it hurts. I'm not into that kind of kinky stuff." Barker shut his lips, unaware that he had been biting her. "What are you, some kind of vampire?"

"Aaaaagh," he said.

She whispered something he couldn't hear as he entered her, deciding at the same moment that she was as cold as a frozen fillet of haddock. He wondered if his breath stank, the way she averted her face. "My God, you're wet," he said. He hadn't yet come and was teetering at the brink when she said, "Oh, shit, I just got my period!"

"What are you talking about?"

"My menstrual period. I never know when I'm going to get it. Sometimes I go for months. I'm dysmenorrheic. It's because of the soccer and all the running I do—seven miles a day. That's pretty good, you know."

Barker flopped on his back, his prick deflating like a balloon with a hole in it. He ached all over; even his toes, for some reason, started tingling to the point of pain. He closed his eyes and found he was weeping.

"What's with you?" she said, pulling up on one elbow and

staring at him. "Freaked by a little blood?" Her reluctance had turned inside out; she was *shameless*.

Barker couldn't answer, anymore than he could understand why he was crying. "I don't know," he managed to whisper.

"And I don't understand why guys are so grossed out by period blood. And especially you. I mean, God, you being Professor Romeo. . . ."

"Please," he said weakly. "I'd rather you didn't call me that." Panic swept into the space behind his breastbone. He heard Kathy leave the bed and pad over to the other side of the room.

"Oh, shit!" Kathy said. "I don't have any tampons with me."

Barker opened his eyes and saw a red line on the inside of Kathy's left thigh. She looked at it, too, and shrugged.

"Jesus Christ, Kathy," he said. "Get the hell in the bathroom before you bleed all over the rug."

Kathy fled into the bathroom. Barker looked down at where she had been standing. A couple of drops of her blood were soaking their way into the expensive gray pile. He shook his head, got up, and began to put his clothes back on. The skin of his prick was pinkish. He didn't want to go into the bathroom, so he pulled out his pocket handkerchief and wiped off as much of the blood as he could. Then he pulled his shorts over his hips and stepped into his trousers.

"Hey, Professor, will you go down and buy me a box of Tampax? I can't leave here like this." The bathroom door was shut.

"Christ," he said. "Can't you use a towel or something?"

"Are you putting me on?" she said. "You mean you won't go down to the drugstore while I'm sitting here pouring buckets? Come on, man, get real."

It was obvious he had no choice. But his reluctance was a wire strung neck-high across the room, blocking the exit. Barker took a deep breath, snipped the wire, and went down to the pharmacy, where, along with a box of Regular Tampax, he picked up several items for camouflage: a pocket-sized package of Kleenex, a tube of Crest toothpaste, a roll of lime Lifesavers, and a bar of Jergen's soap, placing them on the counter. The woman standing on the other side of it dropped them one by one into a crinkled plastic bag without appearing to notice the Tampax. Barker felt silly.

Kathleen was still in the bathroom when he let himself back into the room.

"I thought you'd pulled a fast one on me," she said, as Barker handed the box around the door.

"And you were dead wrong," he said. "Why on earth would I do a thing like that? You must know some pretty odd characters—what sort of man would run out on a girl in your predicament?"

"Gimme a break," she said. He didn't quite know how to take this. "Shit," she said. "You got me Regular. I asked for Super."

"You most certainly did not ask for Super. You didn't say what size you wanted. I got what anyone would have—the size in the middle. And why am I on the defensive here? Don't you think you have things backwards? You should be apologizing to me."

"Listen, Professor Romeo, I never wanted to go to bed with you in the first place; I've got a perfectly good boyfriend. You're not bad-looking for a guy your age, and you're obviously cool about sex, but who needs it? I'm asking you, who needs this? You act as if I got my period on purpose just to tick you off."

"I'm sure you didn't," he said. He thought for a moment of bringing up the Porsche again, then decided against it. All he wanted to do now was get rid of her.

By the time they recrossed the Charles River and were safely back in Cambridge, Barker had convinced himself that the name "Professor Romeo" was Kathy's on-the-spot invention; this made him feel better about what had happened. He was also fully prepared to write off the experience as one of his rare miscalculations.

"Even Homer nods," he murmured as he showered, making sure every last trace of Kathy's menstrual blood disappeared down the drain.

The secretary, or whoever it was fielding Anita Andrews' tele-communications, made Barker wait for at least a minute while she checked to see if Dean Andrews was free. This caused Barker to smile, though not in happiness—a rueful smile, heavy with contrary meanings. But when the clear voice of his erstwhile ladylove came on, he was glad he had called. She still had the ability to lighten his heart.

"Jacob?" she said. "What's up?"

"Nothing's up, Anita. I just wanted to congratulate you on your new job."

"Oh, you saw the *Crimson*? Damn kids, they broke the story. They were supposed to wait. The news office is ticked off; they hadn't planned to release the story till tomorrow. Now it's old news and the *Times* probably won't run it. *C'est la vie*, I guess."

"*C'est la vie*," Barker repeated. "But you posed for the picture, you talked to them. What did you think they would do?"

"Is this the third degree again, Jake? Sounds like old times. If you must know, the boy who interviewed me promised not to run it till he checked with the news office. If you're going to tell me I was naive to believe him, you're wasting your time. I already know that. Is there something else you want to tell me? If not, I'm awfully busy. . . ."

"I should hope so, with that fancy office," Barker said. "Why don't we have lunch sometime?"

"Yes, do let's," Anita said.

Barker very nearly said, "Come back, I want you back." The words were ready to march but he blew them away just in time. He didn't want her back. It was pride that almost spoke the words, not Jacob Barker.

138

"Well, goodbye then," Anita said. He heard the tiniest catch in her voice.

"Anita!"

"What?"

"Just one more thing, have you got a moment? It's about this new job of yours. I mean, it sounds a little like an arm of Public Relations. Female grievances—what the heck does that mean? Female complaints—those I've heard of, but not grievances. Is this what deans do these days? When did they stop being in charge of curriculum? When did they give up overseeing the faculty? I mean, what exactly is going down here? Don't misunderstand, Anita, I'm just curious."

"That's an understatement," Anita said ambiguously. "And I understand you far better than you think I do. You think I'm some kind of window dressing for administration image-makers. Well I've got news for you, Jake, this is serious business. I'm talking sexual harassment here. It's been allowed to metastasize for years because no man wanted to put anything in place to stop it. Martha Stephens and myself—you know Martha, she's the one with the thing about purple clothes, she was a student of yours about ten years ago—we're going to get an apparatus on line, we're working on a set of guidelines that will go out to every member of the faculty. There's going to be a grievance board, so that, at the very least, these poor women will have someone to talk to who won't put them in jeopardy, someone they can trust. And if it turns out they have a case, we're going to punish the man who took advantage of them. And now, my dear, I've really got to get off the phone and do a little work. Thanks again for the congratulations—I really appreciate it."

"How about if a female faculty member harasses a male student?" he said.

"Don't lay that on me, Jake, I've heard it a million times before. It doesn't happen that way."

"I actually know of an incident involving a female teacher."

"Then report it to Martha. Otherwise, forget it."

139

"It happened at Columbia," he said.

"Bye, Jake."

Barker hung up the phone badly shaken. How much did she know, how much suspect? He remembered Martha Stephens all too well. She was one of the few girls he had misjudged; it was her eyes that lied; the eyes of an innocent, they had seemed soft and welcoming. She looked virginal. During a conference in his office late one afternoon, as the Montreal Express roared across Harvard turf and sleet hurled itself against the windowpane, they had sipped oolong tea brewed by Barker and, thigh next to thigh, had gone over an excellent paper she had turned in on eye blinks per minute during testing—or some such subject. But when he casually laid a hand on the purple stuff over Martha's knee, she jumped up and uttered a loud curse. "You asshole" was what she actually said. It pained him to hear her talk like that. He pretended not to understand why she was so ticked and hustled her out as quickly as he could. Teeth flashing, she told him she was going to report him, but he knew her threat to be an empty one—there simply was no one to whom she could snitch. And if she did, in fact, say something to a person in authority, she was too smart not to realize Barker would deny acting improperly; and she would be in danger of having the accusation bounce off him and stick to her. Who was more believable—a full professor at Harvard University or a junior from Paducah, Kentucky, or wherever it was she had escaped from? At that time Barker was safe. Now, after having spoken with Anita, he figured his safety had entered the problematic category. The life jacket was old and the kapok had started to come out through several holes he hadn't noticed.

Barker spun his chair to face the window behind his desk. Across the green a woman was pointing a camera at a man posing in front of the statue of the putative John Harvard; this configuration occurred many times a day, as if Harvard was Abe Lincoln or Mahatma Gandhi. Barker had never understood why anyone would want to have their picture taken with a statue—what was it they hoped to capture in such a pairing? It eluded him even as he assumed it must reflect some universal, albeit primitive, need for association with the sacred. And to anyone who watched it from afar, Harvard was the Vatican, its president the pope. When Barker joined the Harvard faculty, Von Stampler had assured him that he would thenceforth be considered, both by those within it and those not so fortunate, to be a member of the Upper Class. Barker wondered first whether this was true, and secondly whether it was, per se, a good thing to be a member of the Upper Class. To what did that entitle you except a slew of responsibilities and a set of expectations on the part of your fellows? The man and woman now exchanged places; he pointed the camera at her. They would go home and show the pictures to their children, who would, Barker guessed, say "so what?," a response Barker considered not only plausible but altogether rational. Children didn't give a shit about that kind of worship.

While Von Stampler had been laying on Barker his Upper Class riff, Barker had been thinking about the sexual perks that went with the job. He knew men who steadfastly refused the blandishments of their young lady students, all of them smart as whips—at least smart enough to score way up there on S.A.T.'s (which was only one kind of smart, but for a seventeen-year-old eager for a Harvard diploma, a far more negotiable one than smartness about storytelling or phrasing in music). To Barker these men weren't more moral than he was, they just lacked nerve. They were afraid of getting caught, feared the wrath of wife or sweetheart. Barker consigned them to the miserable class of people who won't accept a gift from someone who might, conceivably, require a favor in return.

It took someone blessed with utter candor, a man with an appetite for things untasted and untried, to accept pleasure and return it to its source. Barker was the brave one; the rest were craven. And now Anita, wrapped in a dean's mantle, was trying to turn the equation on its ear and claim that women were victims, men predators. Anyone with any brains knew it took two. Two: boy and girl, woman and man. Not once in all these years had Barker forced himself upon a girl. Barker was working himself up into a sweat of rage and sadness. They misunderstood; they overlooked the essential nature of this most human of exchanges, the thing that enabled him to carry out his work and all the mean and inconsequential tasks that had accumulated, as one's house is suddenly crammed with things one can't even remember having bought.

Barker's phone rang, startling him like a pistol going off next to his ear, so deeply had he sunk in the slough of despond. He took a deep breath and answered. It was Susan Cheng, the publicity girl at Lothar and Bright. "Could you stop by at the office one day next week? Or if you don't have the time, we can talk over the phone."

"Oh, no no," Barker said as sun came pouring in over his troubles. "I'll be there. When?"

Chapter Ten

A LIFELONG Democrat, Jacob Barker tended to blame his low moods on Ronald Reagan. Barker was aware of how useless it was to blame his moods on something as remote as a president. A president had as much to do with him personally as the guy who put the stripe in the toothpaste. And yet Reagan's chilling presence seemed to have frozen whatever was left of life and vitality in America's youth. Barker was crazy about the sixties, though he kept this enthusiasm more or less under wraps—these days it wasn't an opinion you went around shouting. What had happened to all the good and honest liberals? Where were the good guys now? They had shit in their blood; they had crawled back into their holes and pulled the covers over their heads. Barker often felt as if he alone cared. It made him burn to see how the bad guys had not only survived but had prevailed. To be sure, there were moments when Barker was convinced there was no one home inside the Reagan body, that he was only a shell molded in the shape of a tall man with an iguana face. But then this speculation brought up the unpleasant matter of who in hell was minding the store?

The ozone layer of optimism was thinning, depleted by too much anxiety. And what, Barker asked himself as once more he drew the razor blade along his cheek above the beard and glanced into his own eyes, and what had he been so optimistic about? He tried to think. His brain? Well, there was that, it could be that. It was a good brain, a first-rate item; people were constantly picking it, picking at it as at a haunch of leftover turkey, even stealing from it if it came to that—that sumbitch Gershenstein in the wilds of Canada had had the nerve to take one of his experiments, move a single visual stimulator one notch to the right, and pass it off as his own creation. And it wasn't worth going after the fucker, it wasn't worth the aggravation. The thought of Gershenstein's theft plunged Barker deeper into the crater with his name on it. His energy, too, was going, along with the optimism. The energy that used to sit in full tanks waiting to be injected into muscle and nerve, where had it gone? The same place, no doubt, that weight goes when one loses it, joining single socks and unwanted pounds floating free in the ether, the same place the soul goes when one dies. . . . Death, now there was a notion one could sink one's teeth into. Dead souls, missing socks, shed pounds, lost energy, flattened optimism. God, if only one knew how to make use of it all. . . .

Barker had a lecture to prepare, a talk he had agreed to deliver more than a year earlier and thus easy to say yes to; besides, they had promised him a hefty fee—three thousand bucks. He was getting up there. Not quite in the Gordon Liddy category, but perfectly respectable. Now, however, the subject (Age of Mother's Menarche in Respect to Handedness of Subject) no longer interested Barker—it was old stuff, stale, and, what was worse, a questionable line of inquiry, quite possibly leading to a dead end. How the heck was he going to write this talk in good conscience and then get up on his hind legs in their newly appointed auditorium with its soft gray upholstery, scientific lighting, and state-of-the-art acoustics and act as if he gave the damn they were paying him to give?

So strong was the urge not to work that when Barker neared the window that gave out over an ancient Episcopalian graveyard, he stepped back hurriedly, afraid he would throw himself through it onto one of the slanted headstones below. His heart pounding and his temples glistening with sweat, he sat himself down at the desk and took several deep breaths, closed his eyes, and tried to empty his mind. This was not how things should be, not at his age. There was plenty of powder and shot left in the old musket. Maybe his problem was too much undischarged libido. This idea caused Barker to smile; he opened his eyes, got out his Sheaffer fountain pen, and began to write. And then that wondrous thing happened once again: as he began to write, the fog lifted, ideas poured forth as if from a magic, bottomless vessel. Fatigue, angst, misery dropped away in the face of a mad and beautiful energy, and when he next looked at his watch, Barker discovered that if he didn't hussle he was going to be late for his appointment with Susan Cheng at Lothar and Bright. Scribbling some notes so that his train of thought would not be derailed by the interruption, Barker then shrugged himself into his fake Burberry and hurried to the subway for the ten-minute ride to Beantown.

The beauteous Cheng kept him waiting. Out of his last four appointments, three had kept him cooling his heels; the week before Barker might have entered the dread paranoid mode and taken this as a sign of diminishing importance and power (these two items being inextricably locked together in the minds of those who possessed little of either) but today he was supermensch and the waiting didn't matter.

"You may go up now," the receptionist told him five minutes later from behind her glass cage. "It's on the third floor."

"I know that," Barker said. He was sure she gave him a fishy smile, but it touched him glancingly, a bullet off the mighty chest of Superman.

Susan got up as he entered and held out her delicate hand for him to shake. The moment he saw her—it was the first time since she had abandoned him in her office—Barker's core began a meltdown. He was just able to say hello.

She asked him to sit down, then looked at him with a question mark imposed over her rose-petal features. "Are you all right?" she asked.

"I think so," he whispered.

"Can I get you something? Coffee? Water?"

Whiskey? Unfortunately she failed to make this offer. And when he straightened somewhat, emitting a tight little cough and a nod, she got right down to business, opening a folder in front of her—his folder, thick enough, though not nearly so thick as his internist's—and withdrew two pieces of paper clipped together with a blue paper clip. One of these she handed to Barker. It was the schedule of his book tour. He read it rapidly.

"I see you've booked me into a Best Western in Boise," he said with a scowl.

"It's the only place with an available room. There's a cattle-men's convention in town same time you're there. If you'd rather skip Boise . . ." She pronounced it *Boy-see*, and let the last phrase dangle. "There are three bookstores in Boise—and a branch of the state university."

"In that case," Barker said, "maybe I can put up with the Best Western for one night." It was okay for him to make a fuss about being lodged in second-class digs; if he failed to protest now, they'd try to pull this trick again. Bennie had told him to make sure they flew him first-class. "You don't say what sort of plane tickets you got for me."

"Tickets?" she said.

"Yes, you know. How do I travel?"

"The way we send all our authors—economy class. Unless, of course, an organization on the other end is paying for the trip. I believe there are some department stores who can afford first-class tickets. I'm afraid it just isn't in the cards for your book."

She had put him on the defensive and was making him feel

146

stupid; for this lousy state of affairs he blamed Bennie, who had urged him to demand first-class accommodations. Bennie could be a real pain sometimes. Meanwhile, as Barker vowed revenge and studied the schedule, the scent of Susan's perfume—something like gingered fruit—entered his soul and completed the chemical reaction begun the moment his fingers and hers had touched. He pressed his feet into the floor and concentrated on staying conscious. His hands were desperate to grab this creature's face and kiss her open mouth; his fingers were desperate to rip open her blouse and squeeze her modest breasts. Could breasts be said to "beckon"? These surely did.

"Susan," he said weakly.

"No, really," she said, her brow creased. "Are you sure you're not sick or something? Maybe you ought to put your head between your knees. It keeps you from passing out; I know, it happened to me last year when they had to draw some blood and hit something wrong and a big purple lump came up, and I could feel the blood just draining out of my head. The nurse told me to put my head down between my knees, and I did and I was back to normal in a few minutes. The lump took a few hours to disappear, though."

"I'm perfectly all right," Barker said, wondering exactly what he had done to open the verbal floodgates in this exquisite girl. "It's nice of you to be concerned, but I'm fine, I think I may have a touch of the virus that's going around." Susan looked at him dubiously but answered the phone when it rang. This time she told the caller she was busy and would call him back. Barker considered this to be a victory for the good guys.

"We need you strong and healthy," she said.

"A sick author is no better than a dead one, eh?"

"I wouldn't say that," Susan told him. "A dead author can't get better. You know what I mean. . . ." It seemed to Barker that she blushed at her clumsiness.

"I do indeed."

"Last year we brought out this book, a mystery novel. Well,

the author suddenly developed a brain tumor and went out like a light. In three weeks she was dead. Her book was still in production."

"And what happened to it?"

"The book? Nothing. It just died, too."

"That doesn't make much sense," Barker said.

"I know," Susan said. "But that's what happened. Word got out and it threw a pall over everything. If she'd been dead for ten years it would have been different—we could have promoted it differently."

"Long-lost masterpiece published after a decade?"

"Right," said Susan. "How did you know?"

"Lucky guess," Barker said. "I'm not about to croak," he added, smiling at her. And to prove how hearty he was, he got up and, stiff-kneed, touched the tops of his shoes.

She stared. Barker realized he had done the wrong thing— she was embarrassed. What to do, how to change things back? "I'm in fine fettle," he said. "And there's nothing I'd rather do than take you to lunch—if you're free, that is." His heart picked up speed; it felt as if it were about to take off. He hadn't the faintest idea what she thought about him, not the foggiest. This was so unlike him—he almost never dangled bait without making sure first that the fish was hungry. He stood beside her chair in an agony of suspense as she appeared to be mulling over the invitation. He held his breath, literally, while his pulse continued on high and she looked at her desk calendar (a ploy, he figured, as she had to know whether or not she had a lunch date). Finally, after a minute or so, she said, "I *am* free. But I can't take long for lunch. I have someone coming in at one forty-five."

"That's fine with me," Barker said, releasing the air from his lungs a little at a time.

"I also have a meeting at eleven." She looked at her watch, he looked at his. It was now ten-thirty. "I can meet you downstairs at twelve," she said.

"Twelve it is," Barker said, squelching an impulse to fondle her tummy just below the waist.

The Barker conscience would not ordinarily have permitted him to do what he now did but it was sleeping off the effects of the meltdown. Taking advantage of this, Barker phoned his secretary. "Something's come up, Emily, and I won't be able to meet my twelve o'clock class. Would you be a dear and run over to Grimm and put a note up on the door of my classroom?"

"Certainly, Professor Barker. Are you all right? Is there anything I can do for you?"

"I'm just fine," he said. "I'll be in midafternoon." And he hung up before she could ask any more questions.

He looked at his watch again. An hour and a half. There was a book someone had advised him to read—*Beyond God the Father*, by that former nun, Mary Daly, but he just didn't feel like spending any time looking for it; he was sure he wasn't going to like it anyway. Instead, he walked five blocks to Filene's, where he purchased a yellow silk tie with aqua dots the size of camphor balls and a kerchief to match—these two items were marked down from thirty-five bucks to six and a half. Not bad. He went into the men's room, where he pulled off the rust number he was wearing and dropped it on top of a mound of used paper towels even though it was in perfectly good shape. It was a small gesture of contumacy but one that gave him unexpected pleasure. Barker wet his comb and ran it through his hair. He liked what the mirror told him.

Back on the main floor, Barker parked himself against a pillar and watched a woman being made up. She sat on a kind of bar stool, with her legs crossed and her chin tilted upwards. Her eyes were shut and on her face was a look of ecstatic patience. The girl in the pink lab coat applying goo over eyelids and across cheekbones worked with the professional dexterity of a dentist excavating a root canal. Barker's eyes flicked from face to thigh, for her skirt had risen over gray pantyhose in an interesting way, creating a smoky tunnel that drew his imagination into bushy hill country.

"May I help you, sir?"

"What?"

"Is there something I can show you in cosmetics?" A sharp-nosed female wearing a sleek cocktail dress with a rhinestone belt and spoonfuls of makeup stood next to Barker. In spite of an upper-crust accent, the expression on her face said, "Beat it creep, or I'll call the cops." She smiled like an actor selling a purgative on TV.

"As a matter of fact you can," Barker said. "I want to buy my lady friend some perfume. What would you suggest? She's the delicate type—an Oriental. She's small and fragile-looking."

"I'll be glad to get someone to assist you," the woman said.

"I thought you offered to help me yourself."

"I'm not a salesperson," she said.

"Ah," Barker said, warming to the battle, "but you did offer. If I recall correctly—and I have a crackerjack memory—you said, 'Is there something I can show you in cosmetics?' Shouldn't offer if you're not prepared to follow through. It's bad P.R."

"What's your game, mister?" she said, shedding the North Shore.

"My game?" Barker said, scrambling for a next move. "I came in here to buy some perfume and find that I'm being treated like a shoplifter. What's your name, please?"

"Listen, pal, I saw you staring up that lady's skirt. That's enough to qualify for a nuisance arrest. Now beat it, or I'm going to call security."

"You just try it, sister. I have as much right to be here as any man in this store." Anger began to crawl up his calves. Barker turned his hands into fists, which he clamped against his legs so that he couldn't haul off and belt her in the mouth—something he felt very much like doing. She stared at him steadily. For a minute or so the two of them were frozen, each

150

one trying to crush the other. The deadlock broke at an unheard signal and Barker said, "I'm going to leave now but I assure you you haven't heard the last of this. I may not know your name but I've got enough to write a letter to the president of this store and tell him just what transpired here. If I were you, I'd start reading the help-wanted ads."

"The exit is right over there," she said.

Ashamed he had lost his cool, Barker fled from the store. He stood on Washington Street, giddy with anger and something else—self-hatred, that was it, an emotion that seemed to come over him more and more often. He fingered his new tie and went across the street to Jordan Marsh, where (after sniffing several other scents) he purchased an expensive bottle of something called Opium, a somewhat risky selection, but it would tell him what sort of person she was, if she could accept the Oriental reference as the compliment it was intended to be.

After buying the perfume, Barker felt better, the incident with the floorwalker or whatever the lady was called fading fast. Barker was proud of his memory's ability to retain and to empty with equal skill. It was a crackerjack memory—all he had to do was press the right button, the one marked Remember or the one marked Forget—and it would do what it was supposed to do, leaving him free to go about his business.

Barker and Susan went to a restaurant near Lothar and Bright, where they were escorted to a table almost large enough for the two of them. The chairs were armless and the menu featured things that involved at least four ingredients— marinated mussels on a bed of arugula with fungi and artichoke hearts à la Vielle Cracow. It must be some kind of joke, Barker figured, and ordered the angel hair pasta with shrimp, bay scallops, cream sauce, and Romano cheese. He was high; he could feel lustful atoms sweeping and arcing through his system. He talked rapidly and tried to steer the conversa-

151

tion always back to her—girls appreciated that, especially now with the media seemingly bent on showing men to be impossibly selfish. Everybody was selfish, men, women, faggots, what was the big deal suddenly about men? The main difference between now and when he was with one of his students was that with the students it was—at least for him—a game, while with Susan he cared deeply how she reacted to him; it was a matter of the most crucial importance. Barker was in love again.

"I'm going to New York," she told him between bites of "homemade" pizza.

"When?" he asked, in a voice he hoped did not betray the panic her words gave birth to.

"When I have the experience, I need to get a job at Random House or Simon and Schuster. When they won't be able to turn me down."

"And what can you do in New York that you can't do in Boston?" he asked. He had stopped eating; the pasta was too salty anyway. He looked at the gentle bulge of breast beneath her pale rose-colored shirt and felt like weeping. He was as bad as a menopausal woman—on the edge of shattering.

"You're joking, aren't you?" she said.

"I didn't think so," Barker said.

"Well, if you want to know, and I don't think I'm being disloyal, that's where the action is. Besides, they have peculiar ideas here about women. They don't think we can do anything but take orders from a man. In New York they only care about one thing—how much money you can make for the company. It doesn't matter to them what gender you are."

"So," he said. "And you want to make piles of money?"

"You don't understand. I don't care that much about money. I care about not being treated like a moron. I want to rise to my level of competence."

"As you should," Barker said, terrified that he wasn't going to get to first base with Susan, not even to fucking first base.

How her youth appealed to him, how empty she was, just waiting for someone like him to fill her up—not that there was anyone remotely like Jacob Barker to introduce her to the world.

"I have something for you," he said, reaching in back of him where he had hidden the box of perfume. It was wrapped in blood-red paper.

"What's this?" she said, surprise on her face. "You know I can't accept a gift from an author. It's against the rules."

"Whose rules?" Barker said.

"The company's," Susan said. "It might be misunderstood."

"You mean as a bribe? Pardon my French, but that's bullshit."

"Still," she said solemnly. "Last year, Kimberly Kraft, you know we've published over twenty of her young-adult novels? They sell like Popeye's fried chicken. Well, last Christmas she went out and bought all the women in the office silk scarves and the men silver pencils, and they made us give them back. She was so angry and her feelings were so hurt, she almost went over to Ancient House to be published. I mean it was really silly, she was just saying thank you. . . ."

"That's a nasty story," Barker said. "But *my* feelings will be hurt if you don't take this."

"But I've just told you, I can't."

"I'll tell you what, why don't you look at it this way? This isn't a gift from an author, it's a gift from a friend. We *are* friends, aren't we?"

Susan Cheng nodded and half closed her lids over her magic eyes. She seemed to Barker to be struggling.

"I don't know . . . ," she said softly.

"Well, little dear, I know. You just take it. No one at Lothar and Bright need know anything about it. It's just between you and me. I meant it when I said my feelings will be hurt if you refuse."

"I shouldn't be doing this," she said, reaching her hand out and accepting the box, which by this time had the moral weight of twelve pieces of silver. Shyly, she removed the wrapping paper and looked at the box. "My favorite perfume," she said. "How did you know?"

"I didn't," he said. "It was a lucky guess. But I think it's a good omen, don't you? I mean as far as the two of us are concerned?"

Chapter Eleven

To BEGIN with, it was the chase that got Barker's blood up; the scent of prime meat on the hoof. Then there were the glandular fantasies that followed, visions almost as real as when he actually lay between warm thighs. In Barker's preeminent fantasy, he was clothed as a pasha in silk pajamas shot with gold, the trousers billowing about his legs. Sometimes he wore a silk turban, at other times he was bareheaded. He sat against a wall of huge pillows like gigantic mammaries. Musicians—nubile boys gaudily dressed—played music, Bach or Mahler, depending on Barker's mood. Soon a faceless virgin would tiptoe into his tent bringing him things to eat on a large round copper tray: fresh dates, barbecued chicken wings, pita bread smeared with baba ganoush, thin after-dinner mints, dry champagne with a single ice cube floating among the bubbles. When he had sampled this eclectic snack, he would dismiss the lurking servant girls and youths, pull the maiden down to him, and enjoy her until exhaustion put him out of commission.

Not once but many times did Jacob Barker attempt to bring his fantasy more in line both with the nineteen-eighties and, just as importantly, with his own age, barely forty-three. He worked hard, for example, on visions of two adults in love buying a new car together; whipping up a great meal side by side—beef carbonnade, asparagus al dente, pommes frites, raspberry tart—handing each other spoons and knives as needed, opening the oven and icebox for one another, washing pots and pans in a double sink. He tried another one about ice-skating for miles down a frozen river arm-in-arm, yet another featuring a squash game in which he and a lady friend played amicably together, congratulating one another on terrific shots. None of this worked; each time he tried, it slipped back into an Arabian night. The two-tiered banquet kept blotting out the more mature version of life with a helpmeet.

Soon after their lunch together, the face of Susan Cheng began to appear atop the neck of the virgin who served him the dates and chicken wings. Barker's step lightened, his general well-being improved.

"I'm thinking wedding bells," was the way he put it to Bennie, trying not to let Bennie know how besotted he was.

Bennie motioned to Lou, the bartender, to bring him another draft beer; Barker was already on his second brew. They were in a bar halfway between Harvard and M.I.T., the kind of place they went to in order to avoid seeing colleagues and students. The two of them had long ago agreed that in public places they preferred the anonymous company of working folk; and while it occurred to Barker that he could be laying himself open to an accusation of reverse snobbery, who the hell cared? The chances of a Cambridge lady (or, for that matter, a former girlfriend) wandering in here were even more remote than discovering a virgin among the Radcliffe senior class. It was late on a late-winter afternoon. Through the scummy window could be seen people waiting for the bus, going in and out of the five-and-ten, and calmly dealing dope.

"Not really?" Bennie said. "The publishing broad?"

Barker nodded.

"She's very young?"

"Twenty-four or -five. It's a spread."

"My instant calculator says twenty years," Bennie said.

"Not quite," Barker said. The spread seemed to him both cruel and exciting. The idea that a young girl—five or six years old when Kennedy was shot—could love a middle-aged professor enough to marry him was staggering. Each time Barker considered this possibility his heart went into high.

"I wouldn't dream of advising you," Bennie told him.

"I don't recall asking for your advice," Barker said, draining his glass. "And for your information, we've only talked about it once; she was skittish."

"But you have spent the night with her?"

"What do you think?"

"I think yes."

"You're a genius, Bennie."

"That's beside the point. But what's she like?"

"She's adorable. I don't know, she's perfect."

"What sort of brain does she have?"

"How the hell do I know? She's got a decent job."

"I'd like to see you marry again," Bennie said. "You need someone to look after you—buy your ties, cook your meals, put your woollies in box storage."

"I don't wear ties that often," Barker said.

Both men quit talking to watch a woman and man in a booth, the woman opening her mouth wide, like a soprano soloist, and the man dropping his chin lower and lower until it rested against his collarbone. The woman had clearly won. Bennie shrugged and said, "Did I tell you where I'm going next month?"

Barker said he didn't think so.

"Poland," Bennie announced.

"This isn't a joke you're about to tell me?"

"No, it's for real. But do you know why they shut down the zoo in Cracow?"

"Why?"

"The clam died," Bennie said. "I hate Polish jokes. There's no spin on them. About the trip, there's a conference in Warsaw and I thought I'd take a look at the town where my parents' folks lived before the war."

"Roots, eh?"

"It's what you do these days," Bennie said.

"I don't," Barker said. "I can't see the appeal of turning yourself inside out trying to locate your roots, but people seem to get a bang out of it, so there must be something to it."

"It's like finding the body so you can bury it, I guess," Bennie said.

"Sounds plausible enough," Barker said. "But about marrying Susan. Do you think it's a lousy idea?"

"I never said that. You never gave me a chance." The skin under Bennie's eyes was wrinkled and puffy. His hair was deserting him: the scalp revealed was pale and blotched. There was a stiff black hair growing out of his left nostril.

"I'm giving you a chance now," Barker said. "I wonder if I have time for another beer. . . ."

"Aren't you hitting the bottle a little heavily these days?"

Barker laughed. "Not to worry. Three beers do not an alcoholic make. Lou, another if you please." The bartender took a clean tumbler from a phalanx of glasses standing upside down on a dish towel and held it under the draft tap. He put the full glass down in front of Barker.

"Thanks much," Barker said.

"No problem," Lou said.

"No problem?" Bennie said. "Why not, 'Have a nice day'?"

"He'll say that when you're ready to leave," Barker said. "I like 'No problem.' I like portmanteau phrases. Someone takes you to the cleaners; you say, 'No problem.' Someone calls you an asshole; you say, 'No problem.' It's so darn friendly."

"Okay," Bennie said. "By the way, I'd like to meet your new girlfriend. Why don't you arrange a lunch for the three of us so I can meet her? I feel like an idiot talking about someone I haven't even laid eyes on." Bennie edged off his stool and stood next to Barker. "Lucky sucker," he said. "Firm young flesh every night. . . . And now I've got to get home. I promised Patsy I'd be there for Jessie's birthday. But Christ, I can't remember what I'm supposed to be there so early for."

"Happy birthday," Barker told him. "I think I'll sit here a while and meditate."

Bennie plucked his coat from the coat tree and quit the bar. Barker took his beer and the plastic bowl of pretzels, half of them broken, to a table where he sat down to think about marriage. Those who were in the cage wanted out, those outside wanted in. Sometimes Barker saw marriage as an asylum for losers. The best of unions eventually soured. Hadn't even Bennie—all unknowingly—looked regretful at having to go home? And Bennie *liked* his wife. Think of the man whose ardor has grown cold as a frozen hamburger patty. At other times Barker feared marriage not as sharing—the way you were supposed to feel—but as relinquishing: the right to privacy; the right to leave things on the floor and in the sink, to make lousy decisions, and to go to bed whenever you felt like it—fully clothed if that's what turned you on; the right to misspend money and sit for hours in a brown study. The minute you were married you gave up your right to act like a rat. On the other hand, that ineffable warmth beneath a woman's skin, the smiles of gratitude it was possible to arouse. Someone to cut the pain of being alone at night, and worse still, at dusk.

Dusk was the terrible hour. Once in a while Barker wept before he turned on the lights. He would sit in his living room, feeling it grow darker by the second, testing himself to see how long he could stand it, the fumes of loneliness invading his room like carbon monoxide from a faulty stove. "Screw Bennie," he said. "I don't need him to make up my mind. I'll ask her. She might even say yes." The thought that she might refuse him turned his knees soft. But he got up and called Susan from the wall phone next to the men's-room door. It was cold in there; he could feel a piercing draft on his ankles coming from under the door.

"Susan," he said when she picked up her phone. "Can I come over?"

"Now?" she said. "I'm just about to leave the office. I've got to be at the Parker House in ten minutes."

"Nobody goes to the Parker House," he said.

"Jake? You know I'd love to see you, but this is a business thing. I've got to meet a book editor from Detroit. If I don't go and talk to her, she might overlook some of our . . . let's say some of our less accessible books."

"Like mine, you mean? *Cleopatra's Nose* is perfectly accessible."

"Yours is one of them," Susan said. "Detroit's a tough book-town."

"All the darkies . . ."

"Jake, really."

"You know I'm joking, Susan. I don't care what color their money is so long as they buy my book."

"I've really got to go now, Jake. You sound funny."

"Can I come over later? After your meeting?"

Susan hesitated three or four beats while Barker held his breath. Everything to do with Susan had a heightened quality; everything she said or did held meaning for him. If she refused him now, she would be cutting away at his vital organs. "I suppose so."

"Why do you hesitate? Don't you want to see me?"

"Of course I do, Jake."

"Well then, what's the matter?"

"My apartment's messy."

"Do you seriously think that makes the slightest difference to me? I want to see you, not your spotless countertop. I promise not to open the oven door."

"Jake?"

"What is it? Now *you're* the one who sounds funny. How can I help you?"

"Remember what happened the last time you came over?"

"Of course I do. You're not sorry, are you?"

"Not about going to bed with you. But the other thing. I'm so young, Jake, I'm just not sure I'm ready for a heavy-duty relationship. I'm too young to get married. And having great sex mixes me up."

"You're not too young. And what's wrong with great sex?"

"I know this may sound stupid, but I really think that some things don't change. Having great sex is like being drunk and wanting more. It makes it harder to think straight."

"Look, I just want to see you. We won't go to bed, I promise. Okay? I just need to be with you for a little while. Feeling blue, I need you. Do, oh do. Say yes, that is."

"Yes," she said.

Girls' mothers had always been more trouble than they were worth. It seemed as if as soon as a perfectly reasonable, lively, attractive, open-hearted person grew up and became a mother, she developed a nasty streak, a suspicious nature. Often when he entered a room, mothers with daughters quivered and scurried off, dragging the daughters with them. Barker guessed that Mona Cheng's suspicions about him (as conveyed reluctantly to him by Susan) were largely due to her being Chinese—cultural disparity having taken a particular and chilling form. Admittedly, there weren't that many folks who would deliberately choose to have their daughter marry beyond the racial pale, but Barker felt he was also up against intransigence: the Chinese were as rigid as old bones. He wondered if—when he married Susan—Mona might disown her, but he was afraid to ask. Mona Cheng was rich.

On their way to Roslindale, where he was to meet Mona for the first time, Barker discovered that he was nervous. Susan must have sensed this for she said, "My mother will probably give you a hard time. Try not to let her get to you; she loves the smell of blood."

"I can handle your mother," Barker said. "Besides, I'm not the enemy. We both love the same person—that makes us allies." Eyes straight ahead, he reached over and patted her coat where it lay over her left thigh.

"My mother's been in the States since 1942 and she still thinks in Chinese. My two sisters married Chinese boys." Susan smiled shyly as she mouthed the loaded verb. "Mom had someone picked out for me. She doesn't believe in inter-marriage. But you know that. . . ."

"But you've never told me about your handpicked suitor. Who is he?"

"Garrett? He's nice enough. But shallow, if you know what I mean. He designs software. When I told Mom I wasn't inter-ested in Garrett, she stopped talking to me for three weeks. But it was okay after that. She knows I'm as stubborn as she is."

"Stubborn? I wouldn't have said that about you."

"Oh, I am. You just haven't seen that side of me."

Chinese people named their children Garrett? Barker swung the steering wheel sharply to the right. A man crossing the street, whom he almost hit, shouted something—an obscenity no doubt; Barker didn't blame him. He sped on toward the house where Mona, the widow of an importer of pig bristles, lived by herself.

This is what Barker saw as soon as his eyes adjusted to the dimness of Mona's parlor, a room crammed with expensive-looking Oriental objects: seated dolls dressed in bright silk pajamas, porcelain platters and cups, tasseled brocade hang-ings, lacquer trays, cabinets filled with tiny jade replicas of animals and people, rugs with curly abstractions woven into the fabric. As he took off his coat, he peeked into the kitchen and saw a Cuisinart, microwave oven, toaster oven, electric coffee grinder, and restaurant-size range.

"So you're Susan's new young man," Mona said, standing before him. The phrase "squaring off" popped into Barker's head.

"Not so young, as you can see, Mrs. Cheng," he said. Mona was short and fat, which surprised and dismayed him. On second look, he decided cylindrical was an apter description; although fat bulged and rippled, Mona was more or less straight from shoulder to thigh, having lost her waist somewhere in the past. She wore a red brocade dress with stand-up collar and frog closings. There wasn't a single strand of gray visible among glossy black hairs.

Mona asked Barker to sit down, indicating a loveseat covered in pale green silk. "I've made us some tea," she said. "Susan dear, will you give me a hand in the kitchen?" Her daughter jumped to. Barker figured Mona was going to give her a preliminary earful as they gathered the tea things together. They stayed in the kitchen long enough for Barker to do some prowling about the room; his trip revealed nothing but more of the same—literally hundreds of items that made the same historical point. A couple of recent Lothar and Bright books lay on the ebony coffee table. They looked unread, but you never knew; some people read books without disturbing their hymens.

Mona served greenish tea in handleless cups and sweet pastries, one of which Barker bit into and almost gagged on, as it contained almond paste. Barker hated almond paste but he managed to get the first bite down by sending a mouthful of tea after it.

Mona stared at him. "Susan tells me you're a professor at Harvard."

"Yes, ma'am,"

"I'd like to know what you do, please tell me about your work."

Barker was tempted to baffle her by using the sort of language employed by most of his colleagues in print. Serve her right. But it could backfire; she might just be clever enough to see this as a hostile thrust. So he said instead, "We're" (he liked that "we"—it sounded Olympian and at the same time modest) "trying to discover what, if anything, studying the

163

brain activity of infants in a laboratory setting can tell us about actual gender differences. It's a slow process."

"Yes," Mona said. "Right and left hemispheres. I know about that."

"That's partly it," Barker said. "We're also trying to find out what we can predict before acculturation takes place. For instance, male fetuses are more active than female. . . ."

"What does that prove?" Mona said.

"Jacob's written a very interesting book on the subject, Mother. That's how we met."

"Oh yes," Mona said. "Will you have another one of these?" She stretched the plate of cookie things toward Barker who said, "No thanks, I've had one already. They're delicious."

"I think I should have made something else," she said.

"Oh no," Barker said. "I almost never eat pastry. Susan can tell you."

"Really?" Mona said. "You're not worried about your weight, are you?"

"Not exactly. It's more a matter of taste." He sensed she was trying to tree him.

"Mom, please let's talk about something other than Jake's weight. I think we're embarrassing him."

"You're not embarrassed, are you, Professor?"

"Of course not," he said. She'd done it! If he said yes, he'd be siding with Susan against her; if no, the opposite. Outsmarted by a mother. "I'm uncomfortable talking about myself," he said in his most ingratiating tone.

"Then we'll change the subject," Mona announced. "Are you a fan of your president?"

Why was she doing this to him? He hadn't done anything to her yet. He felt like spitting. Frustration crawled up his spine and warmed his ears. "Um. Are you?"

"You're very American," she said slyly. "You answer a question by asking one." She brought her cup up to her mouth and sipped soundlessly. "You haven't answered about Ronald Reagan," she said.

"Well, I'll tell you, Mrs. Cheng. I think I preferred Richard Nixon. As a matter of fact, I think Reagan's the worst president the people of this country have had the idiocy to elect since Woodrow Wilson."

Susan was staring at her feet. "Is that so?" Mona said, ice dripping off her tongue. "I should have thought you would have said Herbert Hoover."

"Hoover was a pussycat compared to Wilson. Of course, that's just one man's opinion."

"Mr. Reagan rescued us from inflation," she said, apparently determined to run this topic until it expired of fatigue.

"That he did," Barker said. "But at what price? Look, Mrs. Cheng," (he was waiting for her to tell him to call her Mona; was he to wait in vain?) "I have idiosyncratic politics—at least in these days. But I'm really a sweet guy. Don't pay too much attention; I'm not about to do anything rash with my opinions."

"Mother, do we have to talk about politics?" Susan said this without looking at her mother.

"Of course we don't have to, Susan, but it's not a bad start."

Start to what? How much did the old lady know? Why was he groveling? Barker hated himself for allowing himself to be messed around with like this. Take a wife and you took her relatives as well; maybe that was what was meant by "for better, for worse"—it meant the relatives. Why hadn't he fallen in love with an orphan?

Susan jumped up and peered inside a cabinet affixed to the wall between two windows so beautifully cleaned Barker had to look twice to make sure there were panes of glass in them. Beyond the windows lay a sea of clipped dead lawn dotted here and there by an island of dirt-encrusted snow.

"This jade mule is new, isn't it? I haven't seen it before."

"Your sister gave it to me when she was here last month. She always brings me something when she visits me."

"Mom," Susan said. "Ellie lives in Oregon. She only comes to see you once or twice a year. Of *course* she brings you

165

something. I visit you once a week. I don't bring you something each time I come. That would be ridiculous."

"Once every two weeks," Mona said.

"I'll bring you a gift next time I come. Would you like that?" Susan said in a voice Barker didn't recognize; it seemed to belong to a ten-year-old.

"Never mind," Mona said, "it has to come from the heart."

"Don't do this to me, Mom," Susan said. Barker saw she was on the edge of tears. He felt protective toward her; her youth and beauty still dissolved his bone marrow. Next to her mother—a giant redwood—Susan was a maple leaf in November. He looked at his watch. "Susan," he said, "we should probably think about leaving."

"You just got here," Mona said.

"We're meeting friends at four-thirty in Boston," Barker improvised. Susan looked at him gratefully.

"We really have to go now. But we'll be back soon, won't we, Jake?"

"You bet," he said, getting up.

"Baby," Mona said, "come and give your old mother a kiss." Susan went over to Mona, bent down, and touched her lips to her mother's cheek. When she straightened, Barker saw that Mona was near tears herself.

He asked himself what the hell he was doing to these two women; he sensed a three-act play with much accusatory subtext. But by the time they were beyond the borders of Roslindale, Barker had convinced himself that Mona's tears had been special-ordered for the occasion—crocodile tears—and his guilt disappeared. "What exactly have you told her about us?" he asked Susan.

"I told her that you were very important to me. I stopped just short of saying we were thinking of getting married. In China, you don't tell your mother things like that. You let it come from her."

"By the way," Barker said, "this isn't China, this is Massa-

166

chusetts. And another thing, orange blossom, your mother doesn't think in Chinese anymore than I do."

"I guess I know that," Susan said.

In the face of their determination, Mona accepted her daughter's apostasy. Barker's privately held opinion was that Mona, like most bullies, caved in rather easily when confronted with superior force. Susan wrote up an engagement notice which, somewhat to their surprise and after two verification phone calls, the *New York Times* printed on a Sunday. While not discounting the Harvard connection, Barker figured that the announcement was appealing largely because of the couple's racial makeup. In its own reticent way, this newspaper seemed to enjoy buzzing its more reactionary readers—denizens of such places as Hewlett, Tuxedo Park, New Canaan—by giving prominence to interesting ethnic crossovers. The daughter of a Baltimore cantor marries the lineal descendant of an original Dutch patroon—a Van somebody. The son of the headmaster of an antique New England prep school gets engaged to the daughter of the manager of a discount appliance store in East St. Louis, a woman of color. Where but in America? Barker smirked as he thought of the clicking of tongues against patrician hard pallets. The Harvard prof and the Oriental publicity girl—good, though not quite as piquant as an oil heiress marrying her chauffeur. They mentioned the name of Barker's book in the announcement. When he called Bennie's attention to the item, Bennie said, "Well done, man. When am I going to meet the lucky lady?"

Guy called him from school and said, "How could you do this, Dad?"

"Do what?" Barker said.

"Get engaged to someone I never even heard of? What the fuck. I ought to have my ass kicked for thinking maybe you were going to start thinking about your family for a change."

167

"Guy—listen, son, I want you to meet Susan. She wants to meet you. Why don't you come in on Saturday and we'll go to a nice restaurant and celebrate?"

"Dad? I can't believe you just said that. I don't want to come in. I've got better things to do. Oh, and by the way, thanks a bunch for getting me out of this fucking school. . . ."

"I tried . . . ," Barker said. But the boy had gone and hung up on him. Guy was right: Barker had completely forgotten to tell his son that he was going to marry again. If Guy were dead he would have given him more thought.

Barker took the subway to Washington Street in downtown Boston, where he bought Susan a pea-sized pearl nesting on a gold band. Later, she told him that her mother had asked, "Why not a diamond?"

"You remind me of a pearl," he said, nuzzling. "Some people think the pearl stands for the soul." Susan's temperature was always a notch or two below his, so that she seemed cool, an outdoor creature continually bathed by winds. He licked her neck, just below her perfect ear.

"I hope not too much," she said.

"What are you talking about?"

"I hope I don't remind you too much of a pearl. I was reading a book that said women should avoid committing to a man who keeps telling them they're something else than what they are. Like you see me as a pearl or someone else always calls his girlfriend a cupcake. That's a silly example, but I can't remember another one."

"Would you like to hear what I think of your book? I think it's full of horse doodoo. I assure you that Adam called Eve a cupcake." He made her laugh. "You read too many books," he said.

"I have to, Jake, it's my job."

"I realize that. But you don't have to believe everything you read. You mustn't try to stop me from calling you pet names. A

168

pearl—you can reassure your mother—is far more beautiful than a diamond; it looks soft but it has intrinsic strength. A pearl attracts by a glow from within, not, like a diamond, by a flashy display of reflected light. I wouldn't put a diamond on that adorable hand."

"Will you please shut up, Jake. You sound like Barbara Cartland. Come on now, we have to get up and go talk to Dr. Lee. If I kiss you you-know-where, will you promise not to take a fifteen-minute shower? We'll be late."

"You worry too much about time," Barker said. "People wait. Especially that windbag of a minister. I don't know why we have to talk to him again anyway—or, rather, listen to him. Where'd he get that phony accent, by the way?" Barker hoisted himself to a sitting position and stared at his knees, then past them down to his feet, which looked like the stringy, marbleized feet of an old man, the two largest toenails thick and rancid-looking, like ancient cheese. They turned his stomach. He didn't want Susan to see his ugly feet. She had snaked an arm around his neck and was depositing a tiny moist spot on his neck.

"I love you, Jacob Barker, and I'm going to be your wife."

"I want to make you happy," Barker said, surprising himself.

The wedding came off without anything major going wrong. Susan's two older sisters came East for the event. The older one, Ellie, was even more beautiful than Susan, and there was a moment—as she was taking off her raincoat and raised an arm and her small breasts rose—when Barker felt a pang of lust that made him quiver, this while his bride-to-be stood by his elbow, her body's scent rising into his nostrils. Dr. Lee took nearly fifteen minutes to trot through a service that touched briefly on a nondenominational God and lingered over such abstract gerundives as "committing," "sharing," and the truly frightening "parenting." Barker found himself awash in perspiration beneath the crisp white cotton shirt that had set him back forty-five bucks. For a moment, terror blinded him.

When this passed, Barker looked at Susan standing at his right; in profile, her lashes seemed thick and sticky over eyes almost shut. She must have read somewhere that brides are demure. (How she cherished advice found in books—as if, once printed, words assumed an immutable authority. It was frightening: the poor girl believed everything she read, and if one book challenged the previous one, she simply believed the latest. Barker stuck a memo into his mental file on the subject of discouraging Susan from mindless adherence to the written word.) Her cheeks were pinker than ever, a slight but noticeable uppage in color. He thought he could feel her trembling. Dr. Lee, wearing an academic robe with a hood, guided his steed through a seemingly endless park of clichés and word packages (Barker kicked himself for not composing the service himself). Barker had to pee. He asked himself, "How much longer, oh Lord?"

At last Dr. Lee's horse grew tired and he secured the knot. The couple kissed, then Barker rushed to the basement of the chapel, where he relieved his bladder in an unheated men's room and said aloud, "Well, chum, you've done it again. Let's see if you can do a better job of it than last time." Barker wasn't all bad. He knew how he ought to act. The trouble was that knowing it and doing it were so rarely on speaking terms. The wish and the act: feuding cousins, forever aiming guns at one another.

When Jacob Barker, awash in sentiment, realized where he was, he said to himself, "She's my wife, Susan's my wife. I love her more than I thought it was possible to love a girl." Life with Susan was a living valentine, sex and love so fused they had liquefied and become one. For Susan's sake, Barker did things he had always disliked—quite simply because he loved her. They took daylong car trips, to New Hampshire, to the Berkshires, to Rhode Island. Never before had he enjoyed being shut up in a car, but now—sealed off from the telephone, from all interruption—he had a wonderful time. They talked and talked. While he drove, his right hand explored her sweet young body—about this activity Susan didn't seem the least reluctant. She answered in wordless kind. They were in automotive heaven.

For almost a year, Barker believed it was possible to start things up again, to feel, once more, refreshed on waking, to experience profound concern for another human being. Then gradually, and with the sadness of mortality, his old, bad old habits, his troubles, began to reappear, one by one. He tried to kiss a student in his office one afternoon, and although she turned and ran out, he was badly frightened, for she looked both angry and determined. He found himself awake when he should have been safely in dreamland; the low-numbered hours, two, three, found him lying beside his adored peach blossom, currents of energy stinging his arms and legs, scrambling his brain. He would get up and read one of the stack of suspense novels he had piled up in his study, until at last his eyes began to close by themselves at four in the morning.

At length, Susan was pregnant. Barker wasn't so sure he wanted a baby in the house, but it was too late; the one time he introduced—in the most oblique way—the notion that there were alternatives to giving birth, she began to cry and accused him of not loving her. It was a woman's trick: if they didn't like what you told them, they said you didn't love them. He gave up. When he told Bennie about the pregnancy, Bennie made a characteristically crude remark concerning shots in Barker's locker.

Barker tried hard to hold on and, as he told himself, was doing a fair job of it. No one else appeared to notice the new wrinkles Barker noticed alongside his eyes and lips. He was a Harvard fixture: his habits—his avoidance of department meetings, a tendency to pick at his beard, his willingness to unleash a caustic tongue—were taken for granted.

171

PART TWO

Chapter Twelve

Thus, while it could be said that Barker had begun to coast
on the downhill part of his journey to the grave, the same could
be said for at least half his colleagues. Besides, he told
himself, analyzing the facts with a clear head, coasting does
pick up speed and can appear quite dazzling. There was really
nothing to worry about, just a trick knee here, a slight loss of
hope there. It was at this precarious moment—partway down
the dark side of the mountain—that Dean Fromme's letter
arrived, citing "allegations" and requesting a meeting at
Barker's "earliest convenience." After having read this message twice and glanced at the guidelines Fromme had thought-
fully provided, Barker slipped them inside his top drawer,
locked the drawer, and pocketed the key. Then he left his
office and walked home slowly through the dusk over cobblestone and cement, his feet scattering oak leaves and maple.
The air had a bite to it. He thought he could smell snow and
ice to come.

Susan was waiting for him in the kitchen of the house he had
recently purchased, thanks to unexpectedly healthy sales of
Cleopatra's Nose. Few members of Harvard's faculty could

afford to buy property in the city their employer was located in. Leaving it in the hands of shrinks, lawyers, high-tech entrepreneurs, investment counselors, and a couple of other lucky authors, these academics settled down and made do in surrounding 'burbs. Somewhat more modest than the Von Stampler place, Barker's house was nonetheless presentable. A late Victorian stained dark brown, it had a mansard roof and a wooden stoop flanked with ornamental railings that required frequent repainting. Associated with the house was a small patch of backyard and a one-car garage. Susan had wanted to buy a younger house further from the center of town, a lighter, airier building, but it was Barker's money, so his choice won. A Harvard senior named Billy Forest lived with them in a converted attic room; in return Billy performed jobs in and around the house: dragging full garbage cans from in back to the front sidewalk, shoveling snow, weeding the minuscule bed of flowers planted by Susan, sorting laundry, occasional shopping, and vacuuming twice a week.

Susan's trim little body lay beneath a pair of jeans and a bright red wool sweater. When her eyes landed on his face, he was sure he could feel them. Although the first blush of passion had faded, each time Barker looked at his wife's eyes, guarded by perfect epicanthic folds, his stomach did something funny. Susan wore an apron that hid the signs of pregnancy. She smiled, tormenting Barker: she was sweet and loving; she trusted him; she had no idea what a skunk he was.

"Hi," she said, drawing out the one syllable to take up the space of three. She put down her chopper and wiped her hands on the apron. On the counter lay small mounds of diced vegetables—bok choy, scallions, red pepper, a couple of other items he didn't recognize; Susan trekked to Chinatown to buy the food she mixed together into fiery meals for the two of them. "You look strange," she said. "Is something wrong?"

"Now why would you ask that?" Barker said. "And where's our beamish houseboy?"

"Billy's upstairs studying for a quiz," Susan told him. "He's a good kid. He fixed that lamp in your study. I didn't even have to ask him."

"Billy's got a good deal here and he knows it," Barker said. "He might try fixing a few more things." Susan lowered her eyes.

"That's not why he's here," she said.

"God forbid he should do a little physical labor," Barker said.

"I think he does a lot," Susan said. "I never asked him to empty the wastebasket in your study. . . ."

"He better be careful," Barker said, "he might get a hernia."

"Why are you so hard on Billy?"

"This conversation is getting boring," Barker said. "Let's change the subject: What do you know, I got a letter today informing me I'm on the short list for a MacArthur."

"My God, Jake, that's fantastic! Why aren't you pleased? What's the matter with you?"

"Short list doesn't mean a thing," Barker said. "I've been there many, many times. I'll wager I've been on more short lists than any other tenured professor in the United States. Short list is bubkas." Barker poured himself a stiff vodka and tonic and sat at the kitchen table watching his wife chop and slice. Her hands were the color of blanched almonds.

"How much money if you get it?" Susan said over her shoulder. "Just think, if you got it you could spend all of your time in the lab—or writing. You wouldn't have to teach." She paused. "We could take a trip. . . ."

"Hold on there," Barker said. "A—I haven't got it yet; B—I like to teach; and C—my lab's in Cambridge, and why would I want to take a trip? Where would we go?" At this moment, and with no trigger other than the hopelessness that came over him in a dark swarm, Barker began to cry. He couldn't stop. He put an elbow on each knee and cupped his face with his hands. He wept in loud, coughlike sobs. Tears seeped through his fingers.

Susan came over to him and pulled his head against her stomach, where their baby bobbed, unthinking, in amniotic fluid. Her fingers smelled of garlic and onion.

"Susan," he said, "you've got to help me. I'm in awful trouble. Stay here, help me. . . ."

That night Jacob Barker lay beside his wife and geared himself to tell her what Dean Fromme apparently already knew. He would not dot the i's and cross the t's, of course, merely suggest the size and shape of his alleged misconduct. But even as he prepared to tell Susan about it, Barker found he could not coax the words out of his mouth. There they were, lined up, ready to march, when they turned and ran, deserted, took to the hills, leaving him mute. "Cowards," he shouted after them. Then, telling Susan he was too exhausted to do anything but sleep— "We can talk in the morning"—Barker fell into the sort of drugged unconsciousness that makes one feel ever so much better in the morning.

Showered and shaved, Barker sat at the kitchen table as Susan, who had come downstairs while he was still in the shower, put the finishing touches on his breakfast. "What's this?" he said. "Sausages," she said, depositing three gray thumbs on his plate with a pair of tongs. "I thought you might like them instead of bacon for a change."

"Thanks," he said. He chewed one and didn't like the taste. She spooned scrambled eggs next to the sausages.

"I'm sorry I lost my cool last night," Barker told her. "I don't know what got into me."

"You work too hard," Susan said. "It makes you antsy. My mother says you need more sleep." She bent toward him, poised like a waitress in a restaurant. Please, not her mother again. "Sit down," he said, "you make me nervous."

Susan sat, blinking away whatever was on her mind. "But why did you cry. . . ?" she began. "And what kind of trouble are you in? You promised we'd talk this morning. . . ." She

178

trailed off as Billy bounced in, wearing a much-laundered rugby shirt, pale blue jeans, and filthy running shoes. His glasses had slipped down his thin Midwestern nose. Avoiding Barker's eyes, he said to Susan, "I was going to make you guys breakfast."

Was Billy about to weep? Barker wanted to shake him. The kid was infuriating: if you asked him to do something, he would try to wiggle out of it. But whenever he proposed something himself—like cooking breakfast or rearranging your books—and you said no thanks, he got all bent out of shape. Susan seemed not to notice—or not to mind. Sometimes Barker would find them chatting together like young girls.

"I like making breakfast for my husband," Susan said. "You can wash up if you like."

Billy's face fell into its semisullen mode. His appearance in the kitchen effectively cut off the likelihood of private talk. But perhaps it was just as well, for in the light of this sparkling winter day, Barker's troubles seemed far less dire than they had the night before. It was amazing how light could affect your mood. Barker took out a small spiral notebook and penned a reminder to himself to try his experiments under different intensities of illumination. Maybe the babies would react as dramatically as he had. His need to confess to Susan had vanished overnight, and he began to think that the hailstorm now threatening him might actually blow out to sea.

Billy said, "Wish me luck, I've got a geology quiz at ten o'clock. Twenty-five definitions."

"Break a leg," Barker told him.

For a moment Billy looked startled, then he smiled. "Oh yeah," he said. "Thanks. Leave the dishes for me, Mrs. Bee, I'll do them when I get back."

"Why does he call you Mrs. Bee?" Barker said after Billy had gone.

"I guess he feels funny calling me by my first name," Susan said. "Why, does it bother you?"

"Frankly, it makes me want to barf. Sounds like some goddamn sit-com on television."

"Billy wants to please you. He admires you."

"I don't think I'm being hard on Billy," Barker said, finishing off a glass of orange juice squeezed by Susan. "And I can't imagine what it is about me he claims to admire. He's opposite to me in about every way I can think of."

"He's a decent kid. He works hard." Susan seemed to be sifting through a mess of keys, looking for the right one. "There's something you're not telling me," she said, opening the door. "You started to tell me about it last night and now you're acting as if last night never happened. You can't do this again, Jake, it's not fair to me. I'm your wife, remember? Wives are supposed to be there to help, not just to cook and screw."

This hurt. "You do help me, Susie, I rely on you; you're always here. And I love looking at your perfect Szechuan face. And it matters that you also feed me my breakfast, and smile when I'm tired. Those things count for a lot; don't underestimate them. You're even a pretty smart cookie." He reached for her rump and palmed it. It was tight and hard. He dug his fingers into it.

"You know when you do this you're sending me away?" Susan said, ignoring his hand. "Maybe that doesn't bother you as much as it does me."

Barker sighed. "Look, Susan, there's nothing to tell. I'm going through a few minor problems at work, things that have nothing to do with you and are extremely boring. Honestly, pet, if there's something to tell, you'll be the first to know."

"Oh, Jake, this isn't working! What can I do?"

Susan was beginning to be a pain in the neck. *"Basta!"* he cried. "I don't want to talk about it anymore. *Capiche?* Understand, little one? No more talk about last night unless I bring it up."

Her eyes brimmed quickly. There were entirely too many tears in this house. Where did they get you? Barker suspected that his own teary display of the night before had damaged him in some irreparable way.

"I'm sorry, I didn't mean to upset you," he said. Her arms slipped down below her waist and crossed one another over her tummy, as if protecting her fetus, a gesture she was probably not aware of. He shouldn't push her around like this, but he just couldn't help it; it was like knowing that if you pried up the scab it would bleed, but being unable to keep your fingernail away from it. Susan had about as much fight in her as a stuffed rabbit. "Aren't you going to finish your breakfast? You've hardly eaten a thing."

"See this?" he said, touching his abdomen. "I've got to lose some of this pronto." In the past six months he had had to move his belt over one hole. The thought of turning into a fat man sickened him. "No more eggs or sausages, Susie, please. Just fruit and coffee in the morning. Okay? Hey, lighten up, pet, you'll make the baby unhappy."

Susan tried to smile but turned away from him as he rose to get ready to leave for work. "When will you be back?" she said.

"I'll call and let you know."

"I don't want to be disturbed for the next hour or so, Emily, so please hold my calls." Barker shut the door to his office, sat down, and looked out of the window. The view reminded him of an upbeat campus movie. Postadolescent boys and girls, variously dressed like Maine loggers, bushwhackers, mountaineers, valley girls, professional athletes—chinos and oxford shirts having apparently dissolved in the acid of time— walked across designated paths slicing lawns still greenish, and headed toward classrooms where they would have their heads stuffed with facts and theories, some of them useful, a lot of it composed of air they were unlikely ever to breathe again. Barker sighed and took out and reread Dean Fromme's letter. "Oh, God," he said in a whisper, "what the hell am I going to do?"

"Jesus," he said, "what's going on here?" Barker jumped up and looked out of the window. Below him, on the cobblestone path that circled the science complex, Bennie waved his arms, then tossed a fistful of pebbles against the glass, where they hit like buckshot. Barker smiled weakly; he had forgotten they were meeting for lunch. In addition to liking him as a friend, Barker admired Bennie for turning down Harvard. Bennie was one of the few first-rate men in any field to have done this (a "handful," Bennie said, "with a couple fingers missing") and gone elsewhere.

But Barker's troubles lay like heartburn against his chest. Lunch, small talk, even an exchange of gossip with his old friend seemed as appealing as the men's room in Boston Garden. Nevertheless, Barker waved to Bennie to come on up. Then, before he had a chance to change his mind, he hit three numbers on his phone, got Dean Fromme's secretary on the line, and asked for an appointment.

"Dean Fromme has a cancellation at three-fifteen, Professor Barker; can you make that?"

"That looks okay," Barker said. "I'll be there." He paused, then plunged on. "Have you any idea what Dr. Fromme wants to see me about?"

He thought she hesitated, but that might have been his imagination. "I really couldn't say." He hated himself for having asked the question.

Inside the Brasserie, a noisy place two blocks from the Harvard Yard and favored by senior faculty members, Barker ordered a whiskey from a woman who claimed to be "Marie. I'm your waitron today."

"Whoa," Bennie said, making a big deal of Barker's drink, "how about that? Mind if I don't keep up with you? I've got a shitload of work to finish this afternoon." Bennie asked for ginger ale.

Barker poured some whiskey down his throat; it hit his stomach like a lick of fire, making his eyes water.

Bennie nodded to a colleague, commenting that the man was "available, I believe, as of next semester. He got himself canned." They traded the mildest sort of academic gossip— they both had the same story with minor variations. Then Bennie cleared his throat and said, "What's up, Jake? You look as if they just discovered you're on the C.I.A. payroll."

"As a matter of fact," Barker said, "I want to ask you a question. Right now I'm trying to decide the best way to put it."

Bennie cracked a breadstick in half and began to chomp on one of the halves. He was going bald from front to back, revealing a scalp protected by a layer of pale, blotched skin. His sideburns were silver. Where was the skinny kid with long soiled hair, razor-edged jaw, and eyes of bright, unmarked blue: gone, withered inside this overweight, stiff-legged gent who sat across from him, downing unneeded carbohydrates, more out of habit than hunger.

"Okay," Barker said. "Here's what I'd like to know. What do you do when one of your students makes it obvious that she finds you, ah . . . attractive?"

"I'm flattered."

"That's not what you do. That's what you *are*."

"No, pal, that's what I *do*. I do nothing. I'm not that anxious to risk my salary or my rep." Bennie frowned into his corn chowder and stuck his spoon into it. Their waitron came back and said, "We're all out of schrod."

Bennie said, "I'll have the red flannel hash.

"I don't really like hash," he told Barker. "I only order it for the name." Barker took a bite of grapefruit from his fruitcup and tried to sneak it past the lump in his throat.

"What do *you* do?" Bennie said.

"That depends," Barker said. He felt his heels sinking into ooze.

183

"Depends on what?" said Bennie.

"Depends on a lot of things. Whether I'm in the mood. Whether or not I like her legs. Whether the Karma's right. I don't know, Bennie, I haven't given it that much thought."

"I'm surprised." Bennie seemed more uneasy than startled. "Not surprised that you haven't thought about it more—surprised that you actually indulge this fancy of yours."

"And you don't?"

"I just told you I don't. Not that the idea hasn't crossed my mind. All that gash—some of them deliberately showing me their little lace bikinis, making goo-goo eyes, practically jumping me in the corridor. Look, there's plenty of pussy around—you can fuck just about any damn female you please. Why mess with your students? Jesus, it's like diving into a pool without first making sure there's water in it."

"I wouldn't have suspected you of such innocence, Bennie. You sound as if you thought I was the only one. I can name at least three men who indulge almost as often as they play tennis or jog." Barker didn't like being put on the defensive, especially by Bennie; you accepted your friends as they were, you didn't try to reform them.

"I don't give a shit about your jogging friends. I care about what *you're* doing. I also don't especially enjoy this judgmental role—it doesn't suit me." He sighed and shook his head. "Look, Jake, you're not a kid anymore; you know what happens to a middle-aged man who does what you're doing? Sooner or later he's going to find himself in extremely hot water. You've got such a terrific head on your shoulders . . . why are you willing to risk everything you've worked for? Can you possibly stop?"

"Stop? You talk about it as if I was an addict. What's with you, Bennie? Look, do you mind if we don't go on with this? I've got enough on my mind."

"Whatever you say," Bennie said, like a woman who needs the last word of an argument. Barker trembled with irritation: Bennie should know better.

It was a while before they spoke again, each man chewing and swallowing as if in a monastery governed by a rule of silence. Bennie finally broke.

"Your wife's a wonderful girl, Jake. You're very lucky."

"What does luck have to do with it?" Barker asked.

"If we wanted to pursue that line of inquiry, we'd probably be at it until the middle of next month. But you know what I mean. I mean, given the first installment, I think you've made a sensible choice. Of course, there is the difference in your ages. . . ."

"That's not luck," Barker said, "that's prudence."

"That's Susan," Bennie said. "She's a rare girl. She has a definite aura."

"Aura? Is this Bennie Goodrich I'm talking to? Since when did you start thinking about auras? I know Susan's beautiful—but aura?"

Bennie grew very serious. "If you ever did anything stupid enough to make her leave you, then you deserve to lose her." Bennie put down his fork and stared at Barker in a way that made it impossible for Barker not to look back. "Jake, look, is there something else you'd like me to know? You and I have waded through an awful lot together."

"You got it, Bennie. I think I'm in deep shit, and frankly, I haven't the faintest idea whether I'm going to be able to crawl out or whether I'm going to drown in it. I've begun to pray for the first time in my life."

"They've nailed you, haven't they? They caught you screwing a student? Jesus, Jake, why didn't you tell me before this?"

"Couldn't," Barker said. "It's a blow. I'm still trying to absorb it. They call it sexual harassment. You know who I feel like? Captain Dreyfus—falsely accused. You understand how these things work: it's never one-sided; the girl is as much to blame as the man. It's a bargain between the two of you. You do understand this, don't you, Ben? And of course, for the last year or so, certain ladies in high places have turned into vigilantes. I'm surprised they don't go around with a hang-

185

man's noose. . . ." Barker was babbling; he could hear it himself. He rubbed his napkin over his palms.

"I understand about the urge. What I don't understand is 'bargain.' Don't you see how *you've* got all the shekels? She's got nothing. How *can* she refuse? She's afraid if she does, you'll lower her grade or some damn thing. If it *is* a bargain it's hardly an even trade. I can't see how this escapes you." Bennie looked stricken himself. "Is there anything I can do?" he said, lapsing unexpectedly into sympathy.

"Can you rewrite history? Can you wipe out two decades of sexual activity? Are you equipped with magic?"

"I'm afraid not, Jake. None of the above. But you can count on me when the time comes."

Nicely put, though ominously vague. "I know that, and I appreciate it," Barker said. He looked at his watch. Not quite one hour of liberty left to him. He sighed. "What did you say that colleague of yours was fired for?"

"I didn't say," Bennie said. "But the rumor is the problem's not unlike your own." Bennie wiped the corners of his mouth carefully, as if afraid that he had dribbled. "Ah, friend," he sighed.

"Ah well," Barker said. He signaled to the waitron to bring their bill so they could get the hell out of there. Then, for some deep underground reason, he was kissed by the same imp of terror who had kissed him as he stood before Susan's Chinese minister waiting for the knot to be tied. Why did everything he undertook start out with such glorious promise and end in a pile of garbage?

Chapter Thirteen

Pₐɪɴꜰᴜʟʟʏ, Barker climbed the curving staircase to the mez-
zanine where Dean Fromme's office lay, surrounded by half a
dozen secretaries performing secretarial tasks with phone,
word processor, typewriter, stamp machine, copier, Rolodex,
file cabinet, wastebasket. Barker lowered himself into a
Breuer chair; if his fucking knee didn't get better soon, he
would have to consult Doctor Greene, something he would
rather go without sex for a month than do; his blood pressure
shot up to the ceiling whenever he walked into a doctor's office.
Today the knee, tomorrow the hip, then every joint in his body,
all of them performing the slow dance of decay. He was just
about to pick up a copy of *Harvard Magazine* when the head
secretary came at him, saying, "Dean Fromme will see you
now." Had she smirked while saying this? Barker got to his
feet, involuntarily straightening his tie and tugging at the hem
of his jacket. "You're in for it now, fella," he told himself. "The
party appears to be over."

"Good of you to come in on such short notice, Jake!" Dean
Fromme thrust a paw at Barker's midsection. Their hands
locked, the Dean's fingers tightened brutally, the hands went

up and down, then burst apart. "Sit down, sit down please. Coffee?"

"No thanks," Barker said. "I just had two cups at the Brasserie. Not all that good for you, you know." He sat in one of three black Harvard armchairs. Fromme's nervousness dismayed him. The man looked as if his own nuts were in the fire instead of the other way around. Should he say something to put Fromme at ease? Rats to that.

The dean fiddled briefly with the vertical blinds strung across a window, then sat down at his desk. A single, unscarred manila folder lay within easy reach of his bone-crushing fingers.

"And how's your wife? I understand she's expecting."

"Susan's just fine," Barker said, supplying her name. "And yes, the baby's due in May."

"Second family, eh?" Fromme said. "Seems to be something of an epidemic around here. Let's see, there's Norman Whykoff in Physics, Slattery in Art History—you should see his wife, Jake, she looks just like that young actress, what's her name? The punk one."

"You mean Madonna," Barker said.

"That's the one," Fromme said. He lowered his lids briefly, as if trying to animate the child-bride behind his eyelids.

How to respond? But Barker didn't have to, for the dean followed this fatuous remark by suggesting that it was time to get to the business at hand. So saying, he flicked open the folder and began to summarize the contents of the first document, a memorandum from Anita Andrews, Dean of Women's Affairs. "Ms. Andrews has sent on several affidavits from young women who claim that you, ah . . ."—here the dean faltered, as if looking around for help, and finding none, he resumed the beat—"with whom they maintain that you and they have engaged in, shall we say, amorous encounters. Some of them appear to think that you offered them a species of bargain."

188

"I don't quite understand," Barker said, going deaf as blood rushed into his ears.

"A bargain, an exchange. They acquiesce to your sexual overtures, you give them the course grade they need. There's got to be some misinterpretation here." The dean paused, but not long enough for Barker to insert a word. "These are merely allegations, you understand, old man, and believe me, it's hardly the first time I've seen a file like yours. Though I must say, if only half of this is true, you must have been a pretty busy fellow. Ah, a regular Professor Romeo!" There it was again. So Kathleen Peters had not made it up; it *was* floating in the Harvard air. However, the dean appeared to think he had invented this humiliating tag, and believed himself to be both clever and funny for having done so. He smiled at Barker, who clenched both fists and ordered himself to remain silent.

Fromme went through a complicated throat-clearing. "Would you like me to go on? I mean, would it help you to know the names of your accusers?"

Barker interrupted. "You mean my alligators."

"What? I'm not sure I follow you."

"I resent the allegations and I resent the alligators. It's just a tired old joke, Ed."

"Oh yes, I see."

"Well," said Barker. Why should he volunteer anything?

"Yes. The names. Let's see now; there's a Patricia Weissman, an Elaine Ferrier and a Kathleen Peters. That's about it."

"Is that it, or is that about it?"

Fromme stiffened. Light bounced off his glasses, flashing twin mirrors into Barker's eyes. "I don't think we're going to go very far with this if you get your back up. I'm on your side, Jake, a thousand percent. I've known you for how long?— twenty years? In my book you're above reproach. These folks"—here he tapped the folder—"who are they? What's their game? So many militant ladies. I ask you, where did they all come from? They're no better than Maoists. I'm deter-

189

mined—and so is President Franklin, incidentally—not to let them turn this university into a battlefield. But listen up, my friend, you've got to cooperate with me." The dean seemed to be getting fuel from an auxiliary source.

Fromme was wearing an *echt* Harvard costume: tweed jacket with leather elbow-patches and threadbare sleeves, rep tie. No doubt his blue shirt collar had been neatly turned by Mrs. F. Barker couldn't see Fromme's feet but he guessed either penny loafers or fifteen-year-old wingtips, polished to a dazzling brightness. He was about Barker's age, give or take a year or two. Fromme had taken the safe road—administration—partly by default when he stumbled during his Ph.D. orals, failing to explicate the twelfth of Pound's Pisan Cantos. It was said that one of Fromme's examiners was out to get him, but in any case, he flunked and immediately applied for a job in the alumni office, from whence he began slow and steady progress toward this three-windowed room, these wrinkle-free secretaries. Fromme had skin trouble; it erupted in red blotches whenever he struggled with a problem. There were pinkish areas now, under his jaw line and over his eyebrows.

"Yes, of course, I understand," Barker said. He knew how Nixon felt as soon as what's-his-name, Butterfield, innocent of face, ultimate WASP, tipped over the container of beans on national television. And from that moment on, it was just a question not of if but of when. "I'll do whatever is required," he said, lapsing into the passive voice.

"Aren't you going to deny the charges?" Fromme said. "I mean, granted these statements are signed, but the charges are largely unsubstantiated. As far as I'm concerned they're absurd. Listen to this." Fromme riffled through the papers and began to read: "Professor Barker requested that I meet him at the Golden Cod Coffee Shop and while there inferred that he would like me to go to bed with him. It got me angry. When I got up to leave he held me by my wrist and said if I did I would

190

not be sorry." Fromme removed his glasses and stared at Barker. "She means 'implied,' " he said.

"Who wrote that?"

"This statement is signed by Patricia Weissman. I believe the year she is referring to is 1968."

"Nineteen sixty-eight, that's nearly twenty years ago! You expect me to remember something that happened nearly two decades ago?"

Ah, but he did remember, and with the clarity of murder. A starved child—Patty had turned him on, and now she had turned on him.

"Patricia Weissman?" he said. "Let me think a moment. Ah, it comes back—a classic case of anorexia nervosa. She couldn't have weighed more than eighty pounds. Probably thought she was fat. They all do. "

"And about her accusation?"

"It didn't happen that way. She was a very needy girl, as I remember. Followed me around asking idiot questions. She wanted something I couldn't give her, God only knows what it was. Thinnest creature I ever saw. No, I'm quite prepared to deny her charges—they're moonshine. "

"Then you did not go to bed with her. "

"That's right. "

"And about these other people, you say you weren't intimate with them either?"

"That's what I'm saying," Barker said. These lies emerged as effortlessly as carbon dioxide in suspiration. If he could do this so simply, God only knew what else he was capable of. Barker was aware of a new, supremely cool man shoving the old Jacob this way and that, trying to take over. It was thrilling; it was sickening.

"Splendid!" cried the dean. "That's exactly what I needed to hear. For a moment there, I was afraid you'd lost that backbone you're famous for. We'll see this thing through together. Of course, it won't end at this point in time; you'll have to submit to a hearing—behind closed doors, of course. But not to worry, it's just a formality."

"Ah . . . do you think I should consult my lawyer?" Barker said, amazed at how steady his voice sounded.

"Can't hurt," the dean said briskly. "Though he won't be permitted to be present at the hearing."

"Really? That doesn't seem quite fair."

"This isn't a court of law, Jake, it's just between us Harvard folks. A family affair, so to speak."

"I see," Barker said, although he didn't. In the last half hour it had come down to whether he would emerge in one piece. Cards stacked against him? So be it. If anything in this life was truly fair, he hadn't yet heard of it. And if he didn't get out of here in the next couple of minutes, his own skin was going to break out. The dean was a perfect ass, of course—how could you respect a man who refused to name the odor of the stinking facts in front of his nose? Barker rose from his chair. "What's the next step?"

"I'll be in touch." Fromme also rose, and coming round the desk, escorted Barker the fifteen feet or so across soft blue carpeting to the door. "I imagine things will move right along from now on. I think you might want to get in touch with your attorney. Forewarned and so on. . . ." Barker looked at Fromme's feet: penny loafers.

In the smoky dusk of the 19th Hole, Barker felt soothed, like a small boy whipped by his father for doing something wrong when he meant to be good and it was all a terrible mistake. And this boy climbs into his tree house, shutting the trapdoor behind him; or slides beneath the porch floor, listening to the thud of feet above his head; or goes down to the cellar to huddle next to a pile of old suitcases. Barker embraced his self-imposed exile as warmly as thoughts of never-ending love, the pain and the pleasure from the pain coming together so closely they kissed.

Patty Weissman? This person was now older than his wife; midthirties and probably thin as a rail; her tits flat as any boy's. How had they tracked her down? Or had she been lurking all these years, waiting in the wings as it were, for the chance to nail him? Unfair. There was, apparently, no statute of limitations on this sort of perverted revenge. Sighing, Barker looked at the Budweiser clock, saw that he had been in the bar for nearly two hours, phoned for a cab, and took off, leaving an area a local columnist had recently referred to as Cambridge's cloaca. The cab skirted the university, huddling darkly behind brick wall and iron gate, and dropped him at his house. The light in his front-of-the-house study was off; their bedroom light was on.

"Jake? Is that you?" Susan's liquid voice came from the kitchen. The woman practically lived there—they might as well not have bothered with a bedroom. Or her study, a small back room overlooking the yard. It was nice and quiet there, sunny. But she didn't use it; she lugged her portable word processor down to the kitchen, where, determined to be a much-published writer (she had quit her job, saying she never liked it anyway), she turned out topicky pieces—on Chinese cooking, part-time work for mothers, living with your aged parent, and other subjects of domestic concern—which she occasionally sold to local papers and magazines. She had an idea for a book on mixed marriages and had started on the first chapter; as far as Barker could tell, she hadn't done sufficient research to bring it off, but he had not yet told her this. The processor's home was a shelf in the pantry, among canned goods and sacks of rice hard by the back door. When Barker asked her why she didn't use her study, she said she preferred the warmth of the kitchen.

"Yes, it's me," Barker said. "I'll be there in a minute. Gotta pee first." He shut himself in the lavatory. Immediately he started counting stars on the wallpaper above the toilet. He had to count at least fifty before he was through or something terrible would happen to him. He was midway in the forties when he lost count, faltered. Terrified, he felt his legs go soft and his head lighten. He pitched against the wall, covering stars. "Help!" he said aloud. "This can't be happening. I'm doomed." The faintness in his head made his feet seem a long way off. Carefully, he tried to straighten up.

"Jake! Are you all right?" Susan, on the other side of the door, tapped insistently.

"I'm fine," Barker said. "I'll be right out." He splashed cold water on his face and patted it dry with a pale linen towel. It was time to face the musicians.

"Have you eaten?" Susan said, as he kissed her cheek. "I'll bet you haven't."

"I'm not hungry," Barker told her. "But I could use a drink."

"I made a small roast," Susan said. "I baked a potato for you. I'm afraid it's cold now."

"Maybe later," he said. "Susan, for crissake, stop fussing over me—I'm a grown man."

She looked demurely down. "Billy's out," she said, a statement unconnected to anything either of them had said.

"That so?" Barker poured whiskey into a tumbler and dumped in three cubes of ice. "Susan?"

"You have something important to talk to me about," she said. "Like the other night when you said you were in trouble and then you wouldn't tell me the next morning. It's still there, isn't it? It didn't go away."

"No, pearl drop, it didn't. It not only didn't go away, it got bigger and hotter. It may burst."

At that moment Susan's beauty was heightened by Barker's terror—as if she might be plucked away by one of those giant birds that hover in Oriental paintings. You could be in love with beauty, it was not only plausible, it was altogether natural. Susan was smooth all over; she had none of the blemishes dotting the epidermis of so many Caucasian girls. Her cheeks were curved planes of ivory touched by symmetrical patches of pink. Her black hair was dense and straight and smelled of

194

sandalwood, the soap she used. She was boneless, satin, the shell God had given her was as close to perfect as anything living that Barker had ever seen. What had she done to deserve what he was about to do to her? Nothing, except to fall in love with him. What sort of person would be dumb enough to fall in love with him? The perfect shell contained a perfectly foolish egg.

"I'm your wife," said Susan flatly. "It's my pleasure to take your troubles and make them my own. That way they may not hurt you so much." Whose voice was she speaking with now? Where had she picked up this archaic inflection? He thought this was a bad start—she was simultaneously arming herself and stepping backwards. "Would you like a drink, honeybee?" he said. Susan almost never drank alcohol.

"I think so, perhaps," she said. He poured dark rum into a glass and added orange juice. "A fruit punch," he said, handing it to her.

"I'm tired, Jake," she said. "And I'm not feeling all that well. I didn't feel right all day." She lowered her eyes to where their baby lay beyond a wall of flesh. "I'd like to go to bed."

"I'm sorry you're not feeling well," Barker said. In spite of her words, she looked at him with the patience of an invalid. "Oh hell," he said. "I might as well get it over with." He paused and swallowed some whiskey. "I met with Ed Fromme today," he began. "It seems that several ladies have accused me of making, ah—I suppose what could be called amorous advances. There's going to be a hearing before I'm cleared."

"Jake," Susan said, on a breath that seemed more drawn inwards than released. She bowed her head. Her crown of hair looked as if it had been liberated from a porcelain doll. "Why have they done this to you?"

"It isn't exactly something they've gone and done. I may have acted, you know, ambiguously and it was taken the wrong way."

"What do you mean, ambiguously? I don't understand. Did you have sex with your students?" She was still talking to her

195

lap. They sat beneath a hooded light dangling from the end of a long cord attached to the ceiling. The rest of the kitchen was in darkness, surrounded by all the gadgets they had bought—coffee grinder, food processor, microwave oven (which Susan was afraid to use), hand mixer, toaster, Cuisinart.

"We have too many things," Barker said, realizing his own kitchen was equipped exactly like his mother-in-law's. "Why do we own so much junk?"

"Please don't change the subject, Jake," Susan said. Now she brought her chin up, as if asking for him to hit her on it. "You've got to tell me. You can't keep it to yourself any longer; it's making me physically ill."

This was a surprise and it made him feel lousy. The thought that she might be trying to hurt him back flashed through his mind, but he dismissed it as so unlikely as not worth considering. "It was long before I met you," he began. "They were extremely needy, waifs, you might call them. They came to me. You know what a devilishly handsome fellow I was in my youth. . . ." Here Barker hoped to coax a smile from Susan; it did not materialize. "I mean, what can a man do? A girl comes on to him and throws herself at him. There was one, for example, who came to my office without an appointment and closed the door and simply started to undress, unzipped her jeans and took off her shirt—"

"And you stopped her," Susan said, cutting him off. "You told her to get dressed again and leave your office."

"That's precisely what I did," Barker said. "But she was one of the people who signed a letter swearing I'd touched her 'inappropriately,' as she put it, that's the new buzzword. It also appears that I promised her an A in my course if she would go to bed with me."

Susan made a face, twisting her ideal features into something ugly.

"They're all little simps," Barker heard himself saying. "And what's more, they've joined in a conspiracy to ruin me—

God knows why. I never did anything to them except try to give them what they wanted." At this, the twin arcs of Susan's eyebrows lifted together. She shook her head ever so gently. None of her hair moved.

"Jake," she said, placing her palm over his hand and then quickly withdrawing it. "I don't know how to respond to all this. I wanted to know what was bothering you, and now I'm sorry you told me. I feel like you just hit me in the stomach; I can't seem to get my breath. I thought I wanted to hear and now I don't think I can listen to anymore."

"Dearest girl," Barker said, "you're overreacting. They're only accusations—which, incidentally, I think say more about the accusers than about me."

"Don't try to turn things around again, Jake, not this time. I'm not going to let you convince me that I'm the one at fault. You've just told me something really awful, shocking, and I'm trying my best to absorb it. I mean, think how would you feel if I told you that I'd been a hooker for years."

"Not comparable," Barker said. "Because, if it were true, it would be in the nature of a confession, while I haven't confessed to anything—just the opposite. What can I say to you? I'm not a hooker. I mean, I'm not a molester . . . I've never forced myself on a girl in my life. You've got to believe me!" Barker now began to believe what he was saying. He was the victim, and they, his accusers, were agents of malevolence. Denial, ancient seducer of truth, entered Barker's soul and comforted him.

"You're an angel," Barker said. "I'm deeply sorry to put you through this." Was he? Was he really sorry or did part of him enjoy watching her suffer? "Are you really sick?" he asked. "Shouldn't you see the doctor?"

"I'm not an angel," Susan said coldly. She seemed to be trying hard not to cry, not to do anything scary, for her perfect brow wrinkled and unwrinkled with a visible pulse. "And I called Karen. She told me not to worry. It's apparently normal

to feel like all your insides are being squeezed together."
Susan got up. Her head was above the lighted area; he could
see her only from the neck down.

"Susan," he said and made a motion to take her around the
waist, a motion she sidestepped in a way that made him unable
to tell if she meant to or not.

"I'm going up to bed now, Jake."

"I think I'll stay down here a few minutes. Maybe I'll even
have a bite of that roast. Is it rare?"

"Rare enough for you," Susan said.

Barker was too upset to eat. He poured himself another
strong whiskey, wondering vaguely if he was turning into an
alcoholic. He stood looking at the wall of blackness beyond
the window, trying to calm himself by resurrecting the eager,
brilliant boy he once had been; the kid whose father spoke to
him only when he had something to criticize and whose mother
spent far too much time behind the closed bedroom door. But
this effort didn't end well, as the smell of his parents' misery
was almost as overpowering as that of his own.

Barker's ears picked up a murmur—sounds unseparated
into sense—from the floor above. Susan was on the phone
again. Next to chopping food into little pieces, Susan loved
talking on the telephone. Barker had suggested that she get
herself a phone implant. It was a good thing her mother lived
in Roslindale and not Shanghai. Deftly, Barker lifted the
receiver from its cradle and put it against his ear.

"Somebody's there! Somebody's listening. Is that you,
Jake?" It was Mona, a woman with wondrous hearing.

"No one's there, Mom," Susan said. "I can't hear anything."
Barker held his breath.

"I swear I heard that husband of yours pick up the phone.
Jacob?"

"Mother, please, there's no one there. I have to see you."

"I'll come over tomorrow. Will he be there?" Mona's voice
inflamed Barker's aural nerve.

"No," Susan said, "I'll come over there. I'm afraid things aren't going so well. . . ."

"It's not the baby, is it?"

"No, Mom, it's not the baby."

"Then it must be that elderly white man you married. He abuses you. I knew he'd get around to it sooner or later. My poor baby—"

"Mom! Please." Barker could sense Susan trying not to lose control. "First of all, Jake's younger than you are. And second, he doesn't abuse me and you know it. And third, I'm not a baby anymore. I'm about to be a mother—remember?" Mirthless laughter followed. Barker couldn't bear to listen any longer. He hung up the phone carefully, by depressing the little bar, then replacing the receiver in its bed attached to the wall. Where had his eavesdropping got him? What did he know now that he did not know five minutes earlier? Not much. Certainly nothing new about what his mother-in-law thought of him. Shit, he wouldn't beat anyone; it wasn't in the Barker bag of tricks. Soon after Susan had first introduced him to Mona, she had said, "That man has empty eyes"—another remark he had overheard. It was clear from the moment she passed him that plate of awful almond cookies and their eyes met that she distrusted him. In silence, Susan's mother and boyfriend had both announced the same thing: "Don't mess around with her."

Mona's antipathy was an old story. What did come as a surprise now was Susan's slight—but significant—shift away from him and toward her mother. His eyes moistened and he wiped at them with the back of his hand. Sighing deeply, he switched off the light over the table and had turned to go upstairs, when the front door opened and Billy came in, shutting it behind him so loudly the Miller's dog woke up next door and began to bark and howl.

"Hi there, Professor Barker," Billy said, grinning.

"What are you so happy about?" Barker said.

"I just watched the Celts beat the Lakers," he said. "Great game."

The kid was lying through his teeth, of course—where would he get his paws on a Celtics ticket? He was happy as a clam at high tide because he'd gotten a whiff of the scandal. Such things never stayed under wraps very long. Fromme's secretary knew, and now Billy—though how it had spread so fast was anyone's guess. Soon *Crimson* reporters would come sniffing around, trying to uncover more dirt. Should he make a run for it? Disappear?

"That's nice," Barker told Billy. "Gives one a nice warm glow to root for a winner, doesn't it?"

"Did I do something wrong?" Billy said.

"Of course not, William. I'm a tad tired, don't quite know what I'm saying. I think I'll turn in now. Please make sure the front and back doors are locked, will you."

"Sure thing, boss," Billy said. "Mrs. Bee in?"

"Yes, she is. She's upstairs. Would you like a word with her?" This mildly sarcastic thrust missed Billy completely, for he merely shook his head and said, "That's okay, I'll see her in the morning."

"Suit yourself," Barker said, forcing himself to swallow the impulse to congratulate Billy on his chutzpah.

Chapter Fourteen

W<small>HEN</small> Susan came back from visiting her mother, she turned her lovely eyes on him and said, "I'm still trying to get used to what's happening. I don't understand it; I believe you when you tell me you didn't do anything, but then why are they making you submit to a hearing, and why are you so *worried?* Won't you please go see someone, I mean someone you could really talk to—professionally."

"A shrink? Absolutely not!" Barker cried. "I wouldn't let one of those fakers wind my watch."

"Please, Jake, don't you see how much it means to me?"

"You think I did those things, don't you? Or why would you ask me to see a shrink?"

"Because you're not yourself."

"That's very interesting," Barker said. "And who am I then?"

"I don't know," Susan said and she began to cry; pearly tears rolled down over her cheeks dragging thin wet tails behind them. It was warm in the kitchen, but Barker's teeth began to chatter as his blood temperature dropped. He sat down, trembling. "Why are you against me, Susan? Why do you believe them?"

"I didn't say I believed them," Susan whispered.

"This is your mother's idea, isn't it, trying to make you believe that I've gone round the bend?"

"My mother has nothing to do with this. As a matter of fact, when I told her about it, she said I ought to leave you. I can't do that, Jake, I'm your wife. But I *am* asking you this—it isn't so much to ask."

If a new, cool fellow, capable of greased lying, had recently taken possession of Barker, then why not a new, strong egg inside the perfect shell?

"I'll think about it," Barker said, startled by the notion that he might have to get used to a different Susan. "But I don't like those people, I don't trust them." To which Susan replied quietly, "And I don't think you have that much choice now." It was poignant, really, her faith in therapy—as if it could truly alter a man's character.

Susan watched Barker carefully, as she might a child exposed to measles. Whenever he tried to talk to her about the touchy subject, she cut him off with a retort: "I don't need to hear," or "I thought we agreed this was a no-win topic," or just "Please shut up." Susan's refusal to talk about what he now had come to think of as "It" relieved him of having to tell fresh lies. Bennie, the one constant in his life, was in Hunan Province transmitting his wisdom to university students and would be doing so for two more months; Barker figured this unfortunate timing to be further evidence of a disastrous and decisive turn in his luck. He wrote Bennie a postcard with a picture of a half-naked female on it, trusting it to get Bennie in a spot of trouble.

Soon Barker began to feel the effects of a psychic backlog. Distracted, he lost his front-door key, forgot an appointment with his dentist, and had to look up his mother's telephone number. He began to slip away to places he would not be recognized, for rumors of his disgrace had started to circulate.

Some of these were worse than the truth. In these, he was an out-and-out rapist. And some were not so bad. In these, his advances had been merely verbal. Still, friends and colleagues looked at him as if his nose had turned into a carrot.

Susan's pregnancy was long past the point of no return—not that either of them had suggested abortion, although Barker wouldn't have been surprised had he discovered that Mona had tried some fast-stepping persuasion on her daughter. Oddly, Susan had also become conspicuously more concerned for his physical well-being, fussing over him: What would he like for dinner? Could she buy him a new pair of pajamas? He needed a haircut; were there any errands she could do for him? At the same time, she increased the emotional space between them by a distance too great for him to shout or even gesture across. She gave him a valentine with one hand, then grabbed it back with the other. A couple of times he had to repeat a question before she even looked at him, and in bed she edged toward her side, leaving a chilly no-man's-land between them.

"Where were you?" Susan said late one afternoon. "Emily called. She said you missed an appointment. Where were you?"

"Little mousie," Barker said, trying to touch her hair, "I was getting a cup of coffee. Emily's hysterical these days. I was gone for less than an hour."

Susan frowned. "She said you left at two-thirty."

"Just what are you suggesting?" Barker said, feeling his stomach tighten. "Do you think I'm messing around with another woman?"

"Jake!" Susan cried. "I didn't say that, I just wanted to know where you were. I think I have a right to ask."

"It's really none of your concern, little kitten," he said, "but I actually did go out for a cup of coffee and then I took a walk by the river. It was very bracing."

It was clear from Susan's expression that she didn't believe him. "Someone from the *Crimson* called again," she said. "I really think you're going to have to talk to them. I mean, your refusing to be interviewed makes them think you're guilty."

"The vultures are after me?" he said. "What did you tell them?"

"I asked them not to bother you at home," Susan said.

Barker guffawed. "That's like asking the pope to say Mass in a sweat suit. God, you're naive."

"That's very likely so," she said. Her eyes fixed themselves on the wall opposite.

"Don't be discouraged, almond blossom," Barker said. "We'll ride this thing out, you and me."

"I wish you'd stop calling me those silly names," Susan said in a rush.

"Whatever you say," Barker told her. "I thought you liked it."

"Well, I don't," she said. She opened the closet door and pulled her jade-green coat off a hanger.

"Where are you going?"

"To my mother's," Susan said. "She's asked my cousin Gina for dinner. She wants me to be there."

"Didn't she ask me?" Barker said, stung by the rejection.

"You hate my mother, Jake, you do everything you possibly can to avoid being in the same room with her. What's the deal here? You wouldn't go if she sent you an engraved invitation."

"Nancy," he blurted, overcome with dizziness, falling into a chair. His wife stared at him.

"You called me Nancy," she said. "Why?"

"I did not," he said. "Why would I call you Nancy when your name is Susan?"

"Oh Jake," she said, pity dripping from her tongue. "If you want me not to go, I won't. Would you rather I didn't go?" Switcheroo again. He couldn't keep up with her lightning-fast changes.

"Of course not," he said. "Go. Give my best to Mona." With a minimal farewell, Susan left. Barker shut his eyes, tired beyond words, beyond thinking about the weariness molten in his bones. The phone rang. Groaning, Barker pulled himself to his feet.

"Professor Barker," the person on the other end said, "I'm Brian Boyer, a reporter from the *Crimson*. I've just interviewed Dean Andrews. I wonder if I could come and talk to you."

"It's after hours, kid," Barker said. "Bugger off."

"So what's the matter with me?" By his fourth visit, Jacob Barker figured Charles Wernick, his therapist, might be ready to indulge in some diagnosis.

"Can't cut the mustard anymore?" Wernick said. It seemed that he put a question mark at the end of almost everything he said.

"Sure I can still cut it. I get dozens of requests for reprints whenever I publish an article. I've turned down at least eight invitations to speak in the last two months. My classes are filled to overflow beginning of every term. I'm a popular man, Wernick. My picture appears regularly in *Nature*, and the headwaiter at the Faculty Club knows my son's name. How else do you measure success?"

"And how many new ideas have you had in, say, the last decade? When was the last time you made a positive contribution to your field, something you're proud of? I'm not talking about leftover ideas—I'm talking innovation."

"May I tell you something, Wernick? I'm not at my best when someone takes an adversarial tone with me. I understood we were going to try to sort through my troubles together, you and me—same side."

The therapist stared at him and nodded slowly, as if to say that he was willing, for the moment at least, to quit badgering.

"Maybe the mustard's getting stronger, I'm not sure. New

ideas aren't exactly a dime a dozen," Barker went on. "I'd like to ask you something else. When was the last time *you* came up with a new idea?"

"But *I'm* not in the new-idea game," Wernick said steadily.

"You are. I'm only going by what you've been telling me for the past month. You're afraid you're running dry?"

"But I shouldn't really expect fresh ideas at my age. Who does?"

"I'm not going to throw Bach and Freud in your face. Still, I think it's safe to say that your age has as little to do with it as the sort of food you eat."

"Well then, what does? You tell me. That's why I'm here. That's what I'm paying you for."

"But you just articulated the dynamic here," Wernick said. "We're in this thing as a team."

Barker groaned.

"It's painful, isn't it? No one said this was easy."

"As my son Guy says, 'It doesn't tickle.' " Barker felt off balance, as if Wernick had removed Barker's clothes and locked them in a closet somewhere deep inside the house. "I work hard," Barker said, half to himself. "My best work is recognized for what it is. That is, I think the general appraisal of it is realistic, not inflated. I think I'm getting closer to defining the essential differences between male and female. Getting closer all the time." While he talked, Barker grew disoriented. The gauzy curtains over the casement windows billowed and fell back like sails in a light breeze. As if he were waking up suddenly in the middle of the night in a strange room, Barker wasn't sure, for a second or two, just where he was.

"No new pathways cut through uncharted jungles, eh? And you mind this. What is it that bothers you so much if, as you say, you've already established your reputation? Why are you so unhappy with a slight falling-off?"

"You've got to be kidding," Barker said. "I don't see how

you can even ask that question. It's so obvious I don't know how to answer you."

"Obvious to you, maybe," Wernick said, "but not to me. Obviously, or I wouldn't have asked you. My time is valuable too. . . ."

Barker could have said he was sorry but did not. He frowned so hard his forehead hurt.

"Every time I ask you a direct question you deflect it," Wernick said. "Are you aware of this? If you're going to continue coming to see me, I'm going to have to insist we keep to the point."

Wernick didn't mince words—whatever that meant. They came out the way they were designed to be heard. Barker admired this, even as they made him writhe. If it worked, if this so-called therapy was successful, he might be able to go on with his life and work unhampered by the woes that daily and nightly afflicted him: insomnia, diarrhea, bouts of anxiety so violent he felt as if he were being hit with volts of electrical current, agitation so strong he could sometimes hear it as a buzzing in his ears. Also, his concentration was shot; often it was a struggle to keep at a task for more than ten minutes. Lord, in the old days his concentration was driven by a Mercedes engine.

"I'll do my best," Barker said, avoiding the therapist's deep brown eyes.

"Fine. Now, can we talk about girls? Can we talk about what these conquests mean to you?"

"I'm not sure what you mean by that."

"Then I'll rephrase the question," Wernick said obligingly. "I'd like you to think about why it is you keep sleeping with your students, considering the enormous risks it entails."

"You make it sound as if I'm deliberately swimming out past my head knowing there are sharks in the water."

"Is that what you believe?"

"I don't honestly know," Barker said. "But it doesn't ring true, somehow. I'm generally a careful, not to say cautious, type. I carry a boxful of change when I use the turnpike. I don't get into accidents, I don't cut or burn myself. . . ."

"Come off it."

"Bottom line? If you really want to know, the risks, Wernick, have never been that great. As a matter of fact, until this year, when Anita Andrews started sticking her nose in other people's business—I told you about her last week—there was virtually *no* risk. Nobody cared so long as you didn't go absolutely public. And I'm nothing if not discreet."

"It's been a long time since I was in school, of course, but I find what you're telling me somewhat hard to swallow." Wernick looked at him like Barker's father used to.

"As far as I can tell," Barker said, trying to ignore Wernick's disapproval, "teachers have always been involved with their students—Héloïse and Abelard, Paolo and Francesca. It's never been much of a problem before now. It's these ladies getting their dander up."

"Stop right there, Professor," Wernick said. "If that were true, how is it that you've been telling me that immediately after bedding one of these young women you suffer from a bout of guilt? I'm not inventing this, it's something you've reported yourself."

"Guilt? You mean that little twinge? I don't call that guilt. It disappears even faster than the proverbial moment of postcoital sadness. I don't remember telling you I feel guilty. How can I feel guilty when there are two of us? I'm not a rapist, Wernick, I can assure you that I've never in my whole life forced myself on a girl."

"Then why are you here?"

Barker sighed. Wernick was getting to be a pain in the ass—he was worse than Susan. Small wonder the shrink trades were in such bad odor—these people were about as helpful as a blind trailguide. "I came here because I promised my wife I would. Along the way I thought you might help me get rid of some physical glitches."

"Oh yes, now I remember." Dr. Wernick recrossed his

knees and pulled out a pipe whose bowl he began to stuff with smashed tobacco leaves that he removed from a yellow plastic wallet. He took out a box of wooden matches, struck one of them against the side of the box, and held it over the bowl while sucking noisily on the stem. Unblinking, he looked over these works at Barker. A phone rang in a muffled sort of way on the other side of the office door. It rang four times and then stopped; Barker figured a machine had answered. Wernick's office was in his home. There were a couple of French racing bikes chained to the garage and a rusted basketball hoop, and the place smelled like a residence in spite of the fact that the office was encapsulated, allowing entry to the clientele only through a doorway cut arbitrarily into an outside wall. Odors of roasting animal flesh and, once, sweet-smelling bread seeped through the cracks. The smells made Barker's mouth water— lucky Wernick, he was married to a woman who liked to cook.

"Yes, I remember. You have trouble sleeping through the night. You have anxiety attacks. Your digestion leaves something to be desired. Your internist can't find anything wrong with you. So you come to me to see whether the symptoms can be cleared up by more cerebral means. Why not? But I need your cooperation, Professor Barker. That's my bottom line."

Round and round they went; Barker felt more circular, less linear all the time.

"I came here because I promised Susan," he said for the nth time. "I'm a man of my word, Wernick. Besides, what have I got to lose? The worst that could happen is that nothing changes. I've lived with this baggage so long, there's no reason why I shouldn't go on as before. I did, however, have hopes: I think you and I are on the same wavelength."

"What makes you say that?" The therapist's pipe had gone out and he busied himself trying to coax a new spark to life.

"Well, for one thing, you don't patronize me. And for another, you don't resort to psychobabble."

"You should hear me sometimes," Wernick confided, "especially when I'm around my colleagues. It's wall-to-wall psychobabble. God, how they love their special little language—their carings and sharings, their borderlines, ambulatories, and object relations, their metaprocesses and acting-outs. It's an enormous relief to get away from it."

Barker felt as if he were being seduced by this man, who knew exactly what Barker needed to hear. He began to like Wernick again and to drop his disapproval.

But was this man, whom he newly liked, doing him any good? And was it possible for *any*one to alter the mold? Now leathery with age, Barker knew something that Charles Wernick could not know about his patient: the man had grown more cunning with every passing day. While it was true his flashes of insight came less often, his appetites and hungers had increased and he was not about to let any shrink, however decent and likable, diminish them. He hated being pushed; he would resist all attempts to move him so much as an inch. Barker was an old-fashioned libertarian who thrived on the risk, on the constant stress attendant upon a life of danger. He sighed. It was a pity, for he and Wernick could, under different circumstances, have been friends. He liked Wernick's clothes; he wore chinos and an old tweed jacket with leather patches over the elbows. He wore running shoes. "I'd like to change, but I doubt that at this late date I can. That's the truth."

Wernick blinked. Barker thought he might be about to shed tears. "Never too late," he said softly. "The other day I had a woman of sixty-five tell me she had just had an orgasm for the first time in her life, thanks to our work."

"Not really," Barker said, impressed.

"Yes, and not long ago a man in his fifties started therapy with me, and for the first time in his life he can get on an airplane without having to pay with a week-long bout of diarrhea. Sounds like an advertisement for myself, doesn't it? I don't mean it to, I merely want to demonstrate that people who really want to change can do so. Actually, they could do it all without me if they trusted themselves and had enough confidence in the method—it's all just self-hypnosis really."

The smoke coming off Wernick's pipe was bluish and sweet-smelling. He looked like the detective in a film noir.

"I wish I could do it," Barker admitted. "But you see how it goes. Every time I get near the dread thing it starts breathing fire and I have to step back."

"What would happen if you didn't?"

"I'd get horribly burned," Barker said. "Maybe beyond recognition, as they say."

"You truly believe that?"

Barker nodded.

"What's the worst thing that could happen to you if you got too close?"

"I just told you. I'd get burned."

"Stop talking in metaphor," Wernick said. "It sounds good but it's useless right now. I want you to drop the metaphor and contemplate the thing it stands for."

"The thing it stands for," Barker repeated. "The thing it stands for." He said it again, hoping it would reveal itself, but whatever it was retreated until it was just a red dot in the vast distance, a glowing point of danger. "I can't really say *what* it is. . . ."

"If you touched it you would die? Is it like the AIDS virus or more like a poison dart? Is it a tongue of flame or the bite of a rattlesnake? Think!" Wernick seemed to be growing larger.

"It can kill me," Barker said. "I don't want to come near it." Barker tightened his throat against the wash of tears that threatened to overwhelm him. The two men sat looking at each other, each waiting for the other to speak. Finally, Barker said, "Do you mind if we open a window?"

"Why not?" Wernick said. "I don't seem to feel the heat the way most people do. Sorry." He got up and cranked open one of the windows. Fresh, cool air swept into the room.

"I'm willing to let that thing, whatever it is, rest undisturbed for a while if you'll promise to try to get a bit closer to it each day. In the meantime, I'd like to get back to the other problem."

"And that is?"

"You really do need to have everything spelled out, don't you? Okay, then—you and your female students."

"That's not a problem, Wernick, that's a perk." He chuckled so that Wernick would realize he was joking, but it didn't work the way he hoped: Wernick was wearing a mucho serious expression.

"Can we talk about sex without making jokes?"

"I love talking about sex," Barker said. "It's my favorite subject. But you know something odd, every time I get in here I seem to get tongue-tied. Maybe if you asked me some questions—pressed the right buttons—it might be easier for me."

"A reasonable request," Wernick said. "Let's begin with what happens when you walk into a classroom. What do you see?"

"Pussy. Acres of pussy sitting there like daisies in a garden. The boys, on the other hand, are weeds."

"Are they all the same, these daisies?"

Barker shook his head.

"Some of them want to be picked, others couldn't care less. The remainder—well, they've got thorns. I know, daisies don't *have* thorns."

"*No* man likes to risk being rejected."

"You can say that again," Barker said. "It makes you feel like shit. Mind you, it doesn't happen to me very often."

"You can tell the good daisies from the bad ones? That's quite a talent."

"You make it sound as if it happens all at once, in an instant. Sometimes it takes weeks or even months, depending on the girl and how flexible or uptight she is."

"And what does it feel like when you have finally bedded her, this daisy?"

"It's the supreme moment. It's what makes life bearable. All the other crap, the stuff you have to swallow all day long . . ." He tried to go on but found he had begun to sob; his eyes closed over tears that burst through and fell down his cheeks.

212

He coughed, trying to recover. His tears surprised him; they had wrecked his careful balance.

Wernick assumed a kindly expression and said nothing. Barker took out his handkerchief and blew his nose into it; there was lots of stuff in his nose. He wiped his eyes.

"Sorry," he said. "Didn't mean to do that."

"Why did you do that?"

"Don't know."

"Are you scared?"

"I don't know," Barker said. He found he was perspiring heavily.

" 'I don't know' is forbidden here. Whenever someone tells me he doesn't know, I'm pretty sure he does know—he just doesn't want to have to think about it."

"Isn't the hour up?"

"You're hoping it is?"

"My knees lock too easily," Barker said, making an enormous effort to regain his footing. "Always have. Even when I was a kid. Every time my father asked me to do something, there was a battle. Sometimes it raged inside me, sometimes I'd get a licking for talking back—my father called it sassing him. Funny, even when it was something I didn't mind doing, like going down to the corner store for a quart of milk, I still put up a fight."

"You wanted to make your own plans?"

"Yes, that's it." Barker sensed that Wernick was retreating, that Barker had outmaneuvered him. He wanted to tell the therapist not to give in so easily. Barker knew this wasn't going to work.

Chapter Fifteen

"It's Dean Fromme calling," Emily said, coming into Barker's office. Her coming in like that, instead of telling him over the phone, alerted Barker to the possibility that she knew something noteworthy was afoot. "He said not to bother you, but would you be available to meet with him in his office at eleven-thirty?"

"Today?" Barker said. His heart went from first gear directly into fifth, nearly choking him.

"Yes, I think so."

"Emily, my dear, is it today or do you merely *think* it is?"

Emily's eyes grew moist. Her chin quivered. Barker looked away, ashamed to be putting her through this but unable to stop.

"It's today," she said, tight-lipped. "Is there anything else?"

"No thanks." He wanted to take Emily's hand, squeeze it gently, and tell her he was sorry—but not enough to actually do it. In order to get her out of the room—surely she was waiting for an apology, she had that doggy look on her face—

he lifted the receiver on his phone and began to punch numbers. She retreated. "Why do I do things like that?" he said aloud.

Barker badly wanted a drink but there wasn't enough time to go to the 19th Hole before his next class. He could picture the regulars, lounging against the bar, having arrived along with the bartender at 10:00 A.M. and drinking their way slowly across the next seven or eight hours. Poor bastards. Barker figured it was time to update his will, a document he hadn't touched in more than ten years. His associative processes were in splendid working order: from emergency meeting to death in one fluid leap.

It was quiet in the building; everyone was busily grinding his brains, turning the gears of thought and imagination— reading, taking notes, or just sitting and looking out the window. One or two of them were no doubt snoozing.

Barker's phone rang. Emily must have put this one straight through. "Jake, this is Nancy."

"I recognize your voice," he said, steeling himself for a skirmish.

"Guy's in the hospital," Nancy said. "He was in an accident."

"What do you mean?"

"Jake, please. He was nearly killed, they had to pry him out of the car."

"Is he all right?"

"I can't believe you, Jake. What do you mean, 'Is he all right?' No, he's not all right. And look, I can't talk to you now, I've got to get over to the hospital. If you feel like coming, he's at Newton-Wellesley. That's where it happened."

"Where?" he said.

"I don't know, near there. What difference does it make?"

"I'll be there right away," Barker said. "Nancy?"

"What is it? Make it snappy."

"Nothing," he said. "I'll be there in half an hour." By the

time Barker had reached the end of this sentence, Nancy had already hung up.

When he stood, Barker found he was shivering as if he'd just spent the night in a walk-in freezer. His teeth were clacking together so violently it was hard to speak. "Emily," he called as he sped past her desk, "My son's been in a bad accident. I've got to get to the hospital. Call Dean Fromme for me, will you, and tell him I won't be able to make that meeting."

"Is he all right?" his secretary asked. Guy's accident had apparently canceled the apology he owed her.

"I don't know," he said. "Don't know anything. I'll let you know. And Emily . . . thanks."

"Oh, Professor Barker, I'm so sorry," she said. "I'm sure everything will be all right. He's a strong boy."

Barker took a cab to the hospital. He spent this twenty minutes or so telling himself to be prepared for the worst—it didn't help. Once inside the hospital, he was instructed by the lady at the information desk to go to the fourth floor, intensive-care unit. As he emerged from the elevator Nancy sprang at him. She looked both distraught and angry. "You got here," she said.

"I took a taxi," he said.

"Guy's in there," Nancy said, pointing to a room beyond two swinging doors that met in the middle. "He's only allowed one visitor at a time." Her voice sounded odd and thin, as if someone were talking for her from another location.

"Before I go in just tell me how he is. I mean, how badly he's hurt."

"He's all bunged up," Nancy said, sniffing back tears. Nancy must have come straight from work—she was wearing a dress-for-success suit, cut severely and, he thought, unflatteringly; her hips bulged beneath the slim skirt. Under the jacket was an off-white blouse with a floppy bow at her throat. Her hair was a mess. "Why don't you sit down?" he said,

216

leading her over to a bank of molded plastic bus-terminal chairs. Nancy pulled out a tissue and held it against her mouth. "You haven't told me what happened or how bad he is."

"Go in," she said, sitting down. "Stop stalling." She blew her nose, then balled the tissue and hid it inside her fist.

"Why do you say things like that?" Barker asked. "I just need to know what to expect. Christ, Nancy, I don't even know if he's conscious or not."

"What difference does it make?" she said, glaring. "Why are you thinking about yourself instead of Guy? I can't believe you, Jake." A nurse behind the nurses' station looked at them and frowned as Nancy's voice picked up volume. "He's in and out," she said more softly. "He's doped to the ears. I don't think he really knows what hit him."

"What *did* hit him?"

"An ice-cream truck. Or rather, he hit the truck. I don't really know the details, Jake. Why are you standing here? If you're too scared to go in and see your son, just say so and I'll go back. One of us should be with him."

Nancy's live-in, odd-job boyfriend, Tony Callisi, walked over to them carrying two paper cups of coffee. He was wearing jeans and a dull green flannel shirt. His running shoes looked as if they had been dipped in mud. He handed one of the cups to Nancy and said to Barker, "Well, I see you finally got here."

"I came right away," Barker said levelly. "And now I'm going in to see my son." He was stingingly aware that Tony had stuck his right hand in his pocket rather than exchange a handshake with him.

It could have been worse, Barker decided, but not by much. Guy's head was wrapped in gauze, like a mummy's. His nose and eyes were surrounded by puffy flesh, much of it purple. His arms were beneath the covers, as was his right leg. The left one was suspended on a contraption of string and chain

217

attached to a track on the ceiling. Barker thought Guy was snoring, but as he bent over he was startled; the snoring sounds were in fact groans, each one emerging with a suspiration. It was a sickening sound. Barker sat down.

There were three other men in the room with Guy, being tended to by two nurses, who kept going from one bed to another, checking vital signs, taking pulses, looking at monitors, fiddling with intravenous bags. The other men were much older than Guy.

One of the nurses came over to where Barker sat stiffly in the chair, trying to compose himself.

"Is he unconscious?"

"Just sleeping," she said. "He's had a mild concussion. We're keeping a close eye on him, not letting him sleep too long. You must be Mr. Barker." As he nodded, Barker noticed a tube running out from under Guy's covers and into a rectangular plastic bag. "We had to give him a saddle block to set the leg," the nurse explained. "It shut down the nerves that control his bladder; it's just temporary. Nothing to worry about. We're going to remove the catheter tomorrow."

"Is there anything else?" Barker said, feeling ill himself.

"You'll have to ask his doctor that," she said crisply. "He should be here soon. Why don't you try talking to your son? It's not good for him to sleep too long."

If it wasn't good for him, why wasn't she waking him up? The boy's measured groaning was far worse than the near-silence of a deep sleep would have been. "He's in pain. . . ."

"I wouldn't be surprised," she said.

She was a woman in her late thirties—a dangerous age for women, as they could go either way, keeping up the hard work involved in looking good or allowing the symptoms of age to take over. Her uniform reminded him of a short-order cook's, with an apronlike thing across her large breasts. She stood close enough to Barker for him to smell her—not a perfume scent, but not unpleasant either, rather like a wintergreen

Lifesaver. He could have touched her, wrapping his arms around her waist and laying his poor frightened head against one hip, but she pivoted away on thick rubber soles and was off to see why a boxlike machine on the other side of the room had suddenly begun to beep insistently.

Barker looked at his son again. Apart from the groans, his breathing seemed normal enough. "Guy," he said in great softness, half hoping that Guy would not wake up and thus put off that moment when they would be obliged to talk together. But the sound of his father's voice apparently plucked the right string, for Guy opened his eyes. "How're you doing, Dad?" He sounded as if he had a mouthful of dentist cotton.

"Hey, pal, how're you doing yourself?"

"Busticated. Didn't do it right."

"What are you talking about?"

"What did I say?" Guy asked, frowning.

"You said you didn't do it right. Do what right?"

"Shut up, Dad. Can't you let me sleep?" And Guy closed his eyes. Then he let out a sound that was the sort of response one would make to a hard punch in the ribs. Barker stood up. "Nurse," he called, "there's something wrong with my son. Will you take a look please?" The nurse responded by coming over and picking up Guy's wrist, which she then held briefly between thumb and forefinger. She removed the stethoscope from where it lay across the back of her neck and listened to Guy's heartbeats. "No change in his vital signs," she reported. "You don't look too good yourself, Mr. Barker. Maybe you should step outside and get a breath of fresh air. You can open the windows in the solarium."

"Are you sure?" he said. He was aware that none of his usual weapons—not guile, persuasion, ambiguity, rank, or even charm—were the least bit useful in this place and under these circumstances. He was no less helpless than the old man across the room with the dead-white face bristling with dead-white hairs and attached to the beeping machine.

219

"Your son's going to be fine," she said. "It's going to take a while is all."

"Do you know, was there anyone else in the car with him?"

"I really couldn't say, Mr. Barker." Her face indicated that the information booth was shutting down for the day; he would have to apply elsewhere.

"Well, I think I'll take your advice," Barker said. The oval of Guy's face was the only part of him not hidden, not draped, bandaged, wrapped, or sheeted. Just that bruised oval. His nose looked broken. Barker sighed as he palmed his way out of the room and went over to where Nancy and Tony were sitting together. He had his hand on her thigh and an arm across her shoulder.

"Well?" Nancy said, looking up at Barker.

"Well what?"

"What do you think?"

"What am I supposed to think? He's in bad shape. The nurse says he's going to be okay. But what does she know?"

"They may have to remove his spleen," Nancy said, beginning to cry.

"I want to talk to his doctor," Barker said. "By the way, who *is* his doctor?"

"I wouldn't expect you to know," Nancy said, making it clear that just because their son was in desperate shape, it didn't mean that she was going to stop jabbing at her ex whenever she found an opportunity.

"Please, Nancy," Barker said. He was exhausted. Sweat had pasted his shirt against his back. For some reason his shoes pinched. He sat down next to Tony, who looked at him sourly. Meanwhile, hospital activities were taking place around them, trays were being trundled down the corridor, nurses held conferences with doctors, visitors approached the nurses' station to ask questions, a black man swung a mop back and forth across the floor in perfect wet arcs.

"What did Guy mean about not doing it right?" Barker said. "What was he talking about?"

"He spoke to you?" Nancy said.

"Briefly," Barker told her. "But I don't like what he said— he said he didn't do it right."

"He's doped to the ears," Nancy said. She spoke across Tony's body as if he weren't there. "Guy doesn't know what he's saying."

"I think he knows," Barker said quietly.

"What's that supposed to mean?" Nancy said.

"It means I think he may have been trying to kill himself."

"Jesus, man, what's wrong with you? What are you trying to do to Nancy? Where do you get off saying something like that without knowing shit about what happened?" Tony stood up as he said this. He was a menace. How could she hook up with someone like this—a wild man?

Barker regretted having stepped into this muck. He knew Nancy well enough to realize that not in a million years and even with overwhelming evidence would she admit that her son might try to end his own life.

"Calm yourself, friend," Barker said to Tony, who was, appallingly, making a fist out of his right hand.

"Don't call me friend," Tony snarled. "We're not friends, not so far as I know."

"Stop it, both of you," Nancy said. "Listen to you. I can't believe how you're acting. You'd think one of you at least would have the sense to behave like an adult. I suppose it's too much to ask the two of you. Animals."

Tony said, "He's a jerk. Your ex is a fucking jerk. Where does he get off saying Guy tried to kill himself? What does he fucking know about Guy? Sees him once, maybe twice a year and all of a sudden he's this fucking psychiatrist. Tell him, Nance."

"Just what would you like her to tell me?" Barker said.

"To keep your trap shut about things you don't know beans about. Guy wouldn't do what you said. Guy's got his head screwed on tighter than you do."

"You really dislike me, don't you?" Barker said.

221

This question drew off some of Tony's fury. Nancy said, "You would both be doing me a big favor if you wouldn't fight anymore—at least while Guy's in there. I don't think I can stand anymore of this." And Barker knew she meant it as she opened her mouth very wide, pulling back her lips. One more second and she would scream.

"I need some fresh air," Barker told Nancy and Tony. "I'm going for a walk. I'll be back in fifteen minutes." And he turned and left, wondering where to find booze in a town reputed to be dry.

Chapter Sixteen

Two days later Guy was wheeled out of the intensive care unit and into a semiprivate room. The man in the next bed was Bud, a pinkish person in his fifties who had a serious heart problem—they weren't sure yet whether he needed bypass surgery. Bud, who was attached by wire to a monitor that graphed his heart's motion twenty-four hours a day, loved to talk about his life (until sidetracked by his illness) as the chauffeur of a well-known local politician. When Barker came to see his son, between meetings with his lawyer and classroom stints, he found that the visits represented islands of anxiety of a much lower order than the other matter, his upcoming hearing. In comparison, it was positively relaxing to sit by Guy's bedside and listen to Bud's stories.

Pleased to have his audience augmented by one, Bud said, "Did I tell you about the time the boss didn't like that one of his so-called friends welched on a bet, so he had this garbage truck come and park in front of the guy's restaurant in the North End from 8:00 A.M. till midnight for three days until he paid up—plus a couple of thousand interest. This guy's in the boss's back pocket for life."

"A neat trick," Barker said, nodding and eyeing his son, who appeared either to have heard this story before or else was untouched by its drama.

"Hey, that's funny," Bud said. "Your name's Guy. Guy means man, right?"

"I know," Guy said numbly. One time, when Bud was off somewhere being tested, Guy told Barker that Bud was homophobic and made cracks about "faggots." Barker said he hadn't detected this trait in Bud, whereupon Guy got angry and accused Barker of insensitivity. The boy didn't seem to be recovering his old zip, although the leg, they said, was knitting nicely and his spleen remained where God had installed it. He was doing his schoolwork over the phone; the Preiss School had even dispatched a young teacher to engage in bedside tutoring. As for the accident itself, whenever Barker tried to talk about it, he was met with a frown of refusal. "I don't want to talk about it," Guy said. "I won't talk about it."

Barker had canceled a couple of classes using Guy's accident as an explanation, but his son was merely an excuse. The real reason was that he was too distracted by the hearing to think coherently.

About to become a father for the second time, Barker wondered why he felt as if he had been lowered into a deep pit whose sides were slick with mud, while an unseen wag stood at the top urging him to climb on out—as if it was his fault and he had chosen to live below sea level.

"We forge our own destinies, do we not?" Barker said to Susan one morning at breakfast.

Susan squinted at him over her plate of wheat toast and honey. "Is that what you really believe?"

"That's what I've been led to believe," he said. Susan's face was fuller these days. Her doctor had said that her body was holding on to more water than was strictly good for her. This

seemed to cause Susan much worry. Barker felt she was showing symptoms of hypochondria; most women got bloated during pregnancy and it didn't kill them. He liked her old face
better than this puffy version.

Barker sighed. "You're feeling scary about things, aren't
you?"

"I'm holding on," Susan said. But the truth was in her face,
which said she was trapped with a man who demeaned her.
Thinking she had married a noble lion, she was discovering
that her mate was a one-eared alley cat with dust in his hair
and a crimp in his tail.

"Do you want out?" Barker said. "Is this too terrible for you?"

Eyes brimming, Susan looked down and shook her head
slowly back and forth. A tear glistened on her plump cheek.
"No, Jake. I married you and I'm having your baby. I still love
you even though you've done things I don't begin to understand—"

"Then you don't believe me!" Barker found he was shouting. "You would rather believe unhappy females you don't
even know than your own husband!"

"No, I don't believe them, I believe you," she said, screwing her delicate features. "But you've changed. You're so hard,
you didn't used to be hard. You said you wanted to make me
happy, but you seem to want to make me miserable. What have
I done? I don't think I've done anything, but you act like I'm
your worst enemy. . . ."

"You're wrong," Barker said, distressed. He didn't know
what he would do if she started crying. Tears made him think
of blood; they terrified him. And of course he knew what she
was talking about—he *had* changed. But what man did *not*
change, once inside a marriage with the door firmly shut and
padlocked behind him? If it came to that, Susan had changed,
too. She probably thought she was being spunky by question-
ing him all the time; to Barker, it was disloyalty.

"Jake, please!" She started to weep, holding her face in her hands as if afraid it would fall off. "I didn't say I didn't believe you."

"Oh yes you did." His anger flared. He picked up his plate and let fly with it. It struck the wall and seemed to hang there for a second. Then it dropped, crashing to bits on the floor and sending splinters of glass and toast crumbs over the vinyl flooring.

"You *are* out of your mind," Susan said in a voice that startled Barker. "What the hell do you think you're doing?"

"I'm doing what any man in his right mind would do when his wife says she doesn't believe him. I'm goddamn angry. I'm furious!" The skin on his face pounded and streams of adrenaline spurted up his legs. "And I'm leaving before I throw anything else."

Billy padded down the back stairs, barefoot. "Everything okay down here?" he said. His face was creased with pink stripes from the sheet or the sleeve of his pajamas. He looked like a child but Barker knew better—there was adult mischief here. Barker was certain that Billy didn't like him.

Without saying anything, Susan turned her face away. It was clear she didn't want Billy to see she had been crying. Barker said, "I was just playing Frisbee with my breakfast plate, Bill. Care to join me?"

"No thanks," Billy said, turning to go back up to his converted attic room. Wise kid, he needed a role in this hairy scene like he needed a C in economics.

"Billy's a snoop," Barker said. "He wants to get something on me."

Susan said words Barker could not hear. "Speak up, Sue, I cain't hear ya."

"I said, I think you're going crazy. Why are you throwing things? Why are you acting like you think Billy's a spy or something? What's *wrong* with you?"

Barker's chest tightened; he wondered if he were having a heart attack. Susan sat with her back arched over and her face

226

hidden. What had he done to her? He'd taken this fragile blossom and pulverized it. Why had he chosen to wage war against this butterfly?

"Susan?" He was encouraged by the flush of sympathy that had unexpectedly replaced his anger. His chest eased.

"Get out," she said. "Can't you see what you're doing to me?"

"Anyone can lose his temper. . . ."

"Please," she said. "Can't you see I don't want you here?"

"You're going to call your mother."

"Probably," Susan said. She stood up. Her belly looked enormous. "And if you won't get out, I will. I can't stand to be in the same room with you." She went through the butler's pantry and out into the front hall. No doubt she was heading for the stairs and the telephone on her bedside table. Barker plucked his jacket off the coat tree by the back door and quit the house, uncertain whether the pain in his stomach was real or imaginary.

He was ambushed as he came around the side of his house.

"Professor Barker?"

"What do you want?" he asked the boy who stood in front of him, more or less blocking his way, holding a spiral notebook.

"I'm Brian Boyer, sir, from the *Crimson*? I'd like to talk to you—about the hearing tomorrow."

"I have nothing to say to you today or any other day," Barker said as he set the pace at a brisk clip. "Not about the economy, nuclear disarmament, American hostages, or the Celtics."

"How about your hearing?"

"My hearing's fine. Nothing wrong with it. Brian, did you say?"

"That's right, sir—Brian Boyer. I'm sorry if I confused you. I meant Dean Andrews' hearing. The one about sexual harassment. You know . . ."

"I have nothing to say about that either." Barker's brave front only seemed to fuel Brian's engine. His face shone with the thrill of pursuit. Barker increased his pace along the

227

sidewalk of the neat broadway flanked by one-family houses constructed around the time of the century's last turn and constantly tended to, looked after, painted and repainted. The kid kept right up with Barker, although his legs were at least two inches shorter.

"Well, I was hoping you'd be able to tell me something about the proceedings. We're going to write it up and we figured you wouldn't want us to get it wrong. I mean, we want to hear your side of it, Professor Barker."

The smarmy youth had learned his trade well. Barker seethed. "How on earth can you write about something you have almost no access to?" he asked. "This hearing's been closed to all but the three or four people directly involved." Barker had not intended to say even this much; it just slipped past his censor.

"There are the witnesses," Brian said.

"Witnesses are just as likely as anyone to lie," Barker said, "maybe more so. I suggest that you discount ninety-five percent of what they tell you. No, ninety-nine percent." Barker meant this as a threat but was not sure it was being received as such. Brian had the cocky look of a winner. "You want to be damn sure, young man," Barker continued, "that you don't print anything libelous. You ought to know I have a hotshot State Street lawyer working for me."

"If you don't mind my saying so, sir, isn't that our worry?"

Barker knew he shouldn't get into a pissing contest with this kid, but how to escape? Barker knit his brow and walked even faster. The boy hopped and skipped at his side to keep up with him. "Are you trying to run away?" Brian said. "I just have a couple more questions." They were now three blocks from Barker's house.

"No more questions and no more answers," Barker said. "I'm late for an appointment."

"In that case, hopefully you won't object if I go back and talk to your wife?"

228

"Mrs. Barker? Now, why would you want to talk to her?"

"You've got to be kidding," Brian said.

"Me, kidding? That's not my style. At least not when I'm dealing with smart-ass reporters from the *Crimson*." Barker stopped walking. They were nearing Harvard Square. Across the street a man wearing green trousers, a blue and white checked shirt, and a baseball cap was busy applying a noisy electric clipper to a box hedge, slicing away at unsightly shoots. Barker had to get rid of this pain in the neck. "Please leave my wife out of this."

But the boy was undeterred, having correctly read the situation as no longer under Barker's control; the situation—whatever that turned out to be—was up for grabs. "I think I'll just go on back to your place and see if Mrs. Barker will speak to me. You see, I'd sort of like to get her opinion of what's going on."

"Let me try to straighten you out, son. Mrs. Barker has no opinions."

At this, Brian Boyer's eyes widened and his mouth dropped open. Had Barker been able to take it back he would have done almost anything; it was the sort of fatuous remark that would surely be passed from one undergraduate to the next until it achieved perpetual celebrity.

Barker nearly wept. How could he let himself do these things? Was this what they meant when they supplied diagnostic concepts like self-destructive? accident prone? suicidal? Ten, fifteen years back, he would have had Brian on his knees, blubbering, pleading for release. One ought, by rights, to get better at intimidation, not worse; it was a skill that should improve with age.

Brian seemed to have got what he was after, for he said cheerily, "Well, thanks for your time, sir. I appreciate your talking to me." He smiled like a dead fish.

"Don't mention it," Barker said.

Brian turned and headed back up the street. Would Susan

let him in through the front door? That depended, Barker realized, on just how angry and hurt she was.

When he reached his office, Barker found a pink While You Were Out slip with a message on it to call Frederick Cross, his lawyer, a man he had gone to college with and had consulted over the years.

He was about to pick up the receiver to make the call when a pretty student thrust herself into his doorway and said, "Professor Barker? If you have a second I'd like to speak with you."

"From the *Crimson*," he said. "You're wasting your time. I just got through talking to one of your cohorts."

"I'm not from the *Crimson*," the girl said. "I'm taking your course, Psych 204B. I need your permission and your signature to drop the course."

"Drop it? What's the matter with it? It's too late anyway."

"I've decided to change my major," she said.

"Really?" Barker said, his blood surging. "From what to what? By the way, what's your name? And for pete's sake, don't hang around like that. Come in, come in."

"Penny Nichols," she said, affixed to where she stood. "I'm switching from Psychology to Government. And I have a class in ten minutes." She held a piece of paper out and said, "All you have to do is sign this."

Penny had thick yellow hair, mostly straight, but at the hairline frizzy, like pubic hair. Her breasts were visible beneath a gauzy white blouse. Barker's tongue prickled and his heart bounced. It was a curse, this inability to simply *be* with a woman without his entire body reverberating. He could control it about as efficiently as he could hunger and thirst.

Barker took the piece of paper, sat down at his desk, and, sighing, signed his name, giving Penny permission to abandon him.

Penny picked up the piece of paper and turned without

saying thank you, or anything else for that matter. Sadly, he watched her Playboy legs carry her away from him and toward a friend waiting beyond Emily's desk. Penny said something and her friend began to laugh. Their moment of hilarity had to do with him; Barker was sure of this. They were mocking him. The whole world mocked him.

Although he knew he should call his lawyer, he stalled, staring unhappily at the heap of papers he had allowed to accumulate on his desk. Here were unanswered letters and a memo requesting his presence at a meeting called to study the question of whether graduate students should be permitted to use faculty rest rooms. Here, too, was a letter from a former student—a male for a change—asking Barker for a letter of recommendation to Leeds University. Barker decided that anyone who wanted to spend three years in Leeds was too stupid to deserve such a letter. Nastiness leaked like serum from his brain. Did this make him feel any less put-upon? Absolutely not; it only delivered more bile to his mouth.

Emily came to the door. "I meant to ask you before, Professor Barker—how is Guy doing?"

"On the mend, Emily, on the mend. Thank you for asking." She retreated. Barker looked at the ceiling, where a large crack meandered from one corner to the other. He'd have Emily get Facilities Maintenance on it. They were remarkably good about fixing things as soon as they needed repair.

Barker heard his lawyer say, "I just got off the phone with Dean Andrews. I think you'd better prepare yourself for a rough morning tomorrow."

"Is your meter running?"

The lawyer laughed. "I like your sense of humor," he said. "What do they call it—black humor?"

"Gallows humor would be closer to the mark," Barker said. "And you didn't answer my question."

"I thought you understood that I'm taking this case on a flat retainer basis. Phone calls are included—within reason, of course."

"There was this lawyer," Barker began, "who was standing up to his chin in a pile of shit. What's wrong with this picture?"

"Not enough shit," Cross said. "For some reason, lawyer jokes leave me cold. I wonder why that is. . . . Do you want to get serious or should I hang up?"

"Okay, old buddy," Barker said, "I'll be good—no more lawyer jokes."

"All right then. This is what's going to happen tomorrow at the hearing." Barker's stomach cramped in anticipation. "It's going to take place in Dean Fromme's office. You know where that is, I presume." Barker said he did. "Your old friend Anita Andrews will conduct the proceedings. Three witnesses are going to testify, one at a time. You may bring your wife with you but not a lawyer—Andrews is firm on this point. And it's in the guidelines. Personally, I think they're heading into some extremely fishy procedural waters here, but we'll allow it to pass for the moment. I think it's important for you to demonstrate a minimum of goodwill and cooperation."

"If it's fishy, why don't we do something about it?" Barker asked.

"Because if you start challenging their rules you have nothing to gain—except maybe more attention from the media. And that's not exactly what we're looking for, is it?"

"Damned if I do, damned if I don't," Barker said. "But I dimly see your point." The scenario was grossly unfair, the setup a farce. He would sit there and listen while three girls depicted him as a monster with fangs. "Say, Freddie, do I have any rights at all?"

"Only the right to face your accusers," Cross said. "By the way, I think it would be a good idea for you to bring a tape recorder along. I'll want to listen to it. After that we can decide what action, if any, seems appropriate."

Barker thought Cross was saying a lot of words without really saying anything at all. "What do you see as their options?" Barker asked, aware he was lapsing into his lawyer's idiom. His pulse began to pound.

"I suggest you reread the guidelines; they can do just about anything they want. It's quite specific: anything from a gentle slap on the wrist to severing you from the university. Remember, they don't want the publicity anymore than you do. If you're fired for sexual harassment, how does it make them look? Unconcerned. Negligent. But this sort of thing, I'm afraid, has built-in drama. It's not in the same hohum class as say, double-entry bookkeeping. This is steamy stuff."

"For your information, friend, this hearing right now is about as secret as the college's endowment. It's topic A in this academic hellhole. People lie in wait for me. They look at me as if my fly was open and my thing was hanging out."

The lawyer cleared his throat but was gent enough not to comment on Barker's image. But he did go on to say, "There's something I'd like to ask you, Jake. Feel free not to answer if you don't want to, but I ought to know—in case we take this to court—what the real story is. Did you do the things you're being accused of?"

"Is this normal curiosity or what?"

"I just told you," Cross said. "It's important for your attorney to know the facts. I'll hold everything you tell me in the strictest confidence—but you already know that."

"Well, I can't tell you what I think you want to hear," Barker said. There wasn't a soul on earth who didn't want to hear or talk about sex. One would think that, given how casually and openly sex had entered and occupied people's lives, it would lose some of its piquancy, its fascination. But no, no other subject came close to it in topical appeal. Ordinary conversation was merely a cover for tales of adultery, of impromptu couplings, speculation about who was doing what to whom— and how and where. Barker figured his lawyer was not telling him the truth—Cross wanted the dirt just like everyone else. "But one thing I can assure you about: I have never in my life forced myself on a girl. I have never remotely considered rape—or considered it to be excusable under any circumstances. If I slept with a student once or twice over all these years, it was not only with her permission, it was because she wanted to as much as I did."

"You're sure about that?"

"What do you want me to do?" Barker shouted. "Write it in blood?"

"Take it easy, Jake," said the lawyer.

Barker mumbled an apology he did not altogether endorse. "I'm antsy," he added.

Cross let it pass. "By the way," he said, "when you go in there tomorrow try to act and sound as rational and unruffled as possible. You want them to think you're a prudent and sage individual. I'm just guessing, of course, but given the climate and other overheated factors in this case, I'd say these ladies are out to mangle your balls. Conciliation isn't on their plate."

"And what do you think I should wear, Counselor? A high-necked black dress with a white collar, white gloves, and a modest little hat with a veil?"

"Always the joker," Cross said. "I'm delighted to see that your famous sense of humor is still intact. You're going to need it."

When Barker came home on the eve of the hearing—having detoured to the 19th Hole, where he downed a couple of whiskeys and enjoyed a few minutes of mindless talk with men who didn't know who he was and cared less—Susan wasn't at her usual post in the kitchen but in their bedroom talking on the telephone; he could hear her voice from downstairs. Barker tiptoed up the stairs and stood in the hallway outside their room, listening. Light spilled into a trapezoidal pool on the pine floorboards, defining the area beyond its rim in hard-edged mystery. To his left was the baby's room, papered in a pattern of bears holding onto balloon strings. The crib was still broken down in its carton waiting for Barker to assemble its

many pieces and parts—a chore he anticipated with dread—
and frilly yellow curtains suspended from wooden rods lay flat
against windows as yet unopened.

Did he really want to listen? Supposing he heard something
that made him feel even worse than he did now, implausible as
this seemed. He wondered why he wasn't hungry. He had
bought a sandwich for lunch and eaten it at his desk; he
couldn't remember whether it was roast beef or chopped liver.

"Please don't start that again, Mom. You know how if you
tell me to do something often enough I do just the opposite?" It
didn't surprise Barker that his wife was talking to her mother
again. The two women were glued together in an unnatural
bonding. A woman Susan's age—she was closing in on the big
Three-O—ought to be free of her mother, and if the mother
was as adhesive as Mona, it was up to the daughter to apply the
shears, do the snipping. The daughter had to do it or it would
never happen. Barker's opinion of a grown woman who
couldn't buy a coat, plan a dinner party, or take a trip without
consulting her mother was that she was as appealing as a child
who would not shut up. He disliked this trait in Susan; she had
a lot of maturing to do.

Susan was silent for what seemed a very long time, while
Barker tried not to move and give his presence away. He
figured Mona was delivering one of her generic lectures;
Barker had no doubt as to its subject—himself, the professor
sans heart, sans prudence, sans mercy.

"No, Mom," Susan said, "I *am* going with Jake tomorrow. I
can't let them think that what he's done . . . no, please."
Susan's voice switched from alto to soprano. "I don't want to
look as if I'm deserting him." The "as if" hit Barker between
the eyes. She listened to her mother for half a minute, then
took up where she'd left off, defending her defense of her
wicked husband. She was holding her own, dear little soul,
brave girl; maybe he was being too hard on her. "Mom," she
said, "I'm sick to death of talking about Jake. That's all anyone
wants to talk about—Jake this, Jake that. What about *me?*

Don't *I* matter?" Her voice thickened with tears. "I'm going to hang up now, it's time for 'Cheers.' Maybe that'll cheer me up."

Barker almost walked into the room, then decided that he didn't have the energy now to deal with his wife's emotions. Moreover, although it would have felt good, he couldn't thank her, as that would reveal that he'd been eavesdropping. So, as quietly as he could, he slipped back downstairs, went to the front door, opened it softly, and slammed it shut.

Her voice came floating down. "Jake, is that you?" She didn't sound exactly overjoyed.

"It's me, Susie-Q, your old man's back from the wars. Where are you?"

She came and stood at the head of the stairs, peering over at him; backlit, she glowed with a dark beauty that ate into his heart like a laser. "Do you mind if I don't come down?" she asked. "I'm beat."

Barker assured her that he didn't mind and told her he was going to the kitchen to get a bite to eat. "I'll be up soon," he said. "Are you okay?"

"I'm fine," Susan said. "I may be asleep when you come up."

They had both, apparently, been promoted at avoidance school and were heading for the graduate program. And yet he loved her, her loyalty swelled his heart with love. In all the world—what was it now, more than several billion souls—those loyal to him had boiled down to a mere two, Susan and Bennie. His spirit felt crushed by the loneliness he had courted, not deliberately but because that was the only way open to him. What he felt now was worse than any physical pain, worse than the time he had broken his wrist in a fall, worse than a decayed molar, worse than the sinus infection he had had as a ten-year-old and didn't tell his mother about, so it went untreated until, one day at school, he passed out from the pain. He wanted to vacate his body without dying, in order to leave the pain behind for just a few minutes.

Barker opened the refrigerator and found a package of

turkey breast. He laid a couple of slices of this on a slice of rye bread, added a leaf of Boston lettuce carefully washed by Susan, topped it with a second piece of bread. Then he pulled out a bottle of Rolling Rock, uncapped it, and took a long swig. He felt as he had the night before his Ph.D. orals, when he knew that one of his examiners didn't like him, thought him a phony, and had been heard to say he was going to "get Barker's ass." This sense of unfairness, coupled with the paradoxical suspicion that a man gets precisely what he deserves, deposited Barker in the land of fearful uncertainty. He deserved the MacArthur—which he knew he could kiss goodbye as soon as the folks in charge heard about the mess he was in—and at the same time he deserved whatever punishment the kangaroo court chose to mete out. He had been bad; he had done things forbidden, taboo, beyond the moral pale. Just as he began to feel a little better—the punishment was perfectly just because he had, in fact, sinned—the unfairness factor reemerged: plenty of men had done what he had; he could name three faculty members whom he was sure of and three more he suspected. Not fair, not fair.

Chapter Seventeen

ON THE morning of the hearing, Barker took longer than usual to dress himself. After putting on the suit he had bought to wear during television and book-and-author appearances on behalf of *Cleopatra's Nose*, a gray number with an Italianate flair and a subliminal gangsterish sheen, he removed it and replaced it with a pair of gray slacks and a five-year-old Harris tweed jacket. To complement this he chose a blue shirt and a blue silk tie with white dots the size of lentils. The look he achieved was inoffensive—precisely the note intended. He looked at himself in the full-length mirror on the inside of the closet door, felt a rush of sadness as the visual truth was revealed: more girth and wrinkles, less hair.

Behind Barker, Susan was also getting dressed. Not today her baggy pants with the large hole in the front to accommodate her swollen abdomen, and a man's XL sweatshirt, but an unbelted dress that hung from her shoulders and fell gracefully over the baby inside. It was the dress she wore whenever they went out or entertained company.

"I see you've decided to come with me," he said over his shoulder.

"Yes." Barker kept his eyes from meeting hers—he knew they would be full of hurt and he couldn't handle it. He fixed instead on her stomach, which looked as if she were ripening a blue-ribbon-sized watermelon inside her. "You didn't think I wouldn't, did you?" Susan asked.

"I didn't know," he said. "Are you sure this is what you want to do?"

"Why do you always ask me if I'm sure? You make me sound as if I change my mind all the time without thinking." She walked toward the door.

"Where are you going?" he said.

"I don't know about you, but I need something to eat before this thing." The phone rang.

"It's Mona," Barker said. "I can tell by the ring."

Susan shot him an acrid look. "Oh really?" she said, going over to answer the phone. "It's for you," she said, holding out the receiver in a way that suggested it was giving off a bad smell. Barker quit studying his shoe collection—he hadn't quite decided between the loafers and the brogans—and took the receiver from his wife.

It was Freddie Cross. "Listen, Jake," the lawyer said, "I want you to be rational, circumstantial, and emphatic in your denial of wrongdoing. Whatever you do, don't lose your cool and don't belittle your accusers—that way lies disaster, it always backfires. Don't get sarcastic. Try to behave as if all this was a minor nuisance born of misunderstanding. By the way, why don't you take a couple of Valium?"

"I don't believe in that stuff," Barker said, figuring that Cross thought his client was going to get the book thrown at him. The trouble was, that, although people knew what lay between the covers of this book, it had never yet been thrown at anyone. Cross's voice took on a patronizing timbre. "I appreciate the advice, Counselor," Barker said, interrupting, "but I've got to finish dressing. I'm running late."

"Jake . . ."

"Yes, sir?"

239

"Break a leg, Jake."

"Right."

"Oh, and give me a call, will you, when the hearing's over?"

"Sure thing, Freddie."

Barker grabbed the loafers and ran downstairs. Susan was waiting for him. She looked waiflike inside her coat; this effect resulting from the fact that the coat gaped over her stomach.

As Barker and Susan climbed the wide stairway to Dean Fromme's office, Barker was sure that Captain Dreyfus felt precisely as he did now; foreboding made his knees buckle and he reached for the banister. He saw Susan watching him do this and wondered what she was thinking. As for himself, he couldn't imagine he had a life beyond noon of this day. He took Susan's arm; her body stiffened. "I don't need any help, thank you," she said. Where was the love she had shared with him? Her eyes were cold.

The dean's reception area was like that of a popular doctor who has trouble with scheduling. Too many chairs, too much waiting. There were not one but three desks, each manned— or, as Anita Andrews would probably have said it, "personned"—at all times. Susan stepped away from Barker, who studied the scene, including seven or eight people broken up into groups of two or three, talking quietly as one does in a doctor's waiting room, or before a funeral service. Among them was Anita Andrews, holding, for crissake, a clipboard, like a soccer coach. Brian Boyer, the *Crimson* reporter, was in evidence, talking to a woman in her late thirties whom Barker recognized but couldn't name. Kathleen Peters gave him an odd look, part smile, part sneer. Elaine Ferrier sat on a couch studying an open folder perched on her knees; she didn't look up at him, relieving him of making a choice between pretending to ignore her and offering her an ambiguous gesture. Susan sat down carefully, as if she were afraid of breaking in half; Brian went over to her, pouncing (she had not, it turned out, let him in

240

through the front door). Barker held his breath as she gave him her best Asian smile, a thin line across the lower half of her lovely face; slowly she moved her head from left to right and back again. Good girl. Nevertheless, Brian hunkered down on his knees and practically laid his head on her lap.

Barker/Dreyfus stood alone; no one came near him. He felt, for a moment or two, invisible, a virus, a whiff of poison gas. Then Ed Fromme bustled out of his office and rushed up to him with a false smile masking his true feelings—whatever they might be. "Glad you're here," he said. "Can we get started? We can go inside. Ah . . . ?" He paused, looking around. "There she is," he said, gesturing toward Susan. "Mrs. Barker," he said.

Brian stood up and rushed over to where Barker stood with Dean Fromme. "No reporters," Fromme said.

"Reporters are permitted at trials."

"This isn't a trial, young man," Fromme said. "You're wasting your time here. Don't you have a class to attend?"

"I think I'll just hang around and talk to a couple of the witnesses," Brian said.

"The witnesses have been instructed not to talk to anyone," Fromme told him.

"Is that so?" Brian said. "Sounds like the old gag rule to me. And, sir? That doesn't wash—they haven't obeyed your instructions. I got a good story from a couple of them—"

"You're way out of line, young man," Fromme said. Barker noticed his pale cheeks coloring as if tiny vessels had burst beneath the skin. "What's your name?"

The reporter pulled out a plastic press card and presented it to Fromme, who looked at it with distaste. Then he handed it back and said, "I don't want to see your face here when we're through. Is that clear?"

"Yes sir," Brian said.

It was obvious to Barker that the dean had here a wonderful opportunity to test his muscle; he could toss the reporter out on his ass and probably get away with it. No one had yet come up with exactly how far freedom of the press went when within the physical confines of a school; it was a tricky business, and although Barker could understand why Fromme didn't want to engage in testing at this moment, he regretted the dean's reluctance to stick it to Brian Boyer. Fromme had shit in his blood—but then so did most people, there was no news in that.

"Dean Andrews," Fromme said, "I think we can get started now."

At first there were just the four of them: Barker, his wife, and the two deans, Fromme and Andrews. An intimate party. Everything suggesting paperwork—save one closed folder— had been removed, as if someone were afraid that things would get tossed around, that there would be destruction. Fromme told them all where to sit and then sat himself down at his desk. Barker felt naked.

"Rather than ask my secretary to take shorthand," Fromme said, "I've brought a tape recorder with me." He pointed to the latest-model Sony on the corner of his desk. "You have no objections?"

"None in the least," Barker said. He reached into his jacket pocket and came forth with his own Sony—last year's model. "As you can see, we're going to be redundant. I assume you have no objections?" Anita frowned. "By the way, what do you propose to do with your tape?" Barker asked.

"It's for the record," Fromme said. "It's not for publication, if that's what you're driving at." Well, Barker most certainly wasn't thinking that. Where did they think they could publish a transcript of this so-called hearing without his permission? Barker looked at Anita, who seemed about to burst with joy, while Susan studied her hands where they lay one atop the other on her lap.

Dean Fromme began to explain how the hearing was to proceed. "There are three young ladies, all of whom have lodged formal complaints with the university and who have agreed to testify this morning. They will, of course, do so one at a time. Dean Andrews is here on their behalf."

Unwilling to start shooting so soon in the battle—Fromme had not yet trumpeted the opening notes—Barker held his tongue and tried to make eye contact with his wife, who, he discovered, wasn't having any. It occurred to him that he couldn't remember whether or not he had ever told her about his romance with Anita.

"I'd like to say something before our first witness comes in," Anita said. It seemed as if this were the moment she had been priming herself for all her life; a regular Athena, she shone with puissance. Barker ground his jaws together.

"This is a first for Harvard," she began. "We don't know exactly where it will lead. We have drawn some guidelines and"—here she turned her eyes on Barker for emphasis—"I assume all of you have read this document, all of you—but they are *only* guidelines. There are no precedents to follow nor any mandatory punishments. We're feeling our way along, so to speak."

"Ah yes," Barker said, trying to steady himself. "When you say 'we,' who exactly are you referring to?"

"The 'we' is me," Anita answered. "And two women in my office."

That left out Edward Fromme, who recrossed his knees under the desk and cleared his throat. "Can we move right along now?" he asked. Barker suspected that Anita was not on the top of Fromme's list of all-time favorites. She had committed a gaffe in not including him in the "we." Could she make up for it during the course of the hearing?

"Very well," Anita said. "Why don't we hear from our first witness."

"Just a minute!" Barker said in a voice louder than the one he had intended to use. "I need to know what my role is here. Am I going to be allowed to question the witnesses? What if they lie?"

Anita glanced at Fromme.

It was inconceivable that these two hotshots had not worked out this wrinkle ahead of time, but apparently it was so. Fromme and Anita huddled briefly, while Barker studied the sky beyond the window above Fromme's desk. Grayish clouds moved across the space rapidly, revolving as they went. A plane crossed the rectangle, followed by the noise of its engines and two thin white streamers.

The huddle broke. "You will be permitted to ask questions and to present your version if and when it differs," Anita told him, "but only after the witness has completed her testimony. In other words, you may not interrupt." She peered at him over half-glasses, a gesture Barker associated with people who had more than the usual measure of self-confidence. You didn't see wimps doing it. Anita's glasses were a new affectation.

Anita went to the door and ushered in the woman Brian Boyer had been talking to ten minutes earlier.

"This is Patricia Lang," she said. "I believe you knew her by her maiden name—Weissman." Barker gaped. Of course it was Patty—nearly twenty years older, but with the same sallow skin and needy eyes. She had gained a few pounds, perhaps even as many as ten; yet she remained painfully thin. Anita indicated a chair fifteen feet from Barker's, and Patty sat down in it, looking as if a dentist were approaching her with a needleful of Novocain. How had they managed to dredge her from the past? What had they promised her in return for her testimony?

"Would you like to begin, please, Ms. Lang?" Anita said.

"Where should I start?"

"How about from the first time you and Professor Barker spoke together?" Anita said.

Patty flinched as the needle's point pierced her gum, while Barker's memory delivered to him Patty, nude in the motel room where they had gone together seventeen years earlier and where they had made love—if that was what one could call it. "I suppose it all got started when I asked him—Professor Barker, that is—a question after class one day."

244

"This was 1968?" Anita said. She had, God only knew where, picked up the style and polish of a courtroom prosecutor.

Patricia nodded. "Everything was, like, in turmoil," she said. "The kids wanted the war to stop—they thought they could stop it."

"And you might also say that barriers between faculty and students were crumbling . . ." Anita prompted.

"Some of them," Patty said. She wouldn't look at Barker. Although he was often able to will people to look straight at him, when he tried this now with Patty, he failed.

"And Jacob Barker, would you say that he was one of the—how shall I put it?—one of the more *accessible* members of the faculty? He enjoyed socializing with his students?"

"I wouldn't know about that," Patty said. "All I know is how he was with me."

"Okay then," Anita said, lowering her eyes briefly to consult her clipboard, "And how *was* he with you?"

"Ah . . . . . ." It seemed to Barker that Patty might be changing her mind exactly halfway across the Atlantic. She could drift in her dinghy until food and water ran out or she could continue. Or she could turn back. Whichever she chose, the trip wasn't going to be one she'd care to take again.

"Perhaps I can help you," Anita said. Fromme started scratching something on a notepad. "You have reported that Jacob Barker maneuvered you into a place where you were convinced that if you didn't give in to his sexual demands you risked a failing grade in his course. Is that correct?"

Barker noticed a few gray strands sprung like wire from the rest of her hair. Patty nodded. "May I ask a question?" Barker said.

"Not until she's finished," Anita said. "May I remind you that you agreed not to interrupt?"

"I just want to ask why you brought this person in almost twenty years after something vague was supposed to have occurred. What happened to the statute of limitations? And

245

how do I know she is who she says she is—I don't even recognize her. What sort of circus is this?"

"I am who I say I am," Patty said, her face still averted from Barker's. "I remember you. I remember how you looked at me, your eyes, they looked right inside me. I thought you were like a god or something. I was so dumb. . . ."

"How did they find you?"

"Quiet!" snapped Anita, losing her cool.

"I see no reason why you shouldn't know," Fromme said. "Mrs. Lang came to us, not the other way around."

"I don't mind telling," Patty said. "I read your book, *Cleopatra's Nose*? I've been into the women's movement since the early seventies. I read a lot of books about women's issues. Your book doesn't sound like you. It sounds like it was written by a feminist." Barker glanced at Anita, his "collaborator," and couldn't help but appreciate the irony of the trap she had set for him.

"We're getting out of sequence here," Anita said. "Please go back and complete your testimony as to what Professor Barker did to you."

All this appeared to be making Patty uncomfortable: patches of bright pink appeared on either cheek. Her hands crept toward each other for comfort, fingers twining with fingers. "Well, ah . . . Professor Barker asked me to meet him in the Square for coffee. I guess I was flattered by the attention. He was kind of good-looking then. I mean not like Tom Cruise or anything, but he had a way of looking at you that made it hard to say no. And everybody said he was a genius . . ."

Anita nodded. "And?"

"I thought he just wanted to talk. I didn't realize how it would end up. . . ." She paused. "You know."

Barker was amazed at how convincing she sounded. She told how, during their meeting in Omar's, Barker had implied that she should major in psychology and that, with his help, she would be able to do brilliant work. "He said I could think 'laterally.' I'd never heard that phrase before but it made me feel great. He thought I was very smart."

"And what made you think that Professor Barker was trying to strike a sexual bargain with you?" Anita said.

"Well, for one thing, he touched my knee under the table."

"I did not!" Barker half rose from his chair, shouting.

"Kindly don't interrupt again," Anita said. Fromme frowned and rubbed his cheek.

"But she's lying," Barker said.

Susan looked over at Barker; her features were shifting as fast as the clouds and he couldn't tell if it was going to rain or not. He didn't know which of them she believed—him or Patty. He felt faint again and wondered if he were having a stroke. He drew in so much air that he began to cough.

"Please go on," Anita instructed Patty.

"He took me to this motel."

"Do you recall the name of the motel?" Patty shook her head. Barker wondered why, since this was not a court trial, it was so important to name the place. By simple arithmetic, if he was the accused and Anita the prosecutor, then Fromme had to be both jury and judge. What sort of punishment was this silly man empowered to administer? A reprimand? A beheading?

"Did you engage in sex?"

Patty closed her eyes and nodded.

"And did Professor Barker say or do anything that led you to believe that he would give you something in return for your sexual favors, something like a higher grade in his course than you knew you deserved?" Once more Patty nodded.

Barker was not sure just where they were going. Was Anita objecting to any sex at all between teacher and student or was it the barter aspect of it she objected to?

"At this point," Barker said, "I've got to break in here. And if you don't permit me to talk I'll simply get up and leave. This is intolerable." As he said this, Susan shifted in her chair. "You have no legal right to keep me here," Barker went on. Again, Anita and Fromme exchanged a meaningful look. And again, they huddled.

"Dean Fromme agrees with you," Anita said after a minute or two. "You may speak briefly—but no speeches, *please.*"

"Thank you," Barker said. "If you're waiting for me to admit that I indulged in what I believe is known as sexual harassment you'll have to wait until hell freezes over. And if you're using me as an object lesson, I guarantee that I intend to make things extremely unpleasant for you."

"And just what are you implying?" Anita said. The old soft version of Anita had disappeared entirely; she had been recruited by the Nazi Party.

"If I may," Fromme said, cutting in. He was, clearly, finding his judge role to be not half so much fun as paring and shaping curriculum; perspiration adorned his brow and he slumped rather than sat in his chair. "Shouldn't we see if we can establish some facts . . . ?"

"How can you establish facts when it's a case of *my* word against *hers*?" Barker said. "To my mind this hearing goes against every rule of Anglo-Saxon law."

"I know, I know," Fromme said. "Technically, you're correct. But how else, may I ask, can we proceed? This matter is one of growing concern; it's a major problem on campuses all over the United States. We have to address this problem head on. . . . Have *you* any suggestions?"

"Me?" said Barker. Fromme's question was so outrageous that Barker had to smile; here was evidence that the man was out to lunch and unlikely to return. Anita went into the kind of agitation caused by a twister in the sky aiming straight for your house.

"If you don't mind, Dean Fromme," Anita said, "I don't think that question is altogether appropriate. Professor Barker was apprised of the rules before he agreed to meet with us. He can leave any time he chooses. I don't believe any purpose would be served were he to tell you how to deal with a problem largely of his own making."

"I withdraw my remark," said Fromme. Barker was tempted to feel sorry for him.

"Now then, I would like to return to the matter of your book, Professor Barker."

What was her game? Barker realized his agility was not up to that of his former girlfriend; she was several fancy steps ahead of him. "Ms. Lang read your book" (unholy emphasis on the word "your") "when it came out. I believe she discussed it with her support group." Anita glanced at Patty, who nodded. "And I also believe that it was because of them, because of their urging, that she came forward."

Barker wanted to know what sort of group Patty had joined up with. AA? Drug Abusers Forever? Lesbians United? Over-eaters Anonymous? He looked steadily at her, trying to read what was there, and all he could see was a perfectly ordinary woman. Her body—what he could see of it—had filled out an inch or two. She was wearing tan linen pants—they looked expensive—a blue silk blouse, and a long loose jacket. There was nothing special about either the clothes or the person inside them. Wickedness was, of course, invisible.

"My group," Patty began, "said it was very important for me to come here. I know what happened was a long time ago, but they didn't think he"—significant albeit brief glance at the accused—"should get away with carrying on like that."

It was a no-win situation and Barker wanted to protest that it was impossible for him to prove he had *not* done something, but what was the use? The monstrous bird fashioned by Anita and her ladies had wings and was going to fly.

"Do we have sufficient testimony from Mrs. Lang?" Fromme asked Anita. "It's getting late. We have two more witnesses to hear from."

Anita looked at her notes, then at her watch. "There were several more questions I wanted to put to her," she said, "but I guess we can skip them and go on to the next witness. You can go now, Ms. Lang. I want to thank you for coming here. I know it wasn't an easy thing to do. We're most grateful. . . ."

"If you really want to know," Patty said, "it was awful. I didn't want to come. The only reason I did was that my group made me. What he did was inexcusable, and I thought that if I could help stop him I would, even though I might lose a lot of sleep. I want him to know that after I left Harvard I had to go into treatment because of him. He probably forgot all about me until this morning but he messed up my life. I thought I was going to go to graduate school and eventually teach, but after what happened I couldn't concentrate on my studies and then I dropped out for a year and waitressed in Hartford. My mom and dad couldn't believe what was happening to me—"

Fromme broke in. "We're sincerely sorry that you've had a rough time," he said. "And I wish we had more time so that you could finish your story. But I'm afraid we're running behind schedule." He got up. Patty rose, frowning, obviously wounded at having been shot down in midhistory.

"How are you doing?" Barker asked Susan. "Did you see the way she tried to blame me for her emotional problems? That girl's life was messed up long before she met me. You should have seen her—she weighed about seventy-five pounds. She looked like a corpse."

"I don't need to hear this, Jake," Susan said. "Where's the bathroom?"

After a short recess they brought in Elaine Ferrier, spectacular in tight designer jeans and a heavy white sweater. In the years since Barker had seen her, Elaine's face had changed only slightly: hard-edged intelligence had replaced the subtle swell of youth. She looked smart in every way; she had it all under control. The fact that Elaine found herself in a situation unlike any other she had ever known—and one she was unlikely to experience again—seemed to exhilarate rather than baffle her. This number could no doubt march out on a stage and make a speech to two thousand reactionaries on the subject of nuclear disarmament without even beginning to perspire.

Elaine sat down in the chair lately vacated by Patty Weissman. Barker wondered if it was still warm. Thinking of the origin of this heat caused Barker a moment of anxiety—would he get an erection? The moment passed safely. Anita asked Elaine to identify herself, which she did in a clear, cool voice. She had gone to Stanford, she said, for graduate work, but had been sidetracked there by what she referred to as "physical problems" and had yet to complete her work for the doctorate. "I also got married," she said. "It only lasted seven months." Unlike Patty, Elaine looked straight at Barker; her gaze made him feel like a stuffed animal behind a glass case.

"Will you tell us, please, exactly what transpired between you and Professor Jacob Barker in March 1981?"

"Well, I was taking his seminar in infant testing. It was mostly for psychology majors. He gave us spot quizzes all the time."

"How many people were in this seminar?"

"Twelve or thirteen, I think. I can't remember exactly. He asked me to have coffee with him."

"That's his pattern," Anita commented. Fromme scowled and wrote something down. "And you accepted his invitation?"

Anita was talking as if it did not, in fact, take two to execute the fancy choreography of love, as if there were not two minds and two hearts, a pair of bodies performing the astonishing dance. Barker sighed, but more loudly than he had intended, for everyone looked at him; while outside, beyond the gates of Harvard Yard, a siren screamed, an ambulance transporting some lucky sucker with a heart attack or broken pelvis to the hospital.

"I did, because I was afraid that if I didn't Professor Barker wouldn't write the letter I needed to get into graduate school."

"And what gave you this idea?"

"He came on to me," Elaine said. "He had this incredible way of looking at you, as if he could see clear into your brain

251

and read your thoughts. He was extremely intense. He asked me a lot of very personal questions. I guess I was silly enough to think his interest in me was because of my mind."

Barker's skin contracted. "May I say something?" he asked.

"Of course," Fromme said, bringing forth a howl of protest from Anita. "The rules!" she cried.

"Make it brief," Fromme said, ignoring her.

"Ms. Ferrier has this backwards," Barker said, turbulence in his voice. "She came on to me. She asked me very personal questions the first time she came in for a conference."

"Just what did she ask you?" Fromme said.

"She asked me if my former wife was related to President Roosevelt."

"And what did that have to do with the price of eggs?" Fromme said.

"Damned if I know," Barker said, trying to catch Fromme's eye.

Optimism surged; Barker was encouraged. "This girl," he began, "made it quite clear that all she wanted was for us to go to bed together." Thus he lied with less difficulty than shaving cream is extruded from a push-button can. But he had to try to protect himself, didn't he? He was a man without advocate; a mute wife was useless. It struck Barker then that he didn't know why Susan had come with him. It was a bizarre situation in any case; had she stayed away, things would have looked even worse—assuming that was possible. He had no doubt Fromme and Anita were keeping four sharp eyes on her at all times.

"There!" Anita said. "There you have it. He's just admitted it."

"What have I admitted? I haven't admitted anything. I merely said the girl made it clear she wanted me to have sex with her. There was nothing subtle about her—still isn't, far as I can tell."

"Are there anymore questions, Dean Andrews?" Fromme said.

"He's lying," Elaine said. "I didn't want to have anything to do with him physically. I had a perfectly good boyfriend. He's telling it this way because he doesn't want you to know that he came on to his students. Why should I make anything up? Do you think I enjoy being here?"

"Is there something you'd like to say before we let Miss Ferrier go?" Fromme asked Barker.

"Yes. Would you mind telling me why you asked me to be present today?"

"To get at the facts."

"How so? It's their word against mine."

"We've been over this, Ed," Anita said.

"I believe Dean Andrews is correct," Fromme told Barker. "There's no point in going over ground we've already covered. Besides, our witnesses have signed affidavits."

Anita seemed to go into another psychic warp as her voice softened. "Okay," she said. "It's perfectly true that it's his word against theirs. Yet I believe *them* and not *him*."

"But is that enough?" Fromme said. "It would hardly hold up in a court of law."

"I, too, wish this were more clear-cut," Anita said. "But it's one of those complex situations where the damage is chiefly emotional and outright misbehavior difficult to pinpoint. It's not like premeditated murder or rape or even slander."

"We all appreciate that, I'm sure," Fromme said.

"I'm not at all eager to punish anyone who's innocent. I'm not that sort of person." As she said this, Anita looked at Barker in a way he remembered from the first days of their romance. Her face, for one split second, seemed awash in love. Then it vanished and the Crimson Avenger slid back behind the wheel.

Susan got up and began to make her way quietly to the door, causing Barker a spasm of anxiety; he read her departure from the room as departure from their life together: she was leaving him forever. She turned and said, "I need some air."

"I think we can use this as a break," Anita said. Catching

up to Susan before she got away, and placing a hand on Susan's arm, she asked, "Are you all right?"

Susan shrugged the arm off. "I'm fine," she said. "I just need some fresh air."

Given Susan's distress, it would have been natural for Barker to leave with her; he considered this for a minute or two. He felt as he did in the middle of an oft-recurring nightmare: he is waist-deep in water and can move his legs only with incredible effort. He doesn't know whether there's an unseen goal impelling him or danger at his back, threatening to overtake him. He wants to cry out that he's too exhausted to go on, but when he opens his mouth it fills with wind and makes no sound at all. He wants to die and get it over with.

Barker went to the men's room, where he splashed cold water on his face, patting it dry with a thick paper towel. As he came out of the bathroom, looking around for Susan, he bumped into Kathleen Peters. "Did you finally get your Porsche?" he said to her, aware that this remark was far too personal. But what the hay, he didn't care anymore. The building was collapsing in slow motion, imploding. Soon gusts would whistle through the ruins.

"What?" she said, looking at him with scary eyes. "Oh yeah, my car. Daddy came through. I totaled it last year, though. Now I'm driving a Celica. What a comedown. How you be, Professor Romeo?"

"You're a hoot, Kathleen," Barker said, feeling a little drunk.

"We probably shouldn't be talking to each other," she said.

"No doubt," he said. The door of the ladies' room swung open and Susan came out, looking miserable. "Are you all right?" he said to her.

"Why do people always ask that when they can see what the answer is," Susan said. "I'm a little uncomfortable."

"Why don't you call the doctor?" Barker asked. "Do you think you're in labor?"

"Of course not," she said. "But I can't stand this, Jake. I didn't know what it would be like. I don't think I can go back in there."

"I don't need you," Barker said. Susan picked up the ambiguity. "That's true, I guess," she said.

"I didn't mean it that way," he cried. "Really, you have to believe me. I meant I didn't need you at the *hearing*. I don't blame you for going—the whole thing is a travesty." Barker tried to touch his wife but she slid away like a child whose aunt with the bad breath wants to give her a kiss. "Call the doctor," he said.

"You're *pathetic*," Susan said.

"Don't say that. I don't want anyone's pity."

"Jake . . ."

Fromme bustled up and said, "We should get started again. This is the last round, old man, you're standing up just fine."

"What do you mean by that?"

"Just that I want you to know that I'm very sympathetic."

Barker decided to stick it out, as there was nothing left to lose. Once you have forfeited your job, your reputation, your standing in society, your amour propre, and the privilege of using the Harvard athletic facilities, what else could be taken from you that mattered?

Once inside the dean's chamber, Barker told them that Susan wasn't feeling well. "I hope this isn't going to take too long."

"Three quarters of an hour, tops," Anita said crisply.

Kathleen acted as if she couldn't wait to begin. She kept opening her mouth like a fish, then closing it again, looking expectantly at Anita, with whom she must have gone through a practice session—they all had, for that matter; you didn't go into something like this cold. "Professor Barker asked me to come in for a conference," Kathleen said. "He wanted to talk about a paper I wrote for his course, which he wanted me to revise."

"You mean rather than simply handing it back with comments, he invited you to come to his office to discuss it?" Anita asked.

"That's right," Kathleen said. "He was hard to say no to. There was something about the way he looked at me. He has these strange eyes. . . ."

"There's nothing unusual about asking a student to discuss a paper in conference . . . ," Barker said.

"Please," Anita said. "You'll have your chance. Go on, Kathy."

"Okay. Well, when we were in his office he closed the door, and a few minutes later he touched me here." She pointed to her right thigh.

"And?"

"Things just went on from there and we ended up in bed together in a downtown hotel. It was one of those new luxury hotels with humongous towels in the bathroom—too big to steal. He had two drinks first, in the bar."

"You mean he was drunk?" Fromme said.

"I didn't say that. He didn't seem drunk. Just laid-back— you know how alcohol sort of chills you out?"

"Indeed," Fromme said, turning disapproving eyes on Barker. He appeared to find the booze part more disagreeable than the sex.

"And in your opinion, Kathy, was it clear that Professor Barker meant to give you a higher grade than you would have earned if you hadn't gone to bed with him?"

"Yes. I didn't really want to, but I didn't know how *not* to—" Here her voice cracked.

"Ask her about the Porsche," Barker said.

"What?"

"I said, why don't you ask Kathleen why she came—uninvited—to my office in the first place. Ask her what her father promised her if she managed, somehow, to graduate with honors, something she deserved about as much as she deserves to be beatified."

"Do you want to speak to this?" Anita asked Kathy.

"I don't know what he's talking about," Kathy said.

"Ah, what's the use?" Barker said, his eyes stinging. He who lies down with dogs wakes up with fleas.

"If you don't mind, I'd like to spend a minute or two more on this," Fromme said. "I have a problem with leaving it up in the air. Please go on, Jake."

"If you insist," Barker said. "This girl's father promised her a rather expensive automobile—a Porsche, I believe—if she was graduated with honors. She informed me of this crass arrangement and offered to make another one, with me— namely, that if she went to bed with me, I would pay her with the grade she needed for honors. Simple arithmetic."

"A double bargain," Anita said. "Ugly."

"He's lying again," Kathleen said. "I don't know what he's talking about."

"It's her word against mine, isn't it?" Barker said.

Fromme looked as if his teeth were being torn from his head.

"She did graduate with a Cum," Anita said, checking her clipboard.

"And she did get her car," Barker said.

"Dean Fromme and I will have to sort this out in private," Anita said. "Whatever way you look at it, your role in her life was inappropriate."

Fromme, whose eye Barker hoped to snag, looked at Anita and nodded slightly.

Barker/Dreyfus cringed as his medals were ripped off, epaulets sliced away, his saber snapped across the knee of the commanding officer. Naked beneath a naked uniform, Barker cried too late for his soul. The star that had blazed so high was going out.

Anita peered at him; there was no love in her face now, just disgust.

Surprisingly, Anita excused Kathy, who, as she walked toward the door, gave Barker a sidelong glance informed with triumph. As soon as she had left the room, Barker rose and went over to the window. A pack of dogs—two elkhounds, a part German shepherd, a couple of scrawny, sharp-nosed pups, and a tan terrier—nosed around the base of a venerable Harvard elm and each other's rear ends. A young woman pushed a stroller, crossing the yard in front of the seated John Harvard without glancing at it.

"Well now," said Anita.

"I really should go look for Susan," Barker said.

Ed Fromme stood and kicked his legs to get rid of the kinks. A bell with a hollow sound rang out; it was noon. "We don't need you here any longer," Fromme said. "We'll contact you as soon as we've reached our decision."

"Can I at least know what the alternatives are?" Barker asked, though he knew well what they were.

"I suggest you reread the guidelines," Anita said. "There is, of course, the possibility that we cannot keep you at Harvard any longer. Dean Fromme and I will confer and get back to you as soon as we can. Let's see, this is Friday, there's the weekend, and Monday's probably a bit too soon—let's say we'll be back to you middle of next week."

Chapter Eighteen

HARVARD PROFESSOR DISMISSED FOR
SEXUAL HARASSMENT

Cambridge—May 11. Jacob Barker, 46, Harvard University Professor of Psychology, and author of *Cleopatra's Nose*, the trail-blazing bestseller about gender differentiation, a book hailed by Gloria Steinem as "the work that sets the record straight; a guidebook for the twenty-first century," was severed from the university yesterday for sexual harassment involving three of his former students. The women, whose names have not been released, testified against Barker in a closed hearing last Friday in the office of Edward J. Fromme, Administrative Dean of Harvard's Faculty of Arts and Sciences.

In a statement issued by Dean Fromme's office, Professor Barker, long-time resident of Cambridge, member of the American Academy of Sciences, and a frequent lecturer on gender differences, was cited for "several clear incidents of sexual harassment" dating back as far as the late sixties. Dean Fromme was unavailable for comment, as was Professor Barker.

Anita Andrews, Dean of Women's Affairs at Harvard, told the *Globe* that this was the first time a tenured professor had been dismissed from the oldest university in the United States for "this particularly odious form of misconduct." Added Dean Andrews: "Professor Barker will not be the last. We will continue our efforts to identify and rid this institution of any persons who behave in a manner offensive to the opposite sex."

There was more to the story, but Jacob Barker let the newspaper drop from his fingers as he let out a howl. "They *didn't* fire me, they allowed me to resign. How could she say that? What more does she want? She removes my limbs and then she kicks me in the groin!" Susan, who seemed to have lost the power of speech since the hearing, looked at him with amazement. The phone rang. It was Bennie.

"I just read the *Globe*," Bennie said.

"Ah," said Barker. "What can I say?"

"It's not as if you just tested positive for AIDS."

"Next best. That virago told the *Globe* I was severed. False. I resigned. They permitted me that one final dignity. What's the use? It looks the same from the outside."

"If you ask me, they're making an object lesson out of you. You're not Black or Hispanic, just good old American WASP stock. You're fair game. They waited for someone like you and pounced. I feel for you, Jake. Was it very rough?"

"You might say so," Barker said. It was good of Bennie to call; none of his other friends had, save Emily, his secretary. You couldn't really blame them for not calling: it was more a matter of finding the right words to say than whether or not to make the call in the first place. Do you walk up to a man sitting with his arms and legs in the stocks and start chatting with him about the Celtics? What do you say to a man who can't keep his hands off his students?

"What are you going to do now?" Bennie asked. Then, as if the question required more of Barker than he might be able to give, he changed the subject. "How's Susan?"

"Holding on. She's dilated a centimeter or something like that. We think it's going to be very soon." In reality, Susan had placed herself beyond him. She was like a movie ghost who, when another character tries to touch her, turns into air.

"I'm thinking of writing another book," Barker said, "or

260

doing the lecture thing in a serious way, like the Watergate crew. There's big bucks in wrongdoing." His deliberate flippancy masked the horrors; he was a man looking out through the bars of a cage and waiting without hope for his next session with the torturer.

"Sounds like an okay idea," Bennie said, though his voice said otherwise. "Are you up for a game of squash? Take your mind off things. . . ."

"Thanks, Ben, I'd love to play. I'm angry enough to win for a change."

Barker had to postpone their squash game because Susan's water broke that afternoon, right after lunch (both of them eating without exchanging a word). When it happened Susan called out to him from the bathroom for help. It wasn't until they were inside the hospital, with Susan sitting in a wheelchair waiting for someone to get her to the labor room, that Barker, glancing through the window of the gift shop, caught a glimpse of the *Boston Herald* and its banner headline: HARVARD PROF IN SEXCAPADE. It took Barker a moment to realize that *he* was the Harvard prof. He didn't deserve this obscenity. He looked at Susan to see if she had noticed, but her face was screwed up in pain. Poor thing, she was in the middle of a contraction, and had had no idea it was going to hurt so much.

Susan refused to let Barker stay with her in the labor room, and when he started to argue his case, burst into tears; the nurse had to tell him to leave. He felt like an outcast, slipping all too easily in and out of anger and self-pity, each mood working against the other. His balance was shot. He waited in an airless waiting room, like expectant fathers of yore, while his wife went through fifteen hours of labor, at the end of which she gave birth to a girl whom she named—without consulting Barker—Lily Yvonne. He wasn't partial to either name—he thought they were silly, limp words—but he wasn't inclined, given the delicate nature of their relationship, to make a fuss over his daughter's names. Nevertheless, it rankled that he had had no say in the matter at all.

They sent Susan home on the third morning. Nancy, Barker recalled, had languished in this same hospital almost five days after giving birth to Guy; something about her stitches not healing well. Susan was weak but extremely happy with her infant: her face, still puffy, radiated dumb maternal bliss.

"What do you think you'll do now?" she asked Barker the morning after the day she came home.

"Do you mean in general or in the next five minutes?" The infant was clamped to her right breast. Lily's hair was silky, black, and very long for a newborn; it covered the tips of her tiny pink ears and reminded Barker of feathers. He longed to touch her but was afraid of Susan's fire; so far he had picked up his child only once—while Susan was taking a shower. Lily had looked up at him with unseeing eyes. He tried to send her a message that had regret and repentance in it, but she only closed them softly. Now Susan looked at him as if she had no idea who he was.

"I meant from now on, Jake. How are we going to live? What are we going to live *on*?" At least she was talking. Moreover she had said "we" rather than "you."

"As a matter of fact, I was just sitting here thinking about getting myself hooked up with one of those big-time lecture agencies; people like me are much in demand. I go out there and warn the folks against speaking to members of the opposite sex. And there's *Cleopatra*. It's still—mirabile dictu—selling reasonably well. We'll manage. You could even go back to work. You were very good at it. I never did quite understand why you quit." Again Barker heard himself talking like a man without a care in the world, when in fact he was tipsy with despair.

They were in the downstairs sitting room, in what was no doubt once known as the front parlor. Susan was in a rocking chair, nursing and rocking, Barker slouched in a low, ivory-colored couch across from her, with his back to the front window. Barefoot, he was wearing only jockey shorts and a bathrobe. The phone rang every few minutes. They had bought an answering machine and programmed it with a stark message: it asked only that the caller leave a message, not even "please." Susan had objected: "What if it's my mother calling?" "If it's Mona," Barker had told her, "I assure you she'll get through."

"Why don't you get dressed?" Susan said. "And you know very well why I quit. You yourself encouraged me to try to write."

"Oh yes, of course."

"Don't say it that way. I've made a start." Susan had recently published a piece about Chinese cooking in *New Woman*. But Barker couldn't see her as a writer; she was too normal.

"I think I'll go over to the fish place and buy us some squid for dinner," Barker said. "Then—I assume you're interested—I'm going to call Mimi and talk over my ideas for a couple of magazine articles. Bennie and I have a squash game at four."

"Where?"

"Where we always play."

"Will they still let you use it?"

"I don't know," Barker said. "It never occurred to me that they wouldn't."

"Maybe you'd better check it out first."

Susan gently removed Lily from her swollen right breast, reversed her, head and foot, and settled her at the left one with the ease of a woman who had done nothing but nurse babies all her adult life.

"Guy hasn't called," Barker said.

"No."

"Maybe I'll give him a ring. The poor kid probably doesn't know what to say to me." For a reason he couldn't identify,

263

watching Susan nurse his child sent waves of sadness skittering around his body; would they stay? He got up and made for the door.

"Guy may not want to hear from you," Susan said.

"That's crap," he said. "Of course he wants to hear from me. I'm his father."

"I don't want to argue. It'll sour my milk."

"Who told you that?" Barker said. "Don't tell me. I think I know."

"Mrs. Bee?" Billy, once more exhibiting his considerable skill at timing, popped into the room without advance notice, suggesting to Barker that he had originated in outer space. Barker wanted to kick him out, but since the baby, Billy had taken over several household tasks, done most of the grocery shopping, and seemed bent on making himself indispensable to Susan. "Anything you need, Mrs. Bee? I have a couple of hours before my next class." Susan pulled a slip of paper from the pocket of her shirt—without disturbing Lily—and handed it to Billy. "If you wouldn't mind," she said, smiling up at him, all teeth, all heart. Barker felt as if he were invisible.

"No problem," Billy said. "How's the little one doing?"

"She's just fine," Susan said. "Eating like a horse."

Disgusted, Barker left the room.

Mimi Caballero liked Barker's ideas but told him he had to write a one-page proposal for each of them. Barker protested, saying that his name ought to carry the ideas, but she said, "Not even Cher gets away with not writing a proposal." So he sat down at his word processor and tried to translate his thoughts into words; what emerged on the screen was almost incoherent, stuff that would have been turned back by a sixth-grade teacher with instructions to "clarify." "Christ," he said, perspiring and angry, "I can't even construct a simple sentence." He went into the kitchen, where he poured himself a beer, which he downed in a hurry, standing at the window.

"What am I going to do?" he said aloud. "This isn't going to work. Susan!" He shouted her name. There was no response.

"Did you call me?" It was Billy again, this time from halfway down the back stairs.

"Does 'Susan' sound like 'Billy'? Maybe it does."

"Sorry, Professor."

"I'll bet you are."

"Beg pardon?"

"Nothing, Billy. You wouldn't happen to know where my wife is?"

"I thought she was down here with you." Billy was barefoot. The sight of his long toes made Barker think of thick white worms. The phone rang. Billy's brow twitched. "Would you like me to get that?"

"No, thanks," Barker said. "That's what we have the machine for. By the way, you haven't once mentioned what's happened around here."

"I guess that's because I don't know what to say. . . ."

"Well, *that's* a first."

"No, honestly, Professor Barker, I feel lousy for you. It's a bummer."

"It's a bummer all right," Barker said.

"It's hard on everybody."

"Especially Mrs. Bee?"

"Yes. I guess."

"Well, it's been nice having this little chat with you, Bill. Now I have to get ready for my squash game. I'll see you later." Billy turned and headed back upstairs, stumbling hard on the fifth or sixth riser. Barker smiled.

The next morning Barker woke before eight, sensing change. It was nothing he could put his finger on, just the slightest alteration in the currents of psychic air that swirled around his family. Susan was behind the closed door of the bathroom and, if he read the sounds correctly, pulling things off cabinet

265

shelves and dropping them into a cardboard carton. She came out dressed, wearing a pair of jeans and a large shirt that reached almost to her knees. On her feet were baby-blue running shoes. She looked as much like the girl he had first seen busily plying her trade in the offices of Lothar and Bright as she did Marilyn Monroe. Barker had seen photographs of women whose husbands beat them up over a long period of time—Susan had that look. He had never hit her, not once, never even threatened her; where did she get off acting black and blue?

As angry as he was, Barker nevertheless pitied his wife for allowing herself to be his victim. Silly child, how was it possible for her not to have known what the place he was leading her to looked and smelled like?

"I'm going to stay with my mother for a few days; she's not very well," Susan said. "I told her I'd go and stay with her until she feels better."

"Is that the real reason you're going?" Barker said. He sat up in bed, reluctant to stand, as he was naked. "When are you coming back?"

"I'm not sure."

"But you *are* coming back?"

"I'm not sure about that either."

"You can't do this."

"Why not?"

"Because I love you. I need you here. Our baby . . ."

"You're crying, Jake!"

"Can't help it. Don't leave me, Susan. I can't stand it."

"I hate this conversation. When you fucked those girls did you think about me? Did you think about *them*, Professor Romeo?"

"Where did you hear that name?" Barker's mouth filled with slime, tears slid over his cheeks, and fell, one drop at a time, onto the blanket, where they were rapidly absorbed.

"I don't know, I just heard it. I heard it a long time ago, maybe last fall. How do you think I feel, knowing that's what

266

they call my husband—my husband!" Susan paused and Barker knew that her rage was expanding. "How did I come to marry you, Jake? How did I come to have your child? I must have been out of my mind. Like those poor girls you seduced. What did you *do* to them with those great googly eyes of yours? You looked at them and they just fell over and spread their legs for you. You're a devil, Jake, and I don't want my daughter to grow up in the same house with you."

"But yesterday you said 'we'. . . ."

"I hadn't made up my mind," Susan said.

"Say you didn't mean what you said about my being a devil . . . ," he pleaded.

"But I *do* mean it, Jake, just as much as if you had horns growing out of your forehead and hooves where your feet should be." Lily began to cry in the next room. "The baby's hungry," Susan said. "I'm going to feed her and then I'm going to leave."

"You can't, Susan. Susan! Don't go!"

Chapter Nineteen

Susan had fled with Lily, taking up temporary residence with Mona. Billy, too, had quit the ship, packing his things on Saturday afternoon while Barker was at Harvard cleaning out his office. Billy left a short note, whose sole message was a forwarding address somewhere deep in Somerville, a street unknown to Barker, who was quite sure neither of them would be back—unless it was to retrieve something overlooked in their haste.

Barker tried to fill the space within the walls of his house with people, but no one except Bennie showed any inclination to see him. Some put him off with elaborate politeness, others curtly. Patsy, Bennie's wife, was frosty on the telephone. "I'll see if he's here," she said to Barker one evening a week or so after Susan had gone. Then, putting her hand over the talking end of the receiver, Patsy shouted, "It's him again." Barker hung up. A minute or so after this, Bennie called him and suggested they have lunch in a place well north of Harvard Square.

Wandering from room to empty room, Barker noticed rat-sized balls of dust skittering like tumbleweed across the polished floor. He picked one of them up and stared at it on his palm; it was weightless. He knew it to be alive with millions of tiny mites, invisible without a microscope. He dropped it over a wastebasket and watched mindlessly as it floated downwards. The house was filling up with these things. Funny, he had never noticed them before.

Barker's study was a mess, so was the kitchen. The sides of the sink were covered with a whitish film and something beneath it smelled to high heaven. Barker turned on the cold water and flipped the disposal switch. There was a grinding noise; glasses in the drying rack rattled as last night's chicken bones were pulverized. He extracted a beer from the refrigerator, his last beer but one, and drank from the bottle. He looked down at himself; his chinos were stained and his shirt, hanging outside his pants, was missing a button just beneath his breastbone.

Taking the beer into his study, where he sat at the desk, Barker tried to work on one of the articles Mimi hoped to sell to *Gentleman's Quarterly,* a magazine that would pay him in bucks rather than in offprints. He wanted to write about what appeared to be a total flip-flop in feminist belief and rhetoric, softening the word "flip-flop" to "revisionism" but meaning the same thing. It was something he was eager to put into words, but when he turned on his P.C. and instructions cueing him to proceed swam out of the void behind the screen, everything in his head went blank and he couldn't remember what to tell the keyboard. He sat looking at the cursor wink at him, wondering what came next. "What comes next?" he said aloud at the same moment as his doorbell rang. The noise seemed to bounce off every wall in the house.

"Another reporter, come to gaze at the wreckage," Barker said. "Not gonna answer. No one at home, pal, they've all gone away. Pestilence inside."

The doorbell rang again.

"Fuck it!" Barker said, getting up. He tiptoed to the front room where, by pasting his cheek against the windowpane, he could see, with one eye, the shoulder and left arm of the person standing on the porch. It was Guy. Barker opened the door.

"Hello," he said. "Come on in. This is a surprise."

Guy stepped across the doorsill. The way he looked around him reminded Barker that he had never been in this house before.

"Nice layout you've got here," Guy said. He was wearing extremely tight jeans, a black sweater, and a tweed jacket at least two sizes too large for him with the cuffs turned up and over, revealing the silk lining.

"It'll do," Barker said.

"You look like you haven't seen daylight in a month," Guy said.

"What can I get you?" Barker asked.

"Nothing, thanks, Dad. Do you have any Diet Coke?"

"Sorry, no Diet Coke. How about a beer?"

The boy shook his head. "Never touch the stuff," he said. "How'd you get here?"

"Philip, a friend of mine, drove me in. He's got a Cherokee."

They were still in the front hall. "Let's go into my study," Barker said, leading the way.

Once inside, Guy said, "I don't see how you can work in this mess."

"Hah!" Barker said. He was sorry he'd left the empty on his desk. "Sit down, son." He made a sweep of the armchair, removing a pile of papers and journals and dumping them on top of a similar pile on the desk. Guy lowered himself warily, as if afraid of sitting on a kitten.

"So?" Barker said. "To what do I owe this visit?"

"I wanted to see how you were doing."

"It's a good thing I was here. I might have been out. You didn't call."

"It's really warm in here, Dad. It smells funny. Can you open the window or something?"

Barker got up and cranked open the casement window.

Spring air blew in, bringing with it the scent of newly burst blossoms, a sweet, nostalgic odor that struck Barker as gloriously inappropriate.

"You didn't come to my graduation," Guy said.

"I tried."

"Sure, Dad. Mom and Tony came."

"You don't believe me," Barker said. "I really tried."

"Why didn't you call or anything?" Guy said. His cheeks were getting red. "Oh shit, it doesn't matter. By the way, I got the English prize for the best essay."

"Congratulations."

Barker and his son stared at each other for moments that seemed to pass with extreme slowness. For all that was being said, infinitely more was left in silence.

Then Guy said, "I've got a job at Mom's tennis club for the summer."

Barker nodded.

"Dad?"

"Guy?"

"Do you want to talk about it?"

"Not especially," Barker said, "if by 'it' you mean what I think you mean."

"Well, I'd like to talk about it," Guy said. He crossed one leg over the other like an adult.

"I can't imagine why," Barker said. And this was true. He wasn't at all sure that his son hadn't come to gloat. There was no mockery yet but it could happen at any moment; Guy was, after all, carrying a heavy load of grievances, most of them justified. How, in fact, do you face a father maimed by public humiliation? The phone rang.

"Aren't you going to get that?" Guy asked.

"I've got a machine that does it for me."

"By the way, where's your wife? Where's the baby? Can I see her?"

"I'm afraid they've quit the prem-eesies," Barker said.

"For good?"

"For their good, apparently," Barker said. "My wife seems to think I'd be a lousy influence on our child. Lily's a cute little thing, by the way, she's got her mother's eyes." At this, Barker felt his throat tighten. His eyes stung.

"Are you two getting divorced?"

"Too many questions," Barker said. "You're putting me on overload."

"I'm sorry, Dad."

"Look, are you sure you don't want a drink or something? How about something to eat? I've got a couple of pieces of Kentucky Fried Chicken in the fridge. . . ."

Guy shook his head. "I just ate."

"There's something I've had on my mind lately," Barker said, grabbing at anything to keep the words rolling. "It's what they're saying these days, women, that is. The latest wrinkle is that they see things differently than men do. It's the new twist to feminism—they not only have a different worldview from us, they also speak in a different voice. What's so ironic about this is that it's precisely what folks of my generation were taught to believe—that men and women were as different from each other as feet and hands. Just a few years ago your card-carrying feminist insisted there *were* no differences. Are you clued into this, Guy? We're right back where we started before these high-powered females put their heads together and came up with the earth-shaking, not to say thoroughly startling, notion that—would you believe it?—men and women are not alike?"

"That's very interesting, Dad, but what does it have to do with you?"

"Nothing, except that it's been on my mind."

"I'm worried about you, Dad," Guy said. "I don't have to ask you how you're managing. Look at you, look at this room. I don't especially want to know what went on at your hearing, but I would like to know whether you were unfairly singled out. I'll bet you were."

"Who's to say?" Barker said. "Besides, it's too late to do anything about it. Yes, I was singled out. No one could

272

seriously believe I'm the only teacher who ever bedded a student. But I don't see what our talking about it is going to accomplish."

"Why don't you fight it?" Guy said.

It struck Barker that his son still had a notion that fairness was an attainable goal. "I'm touched by your concern," Barker said. "But I'll land on my feet. I always have, so far. I'm a man of resources." Bravado: wherever he chose to land (especially if it was another college), Barker knew his moral dossier would follow him—if it hadn't got there first. Guy's face was not happy. "And what about you? Are things coming together somewhat better than they were the last time we had a talk?"

"I've been seeing someone," Guy said.

"I thought you were through with shrinks."

"Gordon isn't a shrink," Guy said. "He counsels gays and lesbians. He's not interested in how you got that way or in straightening you out. He helps you stop feeling like a freak."

"That must be a relief," Barker said. "I wish there was someone like Gordon for what ails me."

"You and I are in the same boat, Dad," Guy said.

"You need to explain that," Barker said. "I'm feeling dumb today."

"A lot of people don't want to have to deal with us; they'd just as soon we disappeared. I know how it feels to have people talk about you behind your back. It's okay to be gay around other gays and people who don't give a shit one way or another, but there are an awful lot of homophobes out there. And now, with this AIDS thing, it's getting worse all the time. Some straights think you've got a tail and keep a pitchfork in the bedroom closet."

"My problem is hardly analogous . . . ," Barker began. He wasn't prepared to admit that he did, in fact, share Guy's sense of dereliction, not so much for what he had done but for the way he was being treated. He had been decisively cast out: no one but his lawyer had phoned, no one but Emily had sent him a note—he might just as well have been atomized beneath the kitchen sink. Even the mailman smirked at him.

"Why don't you face it, Dad? You're in deep shit. You look like a bum—no offense." He stood up. "Maybe I shouldn't have come here."

"Don't go yet, Guy," Barker said. Suddenly, it was terribly important that Guy stay with him a little longer. "You know, the conventional wisdom says that you've got to unburden yourself, let it all hang out, whatever. But that's not my style, Guy; there are some things it's better not to talk about before you're good and ready. You'll just have to go along with me. I'm trying very hard to absorb what's happened and it's rough. But hashing it over this minute isn't going to make it any easier. Okay, son?"

"Whatever you say, Dad."

"It seems to me you'd like me to admit that I've learned my lesson."

Guy nodded.

"Isn't that the way we always want to view a personal crisis? You must have learned something useful from it, or you might just as well retire and pull the covers over your head forever. God, you're young. . . ."

"Please don't pull that you're-too-young-to-understand shit," Guy said, sitting down again.

"Well, you might just be more mature than I've given you credit for." Barker paused. "Do you want to hear me say that I'll make an effort to keep away from young girls from now on?"

"It's real easy," said Guy. "Why don't you find someone nearer your own age?"

Barker smiled. "I've tried. I can't seem to hack it for more than a year or so; they act so tired, they're so wrinkled—like something you find at Goodwill. But both of us avoiding young female flesh, coming from opposite places? It has an interesting symmetry."

"Do you mean it, Dad? Are you going to start acting your age?"

"Step back," Barker said. "Why don't we just leave it at that?"

"At what?"

"At *I'll think about it.*" Guy looked down at his knees. "I've got an idea," Barker said. "How would you like to take a walk with me? Nice spring day. I could use some exercise." For the first time in over a week, Barker felt energized.

Guy looked at his watch. "I'm not meeting Phil for an hour. Sure. Only—Dad?"

"What?"

"Would you mind changing your pants first?"

"What's the matter with the ones I'm wearing?"

"Have you looked in a mirror recently?"

Barker went upstairs to change his clothes, deciding to take a shower as well. As he did this, washing away sweat, dead skin, crud accumulated over three, maybe four days—he couldn't remember precisely—he realized that he had misled his son. His spots would remain the same color, the same shape, forever. He might, for a time, be able to keep his hands off the sophomore in the front row, gazing up at him with wet and wondrous eyes, but to forego forever the ardent chase, the quickening pulse, the verbal foreplay, the heightened fantasies—how could he promise such a thing? He might as well promise to have his gonads removed. Barker rubbed the washcloth over his belly, pleased that it had flattened somewhat. Like Guy, he would honor his true nature. Guy had come to terms with it and so would he, though he was a man despised and shunned. He would lead his life by the only terms he understood, and if that meant sacrifices of the sort he was making now—melancholy in an empty house, the loss of wife and child, the loss of friends—he was willing to make them. Besides, he wasn't sure he had a choice. Stepping over the tub's edge, Barker pulled a towel off the rack and, dripping across the bedroom floor, called to Guy that he would be down in a minute.

Epilogue

W<small>HEN</small> last heard from, Jacob Barker was in Arizona; we know this because Emily Compton received a card from him postmarked Tempe. The card said, "Getting lots of rays, studying the heavens, not missing the Big H. Trust you and the pooch are well." He did not include a return address. Bennie has had a couple of phone calls from Barker; they were circumspect and neutral. Bennie misses his friend, and told his wife he wouldn't be surprised if Jake showed up on his doorstep one of these days.

Guy, shunning Harvard, is at Bowdoin, doing moderately well in his studies and chairing the campus gay and lesbian association—GALA.

Susan moved out of her mother's house and now shares a cramped apartment near Central Square with her daughter Lily and Billy Foster. Billy graduated with a Magna and is attending Boston University Law School. Susan has sold another piece to *New Woman*, this one about the problems connected with being a single mother. Next week Billy is going to suggest that he and Susan get married.

About the Author

Anne Bernays' seven previous novels include *The Address Book* and *Growing Up Rich*. Her work has appeared in numerous magazines and newspapers, and she is currently on the faculty of the Harvard Extension School. Ms. Bernays has three grown daughters and lives in Massachusetts with her husband, biographer Justin Kaplan.